Dangerous Invitation

Fiona Gray

Published by Fiona Gray, 2024.

This is a work of fiction. Similarities to real people, places, or events are entirely coincidental.

DANGEROUS INVITATION

First edition. November 6, 2024.

Copyright © 2024 Fiona Gray.

ISBN: 979-8227720788

Written by Fiona Gray.

Chapter 1: The Unwelcome Guest

The atmosphere crackled with energy, a heady mix of champagne bubbles and the laughter of friends celebrating love. Mia's engagement party was the kind of event you read about in glossy magazines: floor-to-ceiling windows that framed the skyline like a masterpiece, twinkling fairy lights strung from the ceiling, and a live jazz band softly crooning in the background. Guests in tailored suits and stunning gowns swirled around me, their faces aglow with happiness, but I felt like a solitary island in the middle of this glittering sea. I had come to celebrate my best friend, to revel in her joy, yet all I could focus on was the unsettling weight of anticipation.

It was in this moment of blissful distraction that he appeared. Jordan Steele made an entrance that was nothing short of cinematic. He strode through the door like he owned the place, tall and broad-shouldered, with tousled dark hair that looked like it had been styled by the wind. His piercing blue eyes, sharp enough to slice through the party's jovial atmosphere, locked onto mine as if we were the only two people in the room. I felt an involuntary rush of irritation—what gave him the right to upstage a celebration that was supposed to be about Mia?

"Is this the art center girl?" he drawled, his voice a smooth blend of confidence and condescension that made my skin prickle. The smug smirk tugging at the corners of his lips was the icing on a particularly infuriating cake.

"Ah, yes, the voice of the community," I shot back, hoping my words dripped with sarcasm to match his tone. "And who might you be? The self-appointed critic?"

He chuckled softly, the sound almost mocking, and leaned back against the bar, arms crossed over his chest. "Mia's brother. I've heard a lot about you, but honestly, I thought you'd be taller."

"Good thing I'm not a basketball player, then," I retorted, a touch of humor creeping into my own voice as I tried to reclaim the upper hand. The heat of the moment fired my resolve; I was determined not to let this stranger with his infuriating smirk intimidate me.

"Touché," he said, raising his glass in a mock salute. "But really, an art center? You think that's going to change the world?"

I blinked at him, taken aback by the casual dismissal wrapped in his silky tone. "It's not about changing the world. It's about giving kids a safe space to express themselves, to create. But I guess that doesn't resonate with someone like you."

"Someone like me?" he echoed, his brows arching in feigned innocence. "And what would that be? Someone who appreciates a practical approach to life?"

"More like someone who doesn't understand that art has value beyond dollar signs," I replied, my voice firm despite the slight tremor of uncertainty gnawing at the edges of my bravado.

"Practicality is a form of art," he shot back, and I could see the flicker of challenge in his eyes. "What good is creativity if it doesn't pay the bills?"

"Oh, I don't know," I replied, my heart racing with both frustration and an inexplicable thrill. "Maybe the satisfaction of knowing you've made a difference in someone's life?"

Jordan's gaze flicked over the crowd, and for a moment, the air between us crackled with a tension I couldn't quite comprehend. I saw a flicker of something—admiration?—behind his cocky facade, but he buried it beneath a layer of arrogance just as quickly.

"Nice try," he replied, but his smile was different now, more thoughtful. "You're going to need a lot more than that if you want to convince people to invest in your dreams."

I was about to launch into another volley of words, but Mia's laughter pulled my attention. She was sparkling in her engagement ring, radiant as she swirled around with her fiancé, completely oblivious to our growing debate. I envied her ease, her joy. I wanted to enjoy the night, to lose myself in celebration rather than spar with her brother.

"Why are you even here, Jordan?" I asked, a hint of annoyance creeping into my voice. "Shouldn't you be out chasing your next big business deal?"

"Charming," he replied dryly. "But I'm here for Mia, not business. You, on the other hand, seem to relish the fight."

I raised an eyebrow, unwilling to let him get under my skin. "It's a talent, really."

"Maybe you just like to stir the pot," he mused, taking a slow sip of his drink as if he had all the time in the world to analyze me.

"I like to make a difference," I countered, crossing my arms defiantly. "Something you wouldn't understand if it bit you on your perfectly sculpted backside."

He laughed, a genuine, booming sound that made several heads turn. "I'm not sure whether to be flattered or offended. But it's clear you're passionate about this—more than most people, I suspect."

There was an unexpected softness in his gaze, a flicker of respect beneath the bravado. It caught me off guard, causing the frustration swirling within me to dissolve, if only for a moment.

"Passion doesn't pay the bills either, you know," I muttered, suddenly less confident.

"No, but it might just open doors you didn't know existed," he replied, the weight of his words hanging between us like a fragile promise.

Before I could respond, Mia swept over, her cheeks flushed with happiness. "There you two are! I was starting to worry you'd scare away all my guests with your bickering."

Jordan grinned, the tension dissipating as he turned his full attention to his sister. "Just a friendly debate, Mia. You know how much I love a good argument."

I shot him a warning look, but the glint in his eye told me he was just getting started. Little did I know, our encounter that night was just the beginning of a complicated journey filled with unexpected alliances, challenges, and a tension that would unravel into something neither of us could have predicted.

The party pulsed around us, laughter and music melding into a symphony of celebration that I felt increasingly disconnected from. I watched Mia twirl in her elegant dress, sparkling like the diamonds in her engagement ring, while I was stuck in this tug-of-war with her brother, whose very presence seemed to challenge everything I believed in. I could almost feel the tension radiating off us like heat from a flame, both of us unwilling to back down, both determined to defend our ideals as if they were worth more than the glimmering glass of champagne in our hands.

"Look, I'm not trying to be the bad guy here," he said, his tone shifting slightly, a hint of something more genuine creeping into his voice. "But you've got to understand the realities of funding these projects. It's not just about passion; it's about logistics."

"Logistics?" I scoffed, waving my glass dismissively. "You make it sound like running a community art center is akin to launching a rocket. It's about providing a space for creativity and connection, something this city desperately needs. It's not just another line on a budget sheet."

His brow furrowed, and for a brief moment, I thought I saw a flicker of interest behind those icy blue eyes. "And what do you plan to do when the funding runs out? What's your backup plan? There's only so long you can survive on good intentions."

"Do you really think people are that superficial?" I asked, feeling the warmth of indignation rising within me. "Art has a way of bringing people together, of sparking change. Look at all the great movements—they started with a single voice. Why can't that be me?"

"Because most voices get drowned out," he replied, and this time, there was a softness to his tone that caught me off guard. "You can't just charge in without a plan."

"Maybe I don't want to just be another cog in the machine you're so fond of," I shot back, my heart racing with the thrill of our verbal sparring. "Maybe I want to make a difference, however small it may be."

As our conversation continued to escalate, a sudden laughter erupted from a nearby group, pulling my attention away from Jordan's piercing gaze. Mia was surrounded by friends, her joy infectious, and I was reminded of why I had come here in the first place. I forced myself to take a breath, to rein in the tempest brewing within me.

"Excuse me for a moment," I said, nodding toward Mia. "I need to go check on my best friend before she gets swept away by her own happiness."

Jordan's lips twitched, as if he were holding back a smile. "Just don't drown in your good intentions, okay?"

I rolled my eyes at him, a smile breaking through my annoyance. "Not everyone's drowning in cynicism, Jordan. Some of us prefer to swim."

As I walked toward Mia, I couldn't shake the feeling that my brief exchanges with Jordan were like a dance—two opposing forces moving around each other with grace, but always on the verge of colliding. The air crackled with tension, a strange mix of frustration and something akin to intrigue that I wasn't quite ready to dissect.

"Mia!" I called out, my voice cutting through the laughter. "You're glowing! Have you had a chance to breathe, or are you just going to spin your way through the night?"

She spun around, her dark curls bouncing, eyes sparkling with a mix of excitement and nerves. "I've just been caught up in the whirlwind of joy! Can you believe I'm actually getting married? It feels like a dream!"

I grinned, wrapping my arms around her in a tight hug. "And I'm here for every second of it! Even if I have to deal with your brother."

Mia giggled, her eyes darting back to where Jordan was leaning against the bar, still watching us with that infuriating smirk. "Ah, Jordan. He's like a storm cloud on a sunny day—always looming but never quite raining on your parade."

"More like a hurricane," I muttered, grabbing another glass of champagne to steel myself against the memories of our heated exchange. "He has a way of sucking the joy out of the room, even when he's smiling."

"Oh come on, he's not that bad! He just cares too much about his corporate job and forgets how to enjoy life sometimes," she argued, her loyalty evident.

"Caring about the bottom line isn't enjoying life, Mia," I replied, shaking my head. "But fine, let's celebrate you and your fiancé. Where is he, by the way?"

Before she could respond, a tall figure swept over, drawing my attention with his easy smile and warm presence. Mia's fiancé, Eric, stepped in, wrapping an arm around her waist and kissing the top of her head. "There you are! I was worried you two were plotting to take over the world without me," he joked, his voice a melodic counterpoint to Jordan's sharper tones.

"Just a friendly chat," I assured him, though I suspected he could see through my façade. Eric was the kind of guy who saw right through pretense, and I liked him for it.

As the evening unfolded, I lost myself in the comforting atmosphere of laughter and warmth. Yet, every so often, my gaze drifted back to Jordan, still lingering at the bar, an unyielding presence in the periphery of my celebration. I could feel the pull of our earlier conversation like a magnet, the debate still simmering in the air between us, making me feel both unsettled and alive.

At one point, while Mia and Eric were swept away by friends congratulating them, I found myself at the bar, refilling my glass. Jordan appeared beside me, his posture relaxed, but the smirk remained, an ever-present reminder of our clash.

"You know," he said, leaning slightly closer, his voice low enough to avoid the eavesdropping guests, "if you want to make a real impact, you might consider aligning with people who can help you achieve that. I could introduce you to some contacts."

The suggestion caught me off guard, the warmth of the moment coloring my thoughts. "Is that your way of admitting I might have a point? Because you could have fooled me."

"Don't get ahead of yourself," he replied with a chuckle, those blue eyes glinting with mischief. "I'm merely stating facts. If you can harness that passion of yours and funnel it into something that's more... palatable for investors, then maybe you'll actually get something done."

"Wow, thanks for the backhanded compliment, Jordan," I replied dryly, but a flicker of curiosity ignited within me. "What makes you think I'd want your help?"

"Because despite your fiery spirit, I have a feeling you're going to need it," he said, his expression shifting to something more earnest. "It's a tough world out there for dreamers."

I considered his words, the weight of them settling over me like a soft blanket of understanding. Just as quickly as I warmed to his suggestion, I bristled again. "I don't need your pity or your help, Jordan. I'm perfectly capable of making my own way."

His smile widened, revealing a hint of something more genuine beneath his confident facade. "I guess we'll see about that, won't we?"

With that, the night continued its dance of laughter and merriment, but the challenge hung between us like a taut string, ready to snap at the slightest pull. I couldn't help but feel that beneath our bickering, there lay an uncharted territory waiting to be explored, and I had no idea what it would take to get there—or if I even wanted to.

As the evening progressed, the air thickened with unspoken words and unresolved tensions. I had initially thought my confrontation with Jordan was merely a fluke, an explosive start to an otherwise festive occasion. Yet, as the guests mingled and clinked glasses, I felt an undercurrent of curiosity and resentment that seemed to swirl around us, a magnetic pull that both intrigued and frustrated me.

Mia and Eric were swept up in a whirl of congratulations, blissfully unaware of the storm brewing between their families. I took another sip of champagne, trying to drown out my thoughts, but the bubbles only intensified my irritation. Jordan was leaning against the bar, now engaged in a conversation with another guest, his laughter mingling with the music. I forced myself to look away, but the image of him—his relaxed demeanor and that infuriating grin—kept drawing my gaze back like a moth to a flame.

Suddenly, the music shifted to something slow and melodic, a romantic ballad that wrapped the room in a cocoon of intimacy. Couples began to sway, their bodies moving in sync to the rhythm, and I felt a twinge of loneliness settle in my chest. I glanced at Mia, lost in Eric's embrace, her eyes sparkling with joy. In that moment, I wished for my own kind of magic, a partner who would sweep me off my feet instead of bickering with me.

"Feeling left out?" Jordan's voice broke through my thoughts, smooth and teasing. I turned to find him standing close, that infuriating smirk back in place, his eyes glinting with mischief.

"Hardly," I replied, tilting my chin defiantly. "I'm just enjoying the ambiance."

"Is that what you call it?" he said, leaning in slightly as if he were privy to some secret I wasn't. "Because it looks more like you're plotting your escape."

"Maybe I am," I shot back, crossing my arms. "Or maybe I'm just trying to figure out how to avoid another round of unsolicited advice from you."

"Ah, but unsolicited advice is my specialty," he said with a grin that made my heart race despite my irritation. "You should be grateful."

I couldn't help but laugh, the sound surprising even myself. "Grateful? For the guy who thinks my dreams are just a waste of time?"

"Maybe I'm just trying to help you see the bigger picture," he replied, his tone more earnest now. "You're passionate, and that's great. But passion without direction can lead you astray. It's like sailing a ship without a compass—you might end up lost."

"Is that your way of telling me to find a mentor?" I countered, arching an eyebrow. "Because if it is, I can assure you, you're not exactly my ideal choice."

"Fair enough," he admitted, raising his hands in mock surrender. "But don't say I didn't warn you when you find yourself waist-deep in a sea of red tape."

"Maybe I'll be the one navigating these waters," I challenged, a spark of defiance igniting within me. "Or maybe I'll be the one who proves you wrong."

Our back-and-forth was interrupted by the arrival of more guests, and I seized the moment to slip away from the bar, feeling the heat of Jordan's gaze follow me. I needed air, clarity, anything to escape the magnetic tension that crackled between us. Stepping out onto the terrace, I breathed in the cool night air, the city sprawling beneath me like a glittering tapestry of possibilities.

As I leaned against the railing, the distant sounds of laughter and music faded into a pleasant hum, and I closed my eyes for a moment, allowing myself to feel. Just then, I felt a presence beside me. I opened my eyes to find Jordan standing there, the moonlight casting a silver sheen on his features.

"What? You're not going to lecture me about the dangers of the night air?" I asked, attempting to maintain my bravado.

"Only if you're planning to jump off the edge," he replied, his tone light. "But honestly, I came out here to apologize."

"Apologize?" I echoed, skepticism lacing my voice. "For what, exactly?"

"For being an ass," he said, the sincerity in his tone surprising me. "You care about your art center, and that matters. I might not agree with your approach, but I can respect your dedication."

"Well, it's a little late for respect, don't you think?" I shot back, feeling my defenses begin to crumble. "You had your chance to show it back there."

"True," he admitted, leaning against the railing beside me. "But I also think we're more alike than either of us wants to admit."

"Oh, really?" I said, crossing my arms again, though this time the gesture felt less defensive and more playful. "And how do you figure that?"

"We both have big dreams and stubborn personalities," he replied, glancing sideways at me, his expression a mix of challenge and amusement. "We're both just trying to make our mark in a world that doesn't make it easy."

His words hung in the air, and for a moment, I considered the truth behind them. It felt oddly liberating to acknowledge that we both were grappling with our ambitions, even if our paths seemed so different.

"Maybe," I conceded, "but that doesn't mean I'm willing to join forces with someone who belittles my passion."

"Fair point," he replied, the corners of his mouth twitching upward. "So what if we start fresh? No judgments, just a conversation about how to actually make our dreams happen. Call it a truce."

"Is this where you promise not to roll your eyes every time I mention the art center?" I asked, arching an eyebrow, half in jest.

"Only if you promise not to punch me in the face when I offer my 'expert' advice," he countered, laughter lacing his voice.

I couldn't help but laugh, a genuine sound that echoed off the walls of the penthouse. "Deal."

Just as we shook hands to seal our truce, a loud crash echoed from inside, followed by a panicked shout. My heart dropped as I turned to see guests rushing toward the source of the chaos, confusion painted across their faces.

"What was that?" Jordan asked, his demeanor shifting from playful to alert.

"Let's find out," I said, adrenaline surging through me as I pushed past the throng of people, Jordan right on my heels.

We burst back into the penthouse to find Mia standing frozen in shock, her fiancé looking equally horrified. A large vase lay shattered on the floor, glass shards glittering dangerously like jagged diamonds. But it wasn't the mess that caught my attention—it was the figure standing in the doorway, cloaked in shadow, an air of menace surrounding them.

"Who are you?" Mia's voice trembled, her joy quickly replaced by a cold fear that settled over the room.

The figure stepped into the light, revealing a familiar face that made my heart race for an entirely different reason. "I'm here for the art center," they said, their voice smooth and chilling, a smile curling at the corners of their lips. "And I believe we need to talk."

Chapter 2: Collision Course

The sun dipped low on the horizon, casting a warm glow over the café's patio, where the scent of fresh-brewed coffee mingled with the sweet aroma of baked goods. I was perched on my usual stool, the one that overlooked the bustling street, a vantage point from which I could observe the world while pretending to be engrossed in my sketchbook. I was absorbed in capturing the vibrant energy of the café when I felt the air shift, a familiar presence charging into my space.

Jordan appeared, all tousled hair and that infuriatingly charming grin that could disarm a seasoned negotiator. The corner of his mouth quirked upward, and I had half a mind to scowl at him for interrupting my artistic reverie. Instead, I merely raised an eyebrow, marking my territory in this ongoing battle of wits.

"Still sketching your little dreams?" he quipped, plopping into the seat across from me without invitation. "You know, I've been thinking it might be time to find you a more ambitious project. Something that doesn't involve crayons and whimsy."

"Crayons? Really?" I retorted, feigning outrage. "I graduated to colored pencils last week, thank you very much. And what's wrong with whimsy? Some of us appreciate the beauty in a little chaos."

"Oh, chaos, is it?" He leaned forward, the challenge dancing in his eyes. "Isn't that what you call all your art initiatives? What was it this time—paint a mural to distract the townsfolk from their mundane lives?"

His tone was playful, but the jab stung just enough to make my heart race. I had poured my soul into those community projects, infusing them with life and vibrancy in a town that sometimes felt like it was asleep at the wheel. I gathered my thoughts, determined to stand my ground.

"Actually, it's called 'bringing color back to a grey world.' Not that you would understand the concept of inspiration," I shot back, feeling the rush of adrenaline course through me. "Some of us want to make a difference, not just sit back and critique from the sidelines."

"Touché," he replied, his eyes sparkling with mischief. "But let's be honest. It's a noble pursuit, but it's not exactly revolutionary, is it? More like a light breeze in a hurricane."

I could feel the fire in my cheeks, equal parts indignation and something dangerously akin to exhilaration. This was our dance—two opposing forces colliding in a whirlwind of playful animosity. Yet with each clever retort, I felt the simmering tension between us shift, growing more complex and layered.

"Is that your idea of charm, Jordan? Insulting someone's hard work?"

"Only when the work is laughably impractical," he countered, and there was a spark of something else in his gaze. Was it challenge? Was it interest? The line between our animosity and something else entirely seemed to blur with every exchange.

"You wouldn't know practical if it slapped you in the face," I challenged, crossing my arms defiantly. "You think you can come in here and critique my work when your own ideas have all the creativity of a beige wall?"

"Beige is a classic choice," he shot back, laughing softly. "But I have to give you credit. You've got some guts, diving into a world of color while the rest of us are trying to survive in shades of grey."

There was an unexpected sincerity beneath his banter, a recognition that made my heart flutter against my will. It was infuriating and intoxicating all at once. I glanced away, biting my lip to suppress a smile, but my defiance only fueled him further.

"I think you're just scared of what might happen if you let a little color into your life," I said, my voice softer now, curiosity creeping in.

"Scared? Not me," he replied, leaning back in his chair with an air of mock bravado. "I simply prefer my reality to be—how should I put this?—grounded."

As if summoned by the universe, a waitress approached our table with an unyielding plate of freshly baked pastries. She placed them between us, the sweet scent momentarily distracting from our heated discussion. Jordan reached for a pastry, breaking it in half, the warm steam rising between us like the tension in the air.

"Here," he said, extending the half towards me. "Taste this. A little sweetness to go with your bitterness."

I hesitated, staring at the offering in his hand, a conflict brewing within me. Accepting the gesture would feel like a surrender, a concession that I enjoyed his company, but refusing it would mean missing out on the unexpected pleasure of sharing something simple and sweet. The internal struggle flickered in my eyes, and I knew he was watching, savoring the moment.

With a resigned sigh, I reached for the pastry, our fingers brushing against each other, sending an electric jolt up my arm. I quickly pulled my hand back, trying to mask the warmth that spread through me. "Fine," I said, forcing nonchalance, "but this doesn't mean I'm softening on my stance about your critique."

"Good," he grinned, that infuriatingly charming smile now tempered with an undeniable allure. "I prefer my opponents fierce."

We fell into a comfortable rhythm, the banter evolving as our surroundings faded into a blurred backdrop. The café buzzed with life, but it was as if a bubble surrounded us, shielding our conversation from the world beyond. We danced around our respective beliefs, exchanging laughter and barbs, but as the evening wore on, I could feel the magnetic pull between us tightening, igniting something far more profound than mere rivalry.

Jordan's eyes locked onto mine, that intensity sharpening as he leaned closer, the space between us charged with an energy that made my heart race. "You know," he said softly, "I never pegged you for someone who could hold their own in an argument. You've surprised me."

"Maybe you should stop underestimating people, Jordan," I replied, my voice steady despite the thrill coursing through me. "You might find that there's more to me than what meets the eye."

"Or maybe," he countered, his gaze unwavering, "I've only just begun to uncover what's hidden beneath that fierce exterior."

As the evening deepened, I wondered if perhaps this collision course was leading us somewhere unexpected—somewhere filled with the possibility of connection amidst the chaos of our contrasting worlds.

The weeks rolled on, a steady procession of sun-drenched afternoons and starry evenings filled with laughter, community gatherings, and the relentless volley of our verbal sparring matches. I often found myself wondering if the universe had conspired to keep us in close quarters, each encounter becoming a finely woven tapestry of banter and burgeoning tension. Jordan seemed to have a knack for popping up just when I thought I could catch a breath, his devil-may-care attitude and smirk challenging me to engage in yet another round of our unspoken competition.

One Saturday, the local farmers' market sprawled vibrantly in the town square, its stalls brimming with the season's bounty. The air was alive with chatter, the mingling scents of fresh produce, baked bread, and flowers creating an intoxicating atmosphere. I had hoped to enjoy a peaceful morning, perhaps sketching the bustling scene, when I spotted Jordan, leaning against a stall filled with organic vegetables, a look of feigned boredom etched across his handsome face.

"Trying to elevate your culinary skills with those earthy delights?" I called out, lifting my chin defiantly as I approached, my sketchbook tucked under my arm.

"Or I could just admire the scenery," he shot back, his gaze sliding over me with a deliberate slowness that made my heart stutter. "It's not every day I get to see you without your art supplies weighing you down."

"Touché," I replied, attempting to mask the warmth flooding my cheeks. "But unlike you, I'm not just here to stand around looking pretty. I'm here for the good produce."

"Is that what you call the mottled carrots?" he said, pointing to a particularly lumpy vegetable that sat neglected at the edge of the stall. "Looks more like something from a horror film."

"You know, some people appreciate character in their vegetables," I retorted, plucking a slightly crooked cucumber from the display. "This guy has personality. I can relate."

"Personality? Right. Let's just hope your culinary experiments don't involve this sort of 'character,'" he chuckled, his laughter infectious. We fell into a rhythm, our banter punctuated by laughter, but there was a thread of tension still weaving between us, each quip layered with unspoken possibilities.

As I examined the produce, trying to decide what would complement my dinner plans, Jordan leaned closer, the warmth of his presence sending an electric thrill racing up my spine. "You're a complicated woman, you know that?" he murmured, his voice dropping to a conspiratorial tone. "What's the real story behind your art initiatives? They can't just be about bringing color to the world."

I stiffened slightly, but curiosity drew me to answer. "What do you mean?"

"Surely there's a motive buried beneath all the paint and brush strokes," he pressed, his eyes glinting with mischief. "Some hidden agenda."

"Or maybe I just want to make my corner of the world a little brighter," I shot back, folding my arms defensively. "But since you're so interested in digging, tell me—what's your angle? Critiquing the world while standing in a market filled with organic produce? Sounds like a rich man's hobby."

"Let's call it 'intellectual engagement,'" he replied, smirking. "Every piece of art I see makes me think about how disconnected our lives have become. Isn't it easier to shop for fresh carrots and ignore the bigger picture?"

His words struck a nerve, and I fought to keep my expression neutral. "Maybe the bigger picture isn't as black and white as you think. Some of us find value in what we can create here and now."

"Ah, there it is again," he said, eyes dancing with excitement. "You're passionate, and I can't resist a passionate debate."

Just as I opened my mouth to respond, a loud commotion erupted nearby. A group of children burst into the market, laughter ringing out as they darted between the stalls, their energy infectious. One little girl, with pigtails flying, tripped and sent a basket of apples rolling, causing a chain reaction of giggles and chaos. Jordan's gaze softened as he watched the scene unfold, a rare smile breaking through his usual bravado.

"See? This is what I'm talking about," I said, nodding toward the laughter. "These moments matter. They're what make our town feel alive."

"True," he admitted, his voice thoughtful as he observed the children. "But you could argue that art and creativity can be just as chaotic, can't they?"

"Perhaps," I mused, feeling the atmosphere shift slightly. "But chaos can create beauty. It's all in how you frame it."

Jordan turned to face me, the light in his eyes flickering with something deeper. "And how do you frame it, then? With color? Or does it have to be something more?"

For a heartbeat, the world around us faded away. I could feel the weight of his gaze, a mixture of challenge and something softer, something that dared me to explore the edges of our bickering and discover what lay beneath. "It's about embracing the mess, Jordan. That's where real life happens," I finally replied, the sincerity in my voice surprising even me.

"Messy is good," he agreed, his expression growing serious. "But it also scares people. It scares me."

The confession hung in the air between us, charged with unspoken truths. I felt a sudden urge to reach out, to bridge the distance that had grown comfortable over the weeks. But just as I contemplated taking that leap, the moment shattered with the arrival of his friend, a boisterous guy named Derek, who clapped Jordan on the back, interrupting our fragile connection.

"Hey, man! You coming to the game later?" Derek boomed, his presence too loud, too jarring for the atmosphere that had just begun to settle.

"Yeah, I'll be there," Jordan replied, his attention shifting abruptly as he glanced back at me. "You should join us, too," he added, the invitation lingering, a challenge wrapped in friendliness.

"Not my scene," I said, shrugging, but a small part of me wondered what it would be like to step into his world, to witness him beyond our battles of wits.

"Don't knock it until you try it," he countered, a playful glint in his eyes. "You might discover something new."

"Like the art of sitting on bleachers?" I teased, trying to regain my footing. "I think I'll pass."

"Suit yourself," he said with a shrug, but there was an unmistakable light in his expression, as if he were reveling in the push-and-pull of our dynamic.

As the conversation drifted to lighter topics and our banter resumed, I felt the earlier moment slip away, but the spark remained, smoldering beneath the surface. Each encounter was becoming more than just rivalry; it was a dance of discovery, and despite the interruptions, the tension that crackled between us was undeniable.

As we parted ways at the market, the echo of his laughter lingered, a reminder of the whirlwind that was Jordan. I knew then that the game was far from over; the stakes were rising, and I was intrigued by where this collision course might lead.

The farmers' market faded into memory, replaced by the excitement of a late summer fair that transformed our quiet town into a vibrant hub of activity. Stalls brimmed with handmade crafts, delicious food, and the joyful sounds of laughter and music spilling through the air. The scent of caramel popcorn mingled with the sweetness of cotton candy, and my heart danced with anticipation as I strolled through the throngs of people, sketchbook tucked under my arm, the familiar thrill of inspiration tingling in my fingertips.

But it wasn't long before I caught sight of Jordan, flitting through the crowd like a mischievous breeze. His unruly hair caught the sunlight, and for a moment, I felt the unmistakable tug of attraction mixed with exasperation. Just when I thought I could enjoy an afternoon of art and creativity without him hovering nearby, there he was, laughing with a group of friends, his voice rising above the din.

I rolled my eyes, half-amused and half-annoyed, and prepared myself for the inevitable encounter. It came sooner than expected when he spotted me, his gaze locking onto mine with that familiar spark of mischief. "Ah, the artist in her natural habitat," he called out, making his way over with the swagger of someone who knew he was about to stir the pot.

"I was wondering when you'd make your grand entrance," I replied, trying to maintain my composure. "What are you doing here, following me? Shouldn't you be off analyzing the philosophical implications of funnel cakes?"

"Those cakes are serious business," he retorted, a grin breaking across his face. "And I'm merely here to ensure you don't drift too far into your whimsical fantasies. Someone has to keep you grounded."

"Grounded? Is that your idea of charm? Because I'm starting to think you might just be a professional dream-killer," I shot back, my heart racing as I battled the heat creeping into my cheeks.

"Dream-killer? Wow, that's harsh," he said, feigning hurt. "I prefer to think of myself as a reality check. After all, someone has to tell you that finger painting is not going to change the world."

"Oh, please. And your 'grounded' views on life have been so transformative, haven't they?" I tossed back, feeling my pulse quicken as we fell into our familiar rhythm. The playful banter was a dance that always left me breathless.

Just then, a shrill sound pierced the air—a whistle that sliced through our exchange. We turned to see a man with a booming voice announcing the start of a pie-eating contest at the center of the fair. "Ladies and gentlemen! Gather 'round for the most delicious showdown you'll ever witness!" he bellowed, waving his arms animatedly.

"Think you could handle it? I mean, I know you're a pro at inhaling sweets," Jordan teased, nudging me with his elbow.

"Ha! As if you'd stand a chance against me," I replied, a spark of competitive spirit igniting within me. "I could take you down any day of the week, especially with a pie."

"Is that a challenge? Because I'm game," he said, his eyes narrowing playfully.

"Let's make it interesting," I suggested, a mischievous grin spreading across my face. "Loser has to publicly announce their greatest fear in front of the crowd."

"Okay, you're on," he said, excitement dancing in his voice. We joined the throng of people gathering around the contest area, the atmosphere buzzing with energy.

As we took our seats at the long table, a wave of nervousness washed over me. I stole a glance at Jordan, who wore a confident smirk. "You know," I said, trying to lighten the mood, "this is definitely a new low for me. Competing in a pie-eating contest in the name of proving a point."

"Hey, sometimes you have to dive into the absurd to find the truth," he said, winking at me. "Or at least some good pie."

The whistle blew, and the contest began. I dove into the pie with fervor, my competitive nature taking over as I shoved mouthfuls of blueberry goodness down my throat. Laughter erupted around us, and I could hear Jordan's playful taunts mixed with cheers from the crowd.

But as I glanced sideways, I realized something was off. Jordan's focus had shifted from the pie to the crowd, a frown replacing his earlier levity. I followed his gaze and spotted a group of unfamiliar faces at the edge of the gathering, their expressions unreadable, almost sinister. Something in their posture—the way they moved through the crowd—sent a chill racing down my spine.

"Jordan," I said, my voice barely above a whisper as I caught his attention again. "What's wrong?"

"Nothing," he replied quickly, but the tension in his jaw told a different story. "Focus on the pie."

"Easy for you to say," I said, but I couldn't shake the feeling that we were being watched. The laughter of the crowd began to fade into the background as my mind raced with possibilities.

The contest dragged on, and I forced myself to concentrate, yet my instinct nagged at me. Just as I swallowed the last bite, I noticed the group advancing, their eyes trained on us like a hawk tracking its prey. The whistle blew, signaling the end of the contest, and the crowd erupted in applause, but I barely registered it.

"Jordan," I said again, more insistently this time, but he was already standing, scanning the crowd.

"I see them," he muttered, his demeanor shifting from playful to serious. "Stay close to me."

"What's going on?" I asked, my heart pounding, adrenaline coursing through my veins as I followed him away from the table.

"Just—" he started, but before he could finish, the crowd erupted into chaos.

A loud crash echoed through the fairgrounds, and the familiar scent of burnt sugar and popcorn turned acrid as a firework misfired overhead, sending sparks raining down. People screamed and scattered, and I grabbed Jordan's arm, feeling the tension radiating off him.

"Run!" he shouted, pulling me through the throng of panicked bodies. I stumbled after him, my pulse racing in sync with the chaos that surrounded us, adrenaline sharpening my senses.

As we darted behind a nearby stall, I turned to him, my breath coming in short gasps. "What's happening? Who were those people?"

He opened his mouth to reply, but the words were drowned out by a loud bang that reverberated through the air, closer now. The crowd's screams grew louder, and panic surged around us, a tidal wave of fear that threatened to pull us under.

"Jordan!" I yelled, my voice straining against the noise. "What do we do?"

But just as he was about to respond, the group of strangers broke through the crowd, their eyes wild with intent. In that moment, I realized the truth—they were not just spectators; they were hunters. And we were their prey.

Chapter 3: Shadows of the Past

The air was thick with unspoken words as I stood in the fading light of the late afternoon. Shadows elongated across the room, creeping towards me like the very memories I tried to keep at bay. The sun filtered through the dusty blinds, casting stripes on the floor that seemed to mimic the lines in my life, divided by the past I could never fully escape. Jordan leaned against the wall, arms crossed, his dark hair tousled in that effortlessly handsome way that made my heart race and my thoughts scatter like leaves in a windstorm. I could sense the weight of his gaze, steady and probing, as if he were trying to decipher a code embedded deep within me.

"You can't keep hiding, you know," he said, his voice low, yet it cut through the silence like a knife. "What happened to your family? You don't have to carry that alone." There was a softness in his tone that belied the strength I usually saw in him, a quality I had not expected to find beneath the bravado.

Anger flared within me, a familiar defense mechanism. How dare he? I opened my mouth, ready to launch into a defense of my solitude, to explain how easy it was for someone like him—privileged, polished—to offer platitudes about connection and vulnerability when he'd never had to worry about where his next meal would come from or how to navigate a family fractured by secrets. But as I looked into his eyes, something shifted. It was the flicker of understanding, a glimpse into the chasm of pain he carried.

"My parents..." I hesitated, the words feeling like lead in my mouth. "They're gone. Divorced, I mean. My father disappeared into his own world, chasing a dream that left us all behind, and my mother? She's... she's still here, but she's not really present." The confession slipped out, raw and unrefined, but liberating in its honesty.

Jordan shifted, his posture softening. "That sounds... really tough. I get it more than you might think. My family, they expect a lot. You could say we're like a parade of achievements, and I'm just one of the floats—sometimes shiny, but mostly just following the routine."

I blinked, taken aback by his openness. I'd always seen him as the confident son of a powerful family, used to getting what he wanted with a mere flick of his wrist. The idea of him feeling trapped beneath the weight of expectations made my heart ache. "I thought your life was... perfect," I said, my voice barely a whisper.

"Perfect? Hardly. It's just polished," he replied, a hint of a wry smile tugging at the corner of his lips. "My father wants me to take over the family business. He doesn't care what I want, just that I fit the mold. Sometimes I wonder if he even sees me at all."

In that moment, I felt an invisible thread connecting us—a shared sense of isolation that was both terrifying and comforting. The world outside faded away, and it felt as if we were the only two people left on the planet. "So, what do you want?" I asked, the question slipping from my lips before I could reconsider.

He straightened, the weight of my question sinking in. "Honestly? I want to write," he confessed, the light in his eyes brightening with passion. "I want to tell stories, create worlds where people can escape. But that's not what my family wants to hear. They want a business mogul, not a novelist."

"Wow, that's... unexpected," I admitted, my admiration for him deepening. Here was a man who, beneath the surface, had dreams as fragile as my own.

We stood in silence for a moment, allowing the revelation to settle like dust in the sunlight. The tension between us crackled with a newfound energy, something more profound than mere attraction—a connection forged from vulnerability and honesty.

But just as quickly, a wave of apprehension washed over me, pulling me back into reality. "It's complicated for us, isn't it?" I said, my brow furrowing as I remembered our starkly different worlds. "Your family would never accept someone like me."

"Someone like you?" Jordan's voice was sharp, a challenge hanging in the air. "What does that even mean? Just because you come from a different background? You're smart, passionate, and you've survived more than most. That's something to admire, not dismiss."

His words stung, but in a way that felt good. "You don't understand," I said, crossing my arms defensively. "The difference between us isn't just the money. It's the expectations, the legacy. You're expected to succeed, to follow a path laid out for you, while I'm just trying to carve out a space where I can breathe."

Jordan took a step closer, the air thickening with an unspoken challenge. "Then let's carve out that space together," he urged, his voice low and insistent. "Why not? Why let the past dictate our future?"

The sincerity in his eyes sparked a fierce desire within me, the wish to leap into the unknown. But doubt crept in like a fog, obscuring the path ahead. What if our connection was only an illusion, a fleeting moment in the vast expanse of our realities?

Before I could respond, the distant sound of laughter echoed down the hall, pulling me back into the present. The world outside this room buzzed with life, and I could almost feel the weight of expectations pressing down on my shoulders, suffocating me. "I need to think," I said, my voice trembling with the uncertainty of what lay ahead.

"Take your time," he replied, but his eyes remained locked on mine, an unyielding anchor in the storm of my emotions. I turned away, the lingering warmth of his gaze sending a shiver down my spine. The shadows of the past were shifting, closing in on me, but in that moment, I felt something stir within—a glimmer of hope that perhaps, just perhaps, the future was still unwritten, waiting for us to take the first steps into the light.

The next few days blurred into a whirlwind of half-hearted smiles and forced laughter. I threw myself into my work, trying to drown out the echoes of that conversation with Jordan, yet the memory lingered like a haunting refrain. Every time I caught a glimpse of him across the office, a pang of longing shot through me, sharp and unwelcome. It was as if he had pried open a door I thought was locked, revealing a world of possibilities I had not dared to imagine. I had always been the cautious one, tiptoeing around the edges of relationships like a cat avoiding water, yet Jordan's presence stirred something in me that felt dangerously exhilarating.

One evening, while I organized files in the small, cluttered break room, I was jolted from my thoughts by a loud crash. My head whipped around to find Jordan sprawled on the floor, a stack of paperwork cascading around him like confetti. He looked up at me, sheepish, his cheeks flushed with embarrassment. "I was going for a dramatic entrance, but clearly, I need to work on my timing," he quipped, a grin breaking through his faux-seriousness.

"Or maybe you should stick to the written word," I replied, unable to suppress a smile. There was a lightness to his presence that I found irresistible. He scrambled to gather the scattered pages, and I joined him, our fingers brushing as we reached for the same document. I felt a spark—electric, undeniable.

"Just trying to save you from drowning in bureaucracy," he said, feigning earnestness as he straightened up, a few papers still crumpled in his hands. "What's worse than drowning? Being buried in a mountain of paperwork. It's like quicksand, only less dramatic."

"Less dramatic? I think I saw a minor meltdown on your part back there." I gestured toward the remnants of his messy entrance.

"You might want to rethink your approach. Maybe a bow next time?"

His laughter filled the small room, brightening the dull surroundings. "A bow? I don't know; I'd need a full costume for that. Perhaps I could rent a cape." He struck a mock pose, arms outstretched as if preparing to take flight.

I laughed, the sound surprising even me. "Just don't trip again. We're not equipped for workplace injuries."

His eyes sparkled with mischief. "You'd make a great supervisor—bossy yet charming."

"Bossy? I prefer 'assertively guiding.'" I shot back, my heart racing at the playful banter, the tension between us charging the air with unspoken possibilities. "But really, you should be more careful. We don't want to scare the office supplies."

He moved closer, the warmth of his presence wrapping around me like a cozy blanket. "Let's be honest; the office supplies aren't going anywhere. They're too busy being dull. But you? You bring a little spark to the day."

The compliment lingered in the air, a subtle invitation that made me question what lay beneath his words. Was this flirting? Did he feel the same pull I did? But as quickly as the thought crossed my mind, I shoved it aside, reminding myself of the walls that divided us.

As the workweek progressed, I found myself looking forward to our encounters. We settled into a routine of banter, little moments that felt stolen from a world where nothing else mattered. Lunch breaks turned into laughter-filled escapades, and brief exchanges became the highlight of my day. But beneath the surface, the specter of my family's history loomed like a storm cloud, threatening to overshadow the light he brought into my life.

One Friday evening, as we wrapped up the week, Jordan suggested we grab dinner. "Let's ditch the takeout and actually enjoy a meal," he proposed, a playful glint in his eyes. "I know a little place with the best pasta in town."

"Pasta? Now you're talking my language." I could hardly contain my enthusiasm, but then reality set in. "Wait—what if someone sees us?" The words slipped out before I could think. I hated myself for sounding paranoid, but the implications of being seen together sent a wave of panic through me.

Jordan shrugged, his expression unfazed. "Let them see. What's the worst that could happen? We'll just be two people having dinner. Besides, who cares what they think?"

"But your family..." I began, but he cut me off.

"My family doesn't dictate my choices. And neither should yours. Let's not live in the shadows of their expectations. You deserve to enjoy yourself, and so do I."

His conviction tugged at my heart, but the knot of fear tightened. It was all too easy for him to dismiss the potential fallout. I had built my life around avoiding trouble, a delicate dance of keeping my head down and my past hidden. "I'm not sure..." I hesitated, but the glimmer of hope in his eyes made it difficult to say no.

"Meet me at seven?" he asked, leaning closer, the warmth of his breath brushing against my skin like a soft caress.

I felt my resolve wavering. "Fine. Seven it is. But if this goes horribly wrong, I'm holding you responsible."

His laughter echoed as he stepped back, a teasing light in his gaze. "Deal. But I promise, you won't regret it."

As I left the office that evening, my heart danced in my chest, a mix of exhilaration and trepidation. The prospect of a simple dinner held more weight than it should have. What would it mean if we crossed that line? What if his family's expectations came crashing down around us? Yet, the thought of spending time with him, away from the prying eyes of the office and the burdens of our pasts, ignited a fire within me that I couldn't ignore.

Later that night, I stood in front of the mirror, studying my reflection with a critical eye. I pulled on a navy blue dress that hugged my figure just right, the fabric soft and comforting against my skin. I fiddled with my hair, trying to tame the rebellious strands that always seemed to defy order. "You've got this," I whispered to myself, a weak but necessary affirmation.

The evening air was crisp as I made my way to the restaurant. The streetlights flickered to life, casting a warm glow that made the world seem a little more magical. When I entered the restaurant, the familiar scents of garlic and basil enveloped me, wrapping me in a comforting embrace.

Jordan was already there, his presence commanding yet inviting. He looked up as I approached, his eyes widening in surprise and admiration. "You look incredible," he said, his voice genuine and warm.

"Thanks," I replied, feeling a blush creep up my cheeks. "You clean up nicely yourself." He was dressed casually, yet somehow he managed to exude an effortless elegance that made my heart flutter.

We settled into a cozy corner table, the ambiance alive with laughter and the clinking of glasses. Conversation flowed easily, a rhythm that felt natural, as if we had known each other for far longer than we had. We shared stories, our dreams spilling into the space between us like the wine in our glasses.

"Can you believe some of our colleagues?" he asked, shaking his head with mock disbelief. "I overheard Tim trying to convince Susan that pineapple belongs on pizza."

I laughed, unable to contain my amusement. "A culinary travesty! How dare he tarnish such a sacred dish!"

Our playful banter continued, but beneath it simmered an unacknowledged tension, a current of desire threading through our words and glances. The intimacy of the moment drew me in, wrapping around me like a silk ribbon, binding us closer together.

Yet, as the evening wore on, shadows crept in once more. The laughter felt a little too loud, the clinking glasses a stark reminder of the world outside this bubble we had created. I could feel the weight of expectations pressing down on me, threatening to break the fragile connection we had built.

"Hey," Jordan said, his voice cutting through my thoughts. "You okay? You look a bit distant."

I forced a smile, but the tremor in my voice betrayed my unease. "Just thinking about… everything, I guess."

"Like what?" He leaned forward, genuine curiosity in his eyes, his earlier playfulness replaced by sincerity.

My heart raced, and I felt the familiar walls rising. "About how this is probably a bad idea. I mean, we both have so much to lose."

He reached across the table, his hand brushing against mine, and the warmth of his touch ignited a flicker of hope. "Maybe, but sometimes the best ideas are the ones that feel the riskiest."

His words hung in the air, and for a moment, time seemed to stand still. I wanted to believe him, to leap into this unknown with him by my side, but the past held me back like an anchor dragging me into the depths of despair.

"Let's not get ahead of ourselves," I replied, my voice barely a whisper. "What if this is just another dream, one that crashes and burns like all the others?"

Jordan's expression softened, and in that moment, I saw the depth of his understanding. "Then we'll build new dreams together. We'll figure it out."

His determination washed over me, soothing the tumult within. But as I looked into his eyes, I knew the battle within me was far from over. The shadows of my past whispered caution, but perhaps—just perhaps—this was the moment to break free and embrace whatever the future held.

The meal unfolded with an air of intimacy that felt both exhilarating and terrifying. As the night wore on, I found myself leaning in closer to Jordan, drawn not just to his words but to the palpable energy that crackled between us. Each shared laugh peeled away another layer of my reservations, leaving me feeling strangely liberated in a way I hadn't experienced in years.

"So, what's your favorite guilty pleasure?" Jordan asked, his eyes sparkling with mischief as he sipped his wine.

I couldn't help but chuckle, considering my options. "Hmm, that's a tough one. Maybe a tie between reality TV and cheesy romantic novels? There's nothing like a good love story to drown out reality."

He raised an eyebrow, a playful smirk forming on his lips. "Romantic novels? I would have pegged you for more of a classic literature type. You seem too sophisticated for the kind of escapism that comes from a love triangle involving a vampire."

"Oh please," I retorted, a grin breaking through my mock indignation. "Vampires have nothing on my high school drama. Besides, it's all about the escapism! Who doesn't want to dive into a world where love conquers all, preferably with some kind of supernatural twist?"

"Touché," he conceded, laughing. "But seriously, I think it's brilliant. Escaping reality is a necessary skill in this life."

The conversation flowed effortlessly, weaving through topics ranging from our favorite films to the absurdities of office politics, all the while, a deeper undercurrent simmered just beneath the surface. I caught myself stealing glances at his hands, resting casually on the table, and my heart raced at the thought of reaching out to him.

Just as I was about to lean in for another quip, the atmosphere shifted. The door swung open, and in walked a group of well-dressed patrons, laughter spilling into the intimate setting. They were boisterous and loud, their energy cutting through the warmth we had cultivated. One of them, a striking woman with platinum blonde hair and a tailored suit, caught Jordan's eye, her gaze lingering a beat too long before she approached our table.

"Jordan!" she exclaimed, her voice high and cheerful, tinged with a hint of familiarity. "What a surprise to see you here! And who's this?" She flashed a bright smile at me, the kind that could light up a room but also felt like an unwelcome spotlight.

"Just a friend," Jordan replied quickly, the shift in his demeanor subtle yet noticeable. I sensed an unease behind his casual facade, and my heart sank. Why did it feel like an introduction to a more complicated world?

The woman's eyes sparkled with curiosity, assessing me with an intensity that felt like an unwelcome invasion. "Oh, I see. You're not just here for the ambiance. You're keeping the great Jordan Hart company." Her tone dripped with implication, and I couldn't shake the feeling that I was being measured against an invisible standard.

"I'm actually just trying to enjoy a quiet dinner," he said, a hint of irritation breaking through his otherwise smooth demeanor.

"Right, right," she said, waving her hand dismissively. "I'm sure you are. Anyway, it's good to see you! We should catch up soon." With that, she flitted away, joining her friends who seemed oblivious to the momentary tension that had filled the air.

"Wow, what a whirlwind," I said, forcing a lightness into my tone as I tried to shake off the discomfort.

"Yeah, that was Claire," he said, exhaling sharply, his expression shifting back to one of guarded neutrality. "We used to date. Or at least, it was more of a 'see where it goes' situation."

The words felt heavy, settling between us like an unexpected stone in my stomach. "And that went well?" I asked, trying to keep my voice steady.

"It was a mess, honestly." He looked away, focusing on the flickering candle between us, and I could see the struggle etched in his features. "She thrives on chaos. The kind of chaos that I'm trying to avoid."

"Sounds like a smart move," I replied, though a flicker of jealousy sparked in the pit of my stomach. "Why was she looking at you like she'd just found the last slice of cake?"

He laughed, a short bark of humor that didn't quite reach his eyes. "She has a way of making everything seem like a competition. I'm just... not interested in that anymore."

"Good to know. I wouldn't want to be compared to a slice of cake," I joked, though the underlying tension left a bitter taste in my mouth.

As we resumed our meal, I couldn't shake the feeling that Claire's arrival had shifted the dynamic in the room, and with it, the course of our evening. Each time I met Jordan's gaze, I was met with a flicker of something raw—perhaps a vulnerability, or maybe it was simply the weight of his past pressing down on us both.

"Hey," he said suddenly, interrupting my spiraling thoughts. "You know, I'm really glad you agreed to come out tonight. I didn't know what to expect, but..."

"But?" I leaned forward, caught in the earnestness of his expression.

"But this feels good. It feels right." His voice dropped to a whisper, each word deliberate as if he were sharing a precious secret.

The gravity of his statement hung in the air, and for a moment, I could feel the world outside receding. It was just us, two souls trying to carve out a space amid the expectations of our families and the pressures of our lives. But the moment was fleeting, slipping away as the chaotic laughter from Claire's group rose again, spilling over into our bubble.

"I'm glad too," I said, my voice steady. But in the back of my mind, doubts clawed at me, shadows whispering that this connection could only lead to heartbreak.

Just then, my phone buzzed on the table, slicing through the atmosphere like a knife. I glanced down at the screen, and my heart dropped. The name staring back at me was my mother's, a name that had come to represent everything I had tried to distance myself from.

"Excuse me," I murmured, trying to keep my voice steady as I swiped to answer. "Mom?"

"Is that you?" Her voice was laced with urgency, a sharp contrast to the warm comfort of the restaurant. "I need to talk to you. It's about your father."

My stomach dropped as the implications of her words settled in. "What do you mean?" I pressed, my heart racing as panic began to seep in.

"Just meet me at home. It's... it's important," she said, her voice trembling.

I glanced at Jordan, whose brows had furrowed with concern. "I have to go," I said, my voice barely above a whisper, the connection we'd just begun to explore slipping through my fingers like grains of sand.

"Is everything okay?" he asked, standing as I rose, urgency tinging his tone.

"I don't know," I admitted, panic clawing at my throat. "I just—she said it's about my father."

Jordan reached for my hand, his grip warm and grounding, but the moment felt fragile, the reality of my family's chaos rushing back in. "Do you want me to come with you?" he asked, his expression fierce with concern.

I hesitated, torn between the comfort of his presence and the tumult awaiting me at home. "No, I need to do this alone," I said, though every instinct in me screamed that this was a mistake.

He nodded, and in that moment, I saw the flicker of hurt in his eyes. "Just... let me know what happens, okay?"

I forced a smile, but it felt hollow. "I will."

As I hurried out of the restaurant, the chill of the evening air hit me like a slap, grounding me in the gravity of my situation. I pushed through the doors, leaving behind the warmth of our connection, my heart racing not just with worry, but with the awareness that my past was about to collide with my present in ways I had tried to avoid.

As I drove through the familiar streets, my mind raced with questions. What had happened now? What could my mother possibly need to tell me that warranted such urgency?

Arriving at home, I dashed up the steps, the echoes of my childhood reverberating around me like ghosts. The door creaked open, revealing my mother's pale face, eyes wide with fear. "You're here," she breathed, relief washing over her features.

"What's going on?" I asked, my voice steadier than I felt.

"It's your father," she whispered, and the world around me faded, the shadows of the past looming large once more.

Chapter 4: A Dangerous Invitation

The gala was a world unto itself, a living, breathing entity that pulsed with the rhythm of jazz and the delicate clinking of crystal. I stood before the mirror, scrutinizing my reflection. The dress was a deep emerald green, fitted perfectly to my curves, with a sweeping skirt that made me feel like I could float rather than walk. My hair, usually a wild halo of curls, had been tamed into soft waves that cascaded down my shoulders, glimmering under the light like polished mahogany. I looked sophisticated, yet I felt like a masquerade mask—beautiful, yet hiding something beneath the surface.

As I stepped into the grand foyer of the Rowen estate, the air thick with perfume and anticipation, I was struck by the sheer opulence surrounding me. A massive chandelier hung overhead, its crystals sparkling like stars against the backdrop of an azure sky painted on the ceiling. The walls were adorned with portraits of stern ancestors, their eyes seeming to follow me as I moved through the throng of elegantly dressed guests.

"Lily! There you are!" A familiar voice broke through the chatter, and I turned to see Jordan striding toward me, his presence commanding yet oddly disarming. Tonight, he wore a tailored suit that accentuated his athletic build, and the playful glint in his eyes had softened the edges of my previous disdain. For a moment, I forgot the chasm between us—wealth and privilege on one side, scrappy independence on the other.

"Looking stunning, I must say," he said, his smile genuine, lighting up his handsome features. It was the first time I truly noticed how striking he was, and my stomach did a somersault as I forced myself to meet his gaze.

"Thanks," I replied, my voice steady despite the fluttering in my chest. "But I'm not sure this is my scene. All this... polish." I gestured vaguely at the crowd, the perfect hair, the perfect makeup, the perfect lives. "It feels a bit suffocating."

Jordan chuckled, a rich sound that resonated with warmth. "Welcome to my life. You get used to the suffocation—eventually, it becomes a part of you." He leaned closer, his voice dropping to a conspiratorial whisper. "But I must admit, you wear it better than most."

"Flattery will get you nowhere," I shot back, but there was no bite in my words. Instead, I felt an unexpected thrill course through me, a spark igniting in the depths of my being. Jordan was more than just a scion of privilege; he was a man who understood the weight of expectation, the pressure of perfection.

As the evening unfolded, I found myself swept away by the charm of the gala, the laughter and music creating an intoxicating atmosphere. We navigated through clusters of guests, where conversations danced around art, philanthropy, and the latest gossip that seemed to ricochet off the marble floors. Jordan introduced me to his family and friends, each interaction a delicate ballet of pleasantries and half-hearted compliments. Yet, with every introduction, I felt my defenses wavering, brick by brick.

In a quiet corner, we found refuge from the crowd. "You don't belong here, do you?" he mused, his voice low. I caught a glimpse of vulnerability behind his confident façade, and it struck a chord within me.

"What makes you say that?" I asked, crossing my arms defensively, though a smile danced on my lips.

"Because you're not pretending," he replied, his gaze piercing. "You're not wearing a mask. You're... real."

His words hung between us, weighty yet buoyant, and in that moment, the divide between our worlds seemed to narrow. The air thickened with unspoken possibilities, but before I could lean into the moment, the facade of the gala cracked.

"Jordan!" A shrill voice cut through the ambiance, and we turned to see a striking blonde, her expression a mixture of fury and concern. "Where have you been? You need to introduce me to the major donors before they leave!"

Jordan's posture stiffened, and he cast me a quick glance, a silent apology flitting across his features. "Right. Duty calls."

I nodded, swallowing the sudden wave of disappointment. "Go on. I'll be fine."

He hesitated, clearly torn, before stepping away, leaving me alone in the swirling crowd. The brief encounter with Jordan lingered like a sweet echo, and I could still feel the warmth of his presence as I wandered deeper into the gala, lost in the elegance and artifice.

But as I navigated through the sea of shimmering gowns and tailored suits, something shifted in the air—a tension that clawed at the back of my mind. The laughter began to sound strained, the conversations sharper. I caught snippets of whispered worries among the guests about missing individuals, strange occurrences in the area that felt too ominous to dismiss.

"Did you hear? Another one has gone missing," a woman whispered to her companion, her eyes darting around the room as if the shadows might leap out at her.

"Who knows what's really happening in this town," her friend replied, glancing uneasily at the exit. "It's like a dark cloud is hanging over us."

Unease snaked through me, the glamorous facade crumbling as I felt a chill seep into my bones. Was this merely an evening of high society, or were we all dancing on the edge of something much darker? The night's sparkle began to fade, replaced by an unsettling sense of foreboding.

As I stood in the midst of the grandeur, surrounded by laughter that felt increasingly hollow, I realized that the gala was merely the surface of a much deeper, more dangerous invitation. I wasn't just at a charity event; I was stepping into a tangled web of privilege, secrets, and threats lurking in the shadows, and I had unwittingly become a part of it. The real challenge would be deciphering what lay behind the glitz and glamour and determining where I truly belonged in this labyrinth of hidden dangers.

The music swelled, a jazzy tune swirling through the air, wrapping around me like a delicate shawl. I stepped further into the heart of the gala, my senses tingling as I absorbed the spectacle. Couples glided across the polished marble floor, their movements as synchronized as a well-rehearsed dance. The lights shimmered, casting soft glows on lavishly decorated tables laden with exquisite appetizers that looked almost too beautiful to eat. I caught a glimpse of an artfully arranged platter of hors d'oeuvres—tiny, vibrant morsels that promised a burst of flavor with each delicate bite.

"Are you going to stand there gawking all night, or are you going to help me save this gala from mediocrity?" Jordan's voice broke through my reverie, and I turned to see him approaching with a playful grin, a glass of sparkling water in hand. He leaned in, the heat of his proximity sending a rush of warmth through me. "Come on, I need someone who can actually converse about something other than hedge funds and country clubs."

I chuckled, the tension from earlier dissolving like sugar in tea. "What do you suggest? I could dazzle them with my knowledge of tie-dye techniques."

"Now that's a conversation starter," he replied, rolling his eyes dramatically. "But how about we discuss something a little more highbrow? I hear the key to small talk at these things is to nod appreciatively while dropping the names of obscure artists. Nothing says 'I belong here' like a reference to a long-dead painter that no one else remembers."

"Ah, yes! Vincent van Who's-He?" I shot back, and he laughed, the sound low and genuine.

With a swift motion, he took my hand, guiding me toward a group clustered near a gleaming sculpture. As we approached, I couldn't shake the feeling of being an outsider, a misplaced puzzle piece desperately trying to fit into this intricate, gilded picture. The conversations around me swirled with terminology that felt foreign and distant, yet there was something undeniably magnetic about being close to Jordan.

"Ladies and gentlemen," he announced dramatically, raising his glass, "allow me to introduce my intriguing companion, the master of the arts—Lily, who knows everything there is to know about the fine art of, uh... expressing herself."

I bit back a grin as I heard the collective chuckles and a few raised eyebrows.

"Right," I said, stepping into the spotlight with an exaggerated flourish. "If anyone needs a guide to the world of fabric dyes and sustainable living, I'm your girl."

Jordan shot me an amused glance, and I could see his relief at the light-hearted atmosphere I had created. As we mingled with the group, the conversation shifted to the latest charity initiatives, discussions of wealth and social responsibility, a tightrope act of moral obligation draped in silk and satin.

At one point, I found myself engaged in a debate with a woman who had the sharpness of a whip and an icy demeanor to match. "But philanthropy is just a way for the elite to showcase their wealth," she argued, her arms crossed defensively, as if waiting for me to misstep.

"Isn't that a bit cynical?" I countered, determined to hold my ground. "Not everyone who donates does it for the accolades. Some genuinely want to make a difference. They just happen to have the means to do so."

Jordan watched the exchange with a mixture of amusement and admiration, his earlier confidence morphing into something softer. I could tell he was impressed that I could hold my own in this arena.

The tension between the socialite and me crackled, and for the first time, I felt a surge of empowerment, reveling in the fact that I could challenge the status quo.

As the evening progressed, I found myself sharing more intimate details with Jordan amid the chaos, peeling away the layers of our personas. "So, what's it like being the golden boy of the Rowen family?" I asked, teasing yet genuinely curious.

He shrugged, a shadow passing over his features. "It's not all it's cracked up to be. Everyone expects you to be perfect, to have it all together. Sometimes, I wonder what it would be like to be someone else, to just exist without the weight of expectations."

"Yeah, but you could be a total rebel! Break free from the shackles of privilege and all that," I teased, trying to lighten the mood.

"Rebel?" he laughed, his eyes dancing with mischief. "Do you really think I could pull off the leather jacket-and-aviators look?"

"Absolutely! It would be a statement."

Our banter was easy, effortless, and for a brief moment, the world around us faded into the background. Then, a chill cut through the warmth of our conversation as I spotted a figure lurking near the entrance, their expression inscrutable as they surveyed the gala with unsettling intensity.

"Jordan," I whispered, leaning closer to him, "do you see that guy by the door? He's been watching us."

I turned to gauge his reaction, only to find his expression shifted from amusement to something resembling unease. "I... I think I know him."

My heart raced, curiosity mingling with concern. "Know him as in... friend or foe?"

"Neither, really. Just someone from the family's social circle. But he's not the type you want to engage with."

"Great," I muttered, scanning the room again. The man hadn't moved; he stood with a confidence that felt predatory, his eyes fixed on us with a chilling intensity that made my skin crawl. "So what's his story?"

Jordan hesitated, his brow furrowing. "He's connected to the business side of things—finance, investments... It's complicated. Just trust me; he's not someone you want to get involved with."

Before I could respond, the man took a step closer, his movements calculated, gliding through the crowd with an ease that was unnerving. My instincts kicked in, a primal urge to distance myself from whatever darkness he embodied.

"Hey, let's grab some fresh air," I suggested, my voice firm as I tugged Jordan along. He followed without protest, clearly sensing the shift in my mood.

We stepped onto the terrace, the cool night air brushing against my skin, soothing the rush of adrenaline coursing through my veins. The stars twinkled overhead, a canopy of distant lights, and for a moment, I felt as though we had escaped the confines of the gala, leaving behind the glittering traps that threatened to ensnare us.

Jordan leaned against the railing, the tension in his shoulders easing as he looked out over the garden. "You okay?" he asked, his voice softer now, concern lacing his words.

"I will be," I replied, though my mind raced with the implications of what I had just seen. "What's going on, Jordan? You said that guy wasn't a friend. Why does he feel like a threat?"

He sighed, running a hand through his hair, a gesture that seemed almost habitual, as if he were trying to wrestle away the gravity of our situation. "Let's just say he's not someone I want involved in my life... or yours."

A knot of anxiety formed in my stomach, a sense of foreboding settling heavily on my chest. "What does that mean for us, then? If he's connected to you... and me?"

His eyes searched mine, a flicker of something serious passing between us. "It means we need to be careful. This night was supposed to be about charity and fun, but sometimes, the most dangerous invitations come wrapped in glamour."

The words hung in the air, a stark reminder that beneath the veneer of luxury and laughter lurked shadows, ready to swallow us whole. I swallowed hard, realizing that I had been thrust into a world that was as intoxicating as it was perilous, and the dangerous invitation extended far beyond the edges of the gala.

The chill of the night air wrapped around us like a whisper of danger, a reminder that our escape from the gala's glittering chaos was temporary. I leaned against the railing, my heart still racing from the unspoken tension that had laced our conversation. The garden stretched out before us, a lush expanse of manicured hedges and blooming night-blooming jasmine, their sweet scent mingling with the crispness of the evening air. Yet, even amidst such beauty, a shadow loomed, darker than the velvet sky above.

"What do you think he wants?" I asked, my voice barely above a murmur. Jordan's expression tightened, the carefree demeanor from moments ago slipping away like sand through my fingers.

"I wish I knew. It's complicated," he replied, looking out into the dimly lit garden as if searching for answers among the shadows. "He's not just anyone. He's connected to some pretty influential people—people who might not take kindly to me stepping out of line."

"Stepping out of line?" I echoed, a mix of curiosity and concern brewing within me. "Is that what you call being yourself? Trying to break free from expectations?"

His gaze shifted to me, and I saw a flicker of something vulnerable—a mixture of frustration and longing. "It's more than that, Lily. The moment I decided to do my own thing, I put a target on my back. The Rowens have a reputation to uphold. If I fail, it's not just my reputation on the line; it's the family's legacy."

The weight of his words settled between us, heavy and palpable. My heart ached for him; he was caught in a web of obligation and expectation, shackled by the very life he seemed to resent. "But isn't there a way to have both? You can honor your family while still being true to yourself."

He smiled, but it didn't quite reach his eyes. "If only it were that simple. But for every dreamer, there's a hundred critics waiting to tear them down."

Before I could respond, the sound of laughter and clinking glasses floated through the open doors, pulling me back into the swirling reality of the gala. I glanced over my shoulder, momentarily distracted by the sight of the partygoers, lost in their own worlds of glitz and pretense.

"Let's go back inside," I suggested, wanting to keep the conversation from veering into darker territory. "I could use another glass of that overpriced sparkling water. Do you think they're still serving the shrimp that looked more like decoration than food?"

Jordan chuckled, a sound that was warming in the coolness surrounding us. "Only if you promise to pretend it's the best thing you've ever tasted."

"Deal," I grinned, pushing off the railing. As we made our way back toward the noise and laughter, I caught a glimpse of that figure again—the man lingering by the entrance, still watching, a predatory glint in his eye. I shivered involuntarily, and Jordan must have sensed my discomfort because he tightened his grip on my elbow, guiding me protectively through the crowd.

Back inside, the atmosphere buzzed with energy, a facade of joy that felt increasingly brittle. We weaved through the sea of guests, Jordan introducing me to a mix of individuals, each more polished and perfect than the last. Their conversations danced around superficial topics—newest fashion trends, vacation destinations, and the latest charitable initiatives. I played my part, smiling and nodding along, yet the looming presence of the man from the terrace gnawed at my mind.

Then, just as I began to relax again, a familiar voice cut through the noise. "Jordan! There you are!" It was Vanessa, an impeccably dressed socialite with a reputation for being both glamorous and cunning. She glided toward us like a swan on a pond, her gaze locking onto me with a scrutinizing glare that sent a shiver down my spine.

"Vanessa," Jordan said with a forced smile, "I was just—"

"Oh, don't worry. I know you're busy charming the peasants," she interrupted, her tone dripping with disdain as her eyes flickered dismissively over me. "But you really ought to be more careful with who you associate with. After all, first impressions are everything, and I can't help but wonder what this one says about you."

I bristled, ready to respond, but Jordan cut me off with a sharp look. "Lily is someone worth knowing, Vanessa. Perhaps if you took the time to look beyond your narrow view of the world, you'd see that."

A flicker of surprise crossed her features before she masked it with a practiced smile. "Well, I suppose everyone has their moments," she replied, her voice laced with condescension. "But darling, be careful not to get swept away. This world can be quite unforgiving."

I clenched my jaw, resisting the urge to throw back a snappy retort that would only fuel her superiority. Instead, I turned to Jordan, who seemed equally irked by Vanessa's intrusion. "You know," I said, the corners of my mouth curling into a playful smirk, "I was just thinking how much I'd love to see you take her on in a verbal sparring match."

He chuckled, the tension momentarily easing. "Trust me, you don't want to witness that. She plays dirty."

"Good thing I have my tie-dye techniques to fall back on," I replied, earning a genuine laugh from him that felt like a small victory.

But Vanessa wasn't done. "Well, Jordan, I must say, if you insist on cavorting with the help, don't forget to remind her of her place." With that, she turned on her heel and drifted away, leaving a cloud of discomfort hanging in the air.

"What a piece of work," I muttered, shaking my head in disbelief.

Jordan sighed, his expression a mixture of annoyance and resignation. "She thrives on this world's approval, and it's a game I refuse to play. But don't let her get to you. You're more than just a guest here; you're something different."

The sincerity in his voice sent warmth pooling in my chest, but the evening's disquiet hadn't vanished. I could feel the undercurrents shifting again, the darkness creeping back in as the figure I'd seen earlier reemerged from the shadows, his gaze unwavering.

"Jordan," I said, my voice urgent, "he's back. The man from before."

Jordan's expression hardened, and he glanced toward the entrance. "We need to move."

Before I could grasp the weight of his words, he led me through the crowd, navigating toward the exit with a determination that sent alarm bells ringing in my head. We pushed through the throngs of guests, weaving past laughter and chatter, Jordan's grip firm on my wrist as we stepped outside into the cool night air.

"Where are we going?" I asked, a hint of panic creeping into my voice.

"Somewhere safe," he replied tersely, scanning the area as if he expected danger to leap out from behind the nearest shrub. The elegance of the gala faded behind us, replaced by the suffocating urgency of the moment.

The distant sound of laughter faded as we moved further from the mansion, and a sudden noise startled us—a rustling in the bushes nearby. I froze, heart pounding, the instinctual fight-or-flight response kicking in.

Jordan stopped too, his body tense. "Stay close."

But the noise came again, louder this time, followed by the unmistakable crunch of footsteps. I spun around, adrenaline surging, only to catch sight of the figure emerging from the shadows, his presence looming like a storm cloud ready to unleash chaos.

"Jordan!" I whispered urgently, but it was too late. The man stepped forward, a smug smile spreading across his lips, eyes glinting with something sinister.

"Going somewhere?" he asked, his voice low and taunting, sending a jolt of fear spiraling through me. The danger I had sensed all night was now tangible, wrapping around us like a noose.

Jordan squared his shoulders, the bravado masking the tension that lay just beneath the surface. "What do you want?"

"Let's just say, I have an invitation of my own," the man replied, his smile widening into something predatory. The air thickened, and in that moment, as the shadows closed in around us, I realized that our evening of glamour had transformed into a deadly game. And I was suddenly desperate to survive the next move.

Chapter 5: Whispers of Danger

The gala was a whirlwind of elegance and chaos, a dazzling display of silk and sequins that hung in the air like perfume. As the last of the laughter and clinking glasses faded, I found myself back in my apartment, the faint echo of orchestral music still lingering in my mind. I was grateful for the quiet, yet it felt oppressive, as if the walls themselves were closing in on me, holding secrets I wasn't yet ready to face.

The next morning, sunlight spilled through my window, gilding the room in warm hues, but instead of comfort, I felt a chill creeping up my spine. It started with a text—just a simple notification that glowed on my phone screen. It read, "You can't escape your past. It's watching you."

The message sent a ripple of unease through me. Who would send something like that? The anonymity was unsettling, a stark contrast to the vibrant faces of the gala just hours before. I brushed it off as a prank, yet the flutter in my stomach lingered. As I moved through my morning routine, the words echoed in my mind, twisting like a serpent.

The doorbell rang, cutting through my thoughts. I opened the door to find Jordan standing there, his dark hair tousled, eyes sharp and intense. He had a knack for appearing when I least expected him. His shirt was slightly wrinkled, as if he'd rushed over, and the hint of an unshaven jaw added a certain ruggedness to his usual polished demeanor.

"Hey," he said, his voice gruff. "We need to talk."

I gestured him inside, the tension in my chest tightening further. The warmth of my living room felt suddenly constricting. "About what? The gala? Or the part where you nearly set my dress on fire?"

Jordan smirked, but it faded quickly as he sat down, running a hand through his hair. "I'm serious, Liz. I've been doing some digging."

"Digging?" I raised an eyebrow, feeling both amused and irritated. "Are we treasure hunting now?"

"No, not treasure," he shot back, his expression darkening. "I've been looking into those messages."

My heart raced. "You think they're connected to the gala? To me?"

He leaned forward, elbows resting on his knees, his gaze steady. "I think someone's trying to send you a message. And it's not a friendly one."

The air thickened with unspoken fears. I was used to Jordan's arrogance, his swagger, but now I could see a flicker of genuine concern in his eyes, a vulnerability that felt almost foreign. "What do you mean?"

"Just—let me show you." He reached into his bag and pulled out a folder filled with papers, clippings that looked suspiciously like a scrapbook of my life. I leaned closer, my pulse quickening as he laid them out. Newspaper articles, photographs, and the kind of grainy images that felt like ghosts from a time long gone.

"This is creepy, Jordan," I said, though I couldn't pull my gaze away. Each page felt like a thread pulling at a fabric I thought was stitched tight.

He tapped a photo of a younger me, standing beside a woman who bore a striking resemblance to me. "Your mother, right?"

"Yes," I replied, my voice barely above a whisper. "What about her?"

"Look at this." He flipped the page, revealing an article about a family feud, decades old, a tangled web of betrayals and scandals. The names jumped off the page, words swirling in a storm of confusion. I recognized the surname immediately; it belonged to the family that had been the talk of the town during my childhood, their riches shadowed by whispered secrets.

"What does this have to do with me?" I asked, my hands trembling.

"It seems like your family was right in the middle of it all. And now, someone wants you to remember."

The weight of his words hung heavy between us. I felt a chill, a creeping sensation that perhaps my past was not as distant as I'd believed. "Why now? After all these years?"

"Because someone wants to settle a score." Jordan's tone was grave. "And if they're sending you messages, it means they know you're vulnerable."

"Vulnerable?" I scoffed, but the truth was undeniable. There was an uncomfortable sense of exposure, a feeling that every corner of my life was being scrutinized.

Jordan's expression shifted. "Look, Liz. I know we've had our differences—more than our differences—but I want to help. We can figure this out together."

"Why would you want to help me?" I countered, suspicion lacing my words.

"Maybe because I don't think you deserve to be scared like this," he replied, his honesty catching me off guard. There was a sincerity in his voice that felt disarming.

I stared at him, the unlikeliest of allies. We had spent so much time bickering, each jab wrapped in a layer of competition and resentment. But now, here we were, two unlikely comrades facing a threat that loomed like a dark cloud overhead. The shift in our dynamic was palpable, the animosity giving way to a burgeoning trust—or at least, a cautious alliance.

"We need to dig deeper," I said, feeling a surge of determination. "If someone is watching me, we have to figure out who it is."

"Agreed," Jordan said, his eyes sparking with newfound resolve. "We'll start with the family feud. Someone out there knows more than they're letting on."

As we plotted our next move, a tension crackled between us, igniting a complicated chemistry that simmered just beneath the surface. It was strange, shifting from rivals to allies, the lines between us blurring in ways I couldn't yet comprehend. But I was drawn to him, not just as a partner in this unexpected investigation, but as someone who had, against all odds, become a beacon in my tangled world.

With the shadows of my past creeping ever closer, I couldn't help but wonder if this partnership would lead us to the truth—or if it would unravel everything I thought I knew.

As the days unfurled after our unsettling revelation, a shroud of unease wrapped around me, thick and suffocating. I couldn't shake the feeling of being watched. Each glance over my shoulder revealed nothing but the mundane: a neighbor walking their dog, a child riding a bike, the world continuing on in its blissful ignorance. But deep down, I knew that something was brewing beneath the surface, an undercurrent of tension that twisted my stomach into knots.

Jordan and I became an unexpected duo, a partnership forged in necessity rather than choice. We met at coffee shops, poring over articles and old news clippings, our fingers often brushing against each other as we exchanged documents. The air crackled with an energy that felt electric, yet I kept it buried beneath layers of practicality and skepticism. Each laugh we shared felt like a secret kept between us, an acknowledgement that, despite the turmoil, there was a spark igniting in the space where our animosity had once thrived.

One crisp Saturday morning, we decided to pay a visit to the local historical society. I had never bothered to explore it, assuming it was merely a dusty collection of artifacts that spoke of lives I didn't lead. But if there were answers to be found regarding my family's hidden past, this was the place to start. The brick building loomed ahead, its entrance adorned with intricate carvings that seemed to whisper secrets of the town's history.

Inside, the air smelled of aged paper and polished wood. An array of framed photographs lined the walls—sepia-toned images of long-forgotten faces and places. I felt a tingle of recognition when I spotted a portrait of my mother, young and radiant, the light capturing her smile like a cherished memory.

"Is that your mom?" Jordan asked, his voice low and reverent.

I nodded, swallowing hard against the swell of emotion. "She was... she was different back then. So full of life."

"Yeah, she looks it." He lingered on the photo for a moment longer, then shook himself out of it. "We should find out more about this feud. It's gotta be in one of these old records."

We wandered through the musty aisles of the society's archives, the hush of the room amplifying the weight of our task. As we sifted through papers and documents, I could sense the tension between us deepening, like the brewing storm outside. With every new revelation about my family's past, I found myself grappling with a growing curiosity about Jordan. What made him tick? Why was he so invested in this when he had every reason to keep his distance?

"Here's something interesting," he said suddenly, breaking the silence, his voice laced with excitement. "This article mentions a charity event that went south between the Harringtons and the Lanes."

I moved closer, peering at the yellowed paper he held. The Harringtons—my family—and the Lanes, a name steeped in the whispers of my childhood. They were the rival family, the ones whose scandals seemed to intertwine with mine like weeds strangling a garden.

"It says here they were supposed to collaborate on a fundraiser, but it turned into a scandal. Allegations flew about mismanagement of funds and... well, it sounds like a classic family feud."

I crossed my arms, unease settling in my stomach. "Classic, sure, but why is this coming back now? I've been out of that world for years."

"Maybe someone isn't ready to let it go," he suggested, a glimmer of concern in his eyes.

Before I could respond, a loud crash echoed through the archives, followed by a flurry of startled voices. We both turned toward the sound, tension spiking as we rushed to investigate.

At the back of the room, a stack of books had toppled over, the librarian—a sweet, gray-haired woman named Marge—struggling to right them. "Oh, dear! These old shelves aren't what they used to be!" she exclaimed, her voice laced with amusement.

Jordan and I exchanged a glance, the moment of fear dissipating, though I couldn't shake the feeling that something else was at play.

"Can we help?" I offered, kneeling to pick up a few books.

"Bless your hearts! Thank you!" Marge said, her smile brightening the dim room. "You two must be here for the history, then?"

"Something like that," Jordan replied, his tone light, though I could sense the undercurrent of seriousness.

Marge's eyes sparkled with knowledge as she began recounting tales of the town's past, her voice weaving stories of rivalries, alliances, and bitter betrayals. Each word painted a vivid picture in my mind, but my focus drifted back to the precarious threads of my own life, now entwined with Jordan's.

As Marge spoke, I caught Jordan's gaze. There was a mix of intrigue and determination in his expression, a silent promise that we would unravel this mystery together. The laughter of children echoed from outside, a reminder of innocence lost in the shadow of my family's legacy.

Hours passed, and with each scrap of information we unearthed, the history felt more and more like a personal burden. Just as I was starting to feel overwhelmed, Jordan leaned closer, whispering conspiratorially, "You know, I never pictured you as the kind to dig up skeletons in the family closet. I mean, you're a lot more... adventurous than I gave you credit for."

I laughed, a genuine burst that startled even me. "Adventurous? More like desperate. It's not every day you get cryptic messages about your life, especially after avoiding it for so long."

"Still," he pressed, a hint of admiration in his tone. "You're handling this better than I would. I'd probably be in a corner crying."

"Hey, I still might be. Just give me time."

As we worked side by side, I couldn't deny the growing sense of camaraderie between us. It was messy, complicated, and laced with a tension that simmered just beneath the surface. Each shared glance seemed to spark a new flame, igniting something that felt both exhilarating and terrifying.

The warmth of our connection deepened as the afternoon sun dipped lower in the sky, casting long shadows through the windows. With the fading light came the realization that we were no longer simply unraveling a family mystery; we were navigating a complex landscape of emotions, the lines of our former rivalry blurring into something that felt unexpectedly intimate.

Jordan's laughter became easier to elicit, and our banter flowed freely, each exchange a dance of wits that hinted at unspoken desires. I wondered, fleetingly, what it would mean if we stepped beyond the bounds of this partnership, this odd alliance built on shared secrets and fears. But for now, we had a mystery to solve, and the truth felt tantalizingly close, hovering just out of reach like a mirage on the horizon.

The following days transformed my life into a whirlwind of late nights and frantic research sessions with Jordan. The air between us pulsed with a blend of curiosity and burgeoning camaraderie, each moment spent together revealing another layer of our personalities. I found myself laughing at his dry humor more often than I cared to admit, our banter a necessary distraction from the looming threat of those anonymous messages.

It was a chilly Wednesday evening when we decided to dive deeper into the labyrinth of my family's past. We met at a dimly lit café that was as much a part of the town's charm as its cobblestone streets. The scent of freshly brewed coffee mingled with the sound of rain tapping against the windows, creating a cozy backdrop that belied the tension swirling around us.

"Okay, Sherlock," I said, sliding a steaming mug across the table toward him. "What's the plan? Are we pulling out our magnifying glasses next?"

He smirked, taking a sip of his coffee. "If only it were that simple. But I think we need to focus on the people involved in this feud. The more we know, the less likely we are to get blindsided."

I leaned in, intrigued. "So, what's our first step?"

"Let's track down some of the old family members. I'm betting they've got stories to tell," he suggested, his eyes sparkling with excitement. "Besides, what better way to annoy the enemy than to have a little chat about family drama?"

I couldn't help but chuckle at his enthusiasm. "All right, then. Let's dig up the dirt."

The next few days morphed into a flurry of activity, with Jordan and I reaching out to various contacts, piecing together a network of the past. With every conversation, the details of my family's history unfurled like the petals of a flower. I learned of the scandals, the secrets, and the deep-rooted grudges that had festered through generations.

One evening, as we sat huddled in my apartment, pouring over a stack of notes, I felt the tension between us shift once more. The air crackled, and I noticed the way his fingers brushed against mine as he reached for a file. It sent an unexpected jolt of electricity through me, forcing me to pull my hand away.

"Focus, Liz," I muttered, shaking my head to clear the thoughts clouding my mind. "We're not here to develop feelings."

"Yeah, because that would just be too convenient, wouldn't it?" he shot back, his tone teasing yet serious. "But seriously, can we talk about how we're starting to make a pretty good team here?"

I couldn't suppress a smile. "As long as we don't let it go to our heads."

Our laughter broke the tension, but underneath it lay a simmering intensity that neither of us acknowledged.

The following week, we arranged to meet an elderly woman named Agnes Lane, a distant relative of the rival family, who had a reputation for being both forthright and feisty. As we approached her quaint cottage, nestled in a garden bursting with autumn blooms, I felt a flutter of nerves. What if she had answers that I wasn't ready to hear?

Agnes greeted us with a sharp gaze that seemed to pierce through my facade. "You two must be the intrepid sleuths everyone's talking about," she quipped, ushering us inside. The walls were adorned with family portraits, their eyes watching like silent guardians.

"Something like that," Jordan replied, taking a seat. "We're hoping you can shed some light on the past. The Harringtons and the Lanes... there's a lot of history there."

Agnes's expression shifted, a glimmer of something akin to bitterness crossing her features. "History? More like a tragic play. But if you want the truth, I suppose it's better coming from me than the gossipmongers."

I leaned forward, captivated. "What can you tell us?"

"Everything started with a betrayal—a young love that went awry," she began, her voice heavy with emotion. "Your mother, dear, was quite the firecracker. She and my brother were in love, but he was drawn into a web of lies by our family's rivals. They twisted the truth, and before long, that love turned into something dark and dangerous."

Jordan and I exchanged glances, the pieces of the puzzle beginning to fit together. "What kind of lies?" I pressed.

"The kind that leads to resentments lasting generations. It was said that your family tried to push him away to protect their reputation, but the Lanes... we don't forget."

As she spoke, I felt the weight of the past pressing down on me, suffocating and real. "And what happened to them?"

Agnes's gaze turned distant, filled with sorrow. "Love was lost, and so was trust. After that, there was a fallout, a split so deep that it carved a chasm between our families. Since then, we've only survived on whispers and shadows."

The atmosphere thickened, the history swirling around us like a tempest. "But why is this happening now?" I asked, urgency creeping into my voice. "Why are these messages targeting me?"

Agnes leaned back, her brow furrowed. "Someone wants to reignite the old flames of hatred. You're not just a target; you're a symbol, a connection to the past that someone wants to use for their own gain."

A chill raced through me, and I could see Jordan's jaw tighten beside me. "Who would do something like that?"

"People who thrive on chaos," she replied cryptically. "The ghosts of our families haven't been laid to rest. They're still fighting, and it seems they've chosen you to carry their burdens."

As we left Agnes's cottage, the autumn air felt heavy with unspoken truths. I turned to Jordan, my heart racing. "What if we're in over our heads? What if this feud is far more dangerous than we thought?"

He placed a reassuring hand on my shoulder, grounding me. "We'll figure it out, Liz. Together. No one's going to drag you into this alone."

But deep down, I couldn't shake the feeling that our investigation was leading us straight into the heart of a storm. Just as I began to find solace in Jordan's words, my phone buzzed violently in my pocket, jolting me out of my thoughts.

I pulled it out, and my heart sank as I read the latest message: "You're not safe. They're watching you."

Panic rose in my throat, a rush of adrenaline as I looked at Jordan, his expression mirroring my own fear. "We need to go. Now."

We turned to leave, the urgency in my steps echoing the turmoil swirling inside me. As we reached the car, a figure stepped out of the shadows, blocking our path. The dim light revealed a familiar face—someone I had never expected to see.

"Going somewhere?" they asked, a wicked smile curling their lips, the darkness of the evening wrapping around them like a cloak.

In that moment, the reality of my situation slammed into me with unrelenting force. We were standing on the precipice of something far more dangerous than a mere family feud. The very shadows of my past had come alive, and they were ready to claim their next victim.

Chapter 6: Betrayal and Revelation

The storm rattled the windows of my apartment, each crack of thunder shaking the very foundation of my thoughts. Rain lashed against the glass like a desperate lover pleading for entry, but I was too preoccupied with the chaos swirling within. My heart raced as I and Jordan sat across from each other at my cluttered kitchen table, a haphazard array of printed emails and scattered photographs strewn about like pieces of a jigsaw puzzle that stubbornly refused to fit together.

Jordan leaned forward, the low light from the lamp casting shadows across his chiseled features. His brow furrowed in concentration, the slight curl of his lips suggesting a mix of frustration and determination. "Look," he said, his voice a low rumble that almost got lost in the symphony of the storm outside. "If we can connect these dots, we might just uncover who's behind this."

I nodded, my pulse thrumming in my ears, but I couldn't shake the nagging feeling that we were being watched. It was as if the walls themselves were eavesdropping on our every word, holding secrets that could drown us in their depths. I glanced at the photographs again, particularly one of me as a child, grinning widely in a sun-soaked park, blissfully unaware of the shadows that would loom over my life in the years to come. "These emails, they all mention someone named Claire," I mused, rubbing my temples as I felt the weight of uncertainty settle in.

"Claire? Your sister?" Jordan asked, tilting his head slightly as if gauging my reaction. There was an intensity in his gaze that both intrigued and unnerved me.

"She's my half-sister," I replied, the words spilling out before I could filter them. "I haven't spoken to her in years. After the accident... well, things changed. Our family was never the same."

Jordan shifted in his seat, his expression softening. "You've been through a lot."

I couldn't allow his sympathy to draw me in. It felt too much like a trap, a siren's song promising safety while hiding jagged rocks beneath the surface. "We all have our stories," I said, attempting to keep my tone casual, but it came out sharper than I intended.

He frowned but didn't press further. Instead, we fell into a heavy silence, the kind that enveloped us like a thick fog, both suffocating and oddly comforting. I couldn't help but steal glances at him—his dark hair falling effortlessly over his forehead, the way his lips quirked when he focused. There was a fierce vulnerability about him, something I felt drawn to yet instinctively cautious of. It was maddening.

Just as I was about to speak, the power flickered, and the room was swallowed by darkness. I instinctively reached for the flashlight I kept in the drawer. The beam cut through the gloom, illuminating our scattered evidence like a spotlight on a stage. The storm roared outside, as if mirroring the tempest within me.

"That's not good," Jordan said, a hint of amusement in his voice despite the circumstances.

I chuckled nervously, my heart racing as I flicked the flashlight off and on, momentarily banishing the shadows. "At least we're not without light," I replied, but the tension was thick enough to slice through.

With a deep breath, I returned to the photographs, staring at the faces of people I once knew. There was a time when laughter had filled those frames—before betrayal had woven itself into the fabric of my life. "What if Claire's involved in this? What if she's the one behind the threats?"

Jordan's gaze darkened, a flicker of something that felt dangerously close to protectiveness flaring in his eyes. "Then we need to find her and figure out what she knows."

"Easy for you to say," I shot back, the words sharper than I intended. "You don't know what it's like to have your own family turn on you."

"I might surprise you," he said, the lightness of his tone dissipating. "Trust me, I've had my share of familial chaos."

I opened my mouth to argue, but before I could form the words, the door creaked, and we both froze, the hairs on the back of my neck prickling in warning.

"Is someone there?" I whispered, the dread pooling in my stomach like a heavy stone.

There was no answer, only the persistent growl of thunder. I felt Jordan shift, a protective instinct radiating from him as he moved closer, his body warm against the cold air that crept in through the gaps in the window. "Stay here," he said softly, his voice a calm amidst the storm's fury.

I nodded, my heart pounding as he crept toward the door. I held my breath, every instinct screaming that something was terribly wrong.

The door swung open with a slow creak, revealing an unexpected figure standing in the dim hallway—Claire, her silhouette backlit by the flickering light of the storm. My heart lurched at the sight of her, a tangled knot of confusion and anger spiraling within me.

"Claire?" I breathed, hardly able to believe it. "What are you doing here?"

"Nice to see you too, sister," she replied, her voice dripping with sarcasm, though her eyes darted nervously around the room. "You really need to be more careful about who you invite into your home."

The tension in the room thickened, and in that moment, the pieces began to click into place like the closing of a trap. Jordan's eyes met mine, filled with a mix of uncertainty and alarm. The night had turned colder, the storm outside echoing the turmoil within as we stood at the precipice of a revelation that could change everything.

The air crackled with tension as Claire stepped into my apartment, her presence igniting a tempest of emotions that swirled within me like the storm outside. The storm's howling winds seemed to echo my own internal chaos. Her face, framed by damp strands of hair clinging to her forehead, was a mixture of defiance and vulnerability. I hadn't seen her in years, and the sight of her stirred memories I had long buried beneath layers of resentment and hurt.

"Nice to see you too, sister," Claire said, crossing her arms, her voice heavy with sarcasm. "I didn't realize you were holding a family reunion."

Jordan shifted beside me, a quiet observer to our familial drama, his tension palpable as he silently gauged the situation. "This isn't the best time for a visit," he said cautiously, his protective instincts kicking in. "We're in the middle of something."

"Really? I wouldn't want to interrupt your little game of detective," Claire shot back, her eyes narrowing as they darted between us. "What are you two trying to uncover, exactly? Maybe I can help."

I felt my stomach twist at her words. "Help? Or sabotage?"

"Excuse me?" She stepped closer, her expression morphing from defiance to genuine hurt. "I'm not here to play games. I came because I heard you might be in trouble."

"And you thought the best way to help was to barge in like this?" I retorted, frustration bubbling to the surface.

Her gaze flicked to Jordan, then back to me, the vulnerability in her eyes replaced by something sharper. "You don't understand. There are people looking for you, and they're not the type to just knock and ask nicely."

The room went silent as her words sank in. I exchanged a glance with Jordan, the implications of her statement crashing over us like the relentless rain outside. "What do you mean, 'people looking for me'?"

Claire hesitated, biting her lip as if weighing her next words. "I've heard whispers—things you wouldn't believe. Dangerous people are after you, and they might already be too close."

"I've been getting threats," I admitted, my heart racing at the thought of the menacing figures lurking in the shadows of my life. "But how do you know about this?"

"I have my sources," she replied, her tone defensive. "What matters is that we need to figure this out together. We're family, whether you like it or not."

"Family," I scoffed, unable to keep the bitterness from my voice. "You were never there when it counted. You left me to pick up the pieces after—"

"After Mom died," she interrupted, her voice rising. "You think I didn't suffer too? I had my own battles to fight."

The air between us was thick with unspoken words, and I could feel the weight of the past pressing down on both of us. I wanted to hate her for leaving, for abandoning me during my darkest moments, but seeing her now, standing before me drenched and defiant, stirred something within me—a flicker of compassion buried beneath layers of anger.

"Okay," I said, forcing my voice to steady. "Let's say I believe you. What do we do next?"

Jordan remained quiet, his presence a comforting anchor amidst the turmoil, but I could sense the tension radiating from him. It was as if he was calculating his next move, unsure of how much he could trust Claire or me.

Claire took a step closer, her voice dropping to a conspiratorial whisper. "We need to find out who's behind these threats. There's a name that keeps coming up—an old family friend who has ties to some unsavory characters. Someone who shouldn't be trusted."

"Who?" I pressed, the urgency of the situation tightening my chest.

"David Armitage," she said, the name rolling off her tongue like a curse. "He was close to Dad—too close, if you ask me. I've seen him lurking around town lately, and it makes my skin crawl."

"David?" I echoed, disbelief washing over me. I remembered him as a charming figure from my childhood, always bringing gifts and laughter to our doorstep. "You think he's behind this?"

"I don't just think it. I know it," she said, the fierceness in her gaze igniting something within me. "We need to confront him. Together."

Jordan's expression darkened at her suggestion, and he interjected, "This isn't just about confronting someone, Claire. It's dangerous. If he's involved with the people who've been threatening her—"

"I can take care of myself," I shot back, my frustration bubbling over. "You don't have to protect me, Jordan. This is my fight too."

Claire raised an eyebrow, a smirk playing on her lips. "Look at you, channeling your inner warrior. You've grown up, haven't you?"

I rolled my eyes, feeling a mixture of annoyance and pride. "Not exactly how I imagined my adulthood, but it'll have to do."

"Let's not get sidetracked with sibling rivalry," Jordan said, stepping between us as if to diffuse the simmering tension. "We need a plan. If David is the link, we should gather information first, see what we're dealing with."

Claire's demeanor shifted, the initial bravado waning as she considered his words. "Alright. We can do that. But we need to act fast."

As the storm raged outside, I felt the atmosphere in the room shift once more—this time towards an alliance of sorts, tentative yet charged with potential. "Fine," I said, a reluctant resolve settling in. "But I'm not letting you dictate this. I want to be part of this plan."

Jordan glanced at me, a mixture of concern and admiration in his eyes. "Deal. But we need to be careful. Trust is a fragile thing right now, and we can't afford to make mistakes."

"Don't worry, I'll be on my best behavior," Claire said, her tone lighter now, but I could see the shadows lurking behind her eyes.

As the storm continued its relentless assault outside, I realized we were at the cusp of something larger than ourselves. The past was colliding with the present, and the choices we made in the coming hours could lead to salvation—or disaster.

The storm howled outside, a furious companion to the chaos brewing inside my apartment. Claire leaned against the wall, arms crossed tightly, a posture that screamed defiance while simultaneously betraying her unease. The tension was palpable, like the electric charge just before a lightning strike, and I couldn't shake the feeling that we were on the edge of something monumental—though whether it was salvation or catastrophe remained to be seen.

"I still can't believe you're here," I said, attempting to pierce the thick air with a hint of levity. "Last I checked, we were more likely to swap awkward family dinners than face danger together."

"Family dinners sound pretty good right now, considering the alternatives," Claire shot back, her eyes sparkling with an intensity that could rival the storm outside. "But let's focus on the task at hand—David. We need to confront him before this spirals out of control."

I glanced at Jordan, who was rubbing the back of his neck, clearly wrestling with his own thoughts. "I agree we need to do something," he said slowly, "but I still don't like the idea of going after him without a plan. We're already in deep, and I don't want to make things worse."

"Worse than what? Worse than the threats? Worse than your shady past? Because right now, I'm not sure how much lower we can go," Claire snapped, the sharpness in her tone cutting through my thoughts like a knife.

"Hey," I interjected, trying to maintain some semblance of peace. "Let's not turn on each other. We're in this together. Whatever history we have, we need to focus on what's right in front of us."

Claire's expression softened momentarily, and she nodded, though the tension in her shoulders remained. "Okay, then. Let's strategize. If David is involved, we need to find out what he knows and how he's connected to these threats. I can't shake the feeling that he's playing a bigger game."

Jordan leaned in closer, the glow of the flashlight catching the determination in his eyes. "I have an idea. We can set up a meeting. Get him somewhere neutral, where we can confront him without him feeling cornered. If we can catch him off guard, he might slip up and reveal something crucial."

"That sounds dangerous," Claire warned, her voice dropping. "He's not someone to take lightly. If he feels threatened, who knows how he'll react?"

"Exactly," I added, the gravity of the situation settling over me like a heavy blanket. "But what choice do we have? We can't just sit back and wait for him to come to us."

As the storm raged on, we crafted a plan that felt both reckless and exhilarating. We agreed to meet David at a small, out-of-the-way café that had always been a refuge for the weary, its ambiance cloaked in low lighting and soft music. It was a place where whispers lingered longer than laughter, where secrets could be shared with less fear of being overheard.

When the night arrived, I stood before the mirror, adjusting my hair and smoothing the fabric of my shirt. I wanted to present an image of calm confidence, but inside, my heart raced like the relentless wind outside. Claire and Jordan were at my side, both equally tense. Jordan shot me an encouraging glance, but I could see the worry etched on his face.

"Ready?" he asked, his voice steady, though I could sense the undercurrent of tension beneath it.

"Ready as I'll ever be," I replied, forcing a smile.

We made our way through the rain-soaked streets, the air thick with anticipation. Each step felt heavy, as if we were wading through the murky waters of uncertainty. The café glowed invitingly ahead, a beacon amidst the storm, yet it felt like the eye of a hurricane, calm but fraught with danger.

Once inside, we took a table at the back, the dim lighting offering a modicum of privacy. As we waited, I sipped on my coffee, the warmth spreading through me, though I couldn't shake the chill of anxiety creeping along my spine. Jordan and Claire exchanged quiet words, their expressions serious as they prepared for the encounter.

Minutes stretched into eternity before David finally arrived, a tall figure with an air of confidence that filled the room like an intoxicating perfume. He strode in, his sharp suit clinging to his frame, every movement exuding an arrogance that made my skin crawl. I felt my stomach drop as I recalled the way he used to charm our family, a smiling snake hiding its fangs.

"Fancy seeing you here," he greeted, his voice smooth like silk, a false warmth wrapping around his words. "Didn't think you'd be brave enough to meet me in person."

"Let's cut the pleasantries, David," I replied, my voice steadier than I felt. "We need to talk."

"Oh?" He leaned back in his chair, a smirk playing on his lips. "About what? The weather? Or perhaps the delightful threats you've been receiving? I do hope you're not scared."

Jordan shifted slightly, his presence a silent reminder that I wasn't alone in this confrontation. "We know you're behind the threats, David. We're not playing games here."

David's eyes gleamed with a mix of surprise and amusement, as if he had just received an unexpected gift. "Interesting theory," he replied, leaning forward slightly. "But theories can be dangerous, especially when they lack evidence."

A jolt of anger surged through me, but I fought to keep my composure. "We're not leaving until you tell us what you know. Who are you working with?"

His laughter echoed in the small space, drawing the attention of nearby tables. "So sure of yourself, aren't you? But do you really think you're in a position to make demands? You should be more concerned about what I might do to you if you keep poking around."

"Why are you doing this?" Claire interjected, her voice firm despite the uncertainty that hung in the air. "You were supposed to be on our side."

"Ah, sweet Claire," David said, feigning innocence. "I'm afraid you've misread my role in this little family drama. I've always been a spectator, not a participant."

Jordan leaned in, urgency creeping into his tone. "Enough of the games, David. This is serious. You're toying with something that's spiraled out of control. You need to tell us who you're involved with."

As the tension in the room escalated, I felt the walls closing in around us. David's demeanor shifted, the humor fading from his expression as he regarded us with a predatory gleam. "You really don't know, do you? You're already in over your heads. This isn't just a game of threats; it's a game of power."

The door swung open suddenly, the wind howling through the café, and I caught a glimpse of something outside—a shadow darting past the window, too fast to identify. My heart raced, adrenaline surging through me as I exchanged a frantic look with Jordan and Claire.

David's gaze flicked to the door, his lips curling into a knowing smile. "And it looks like your friends have come to play."

Before I could react, a loud crash echoed from the entrance, and the lights flickered ominously. The atmosphere turned electric, charged with an impending sense of doom.

In that moment, the precarious balance of the evening shattered, the danger we had been tiptoeing around suddenly tangible and close enough to touch. My heart pounded in my chest, and I felt the world tilt on its axis as the storm raged on outside, mirroring the chaos that was about to unfold inside the café.

Chapter 7: The Line of Fire

The city pulsed around me, a chaotic symphony of sirens and distant laughter threading through the air as I navigated the shadowy alleys that lurked behind Manhattan's glamorous façade. Neon lights flickered overhead, illuminating graffiti-splashed walls, each stroke of color telling stories of rebellion and despair. The scent of street food wafted past, mingling with the unmistakable tang of desperation that clung to this hidden world. My heart raced—not from fear, but from the intoxicating thrill of discovery, the kind that lured me deeper into the chaos that I had once only observed from a safe distance.

Jordan walked beside me, his presence a solid anchor amidst the uncertainty. He had transformed from a mere rival in the high-stakes game we were entangled in to a reluctant ally. Every glance we exchanged crackled with the weight of unspoken words and past grievances, a tension that electrified the air. I couldn't help but admire the way he moved through the underbelly of the city, his instincts sharp and unyielding, as though he belonged here among the shadows and whispers.

"Are you sure this is the right place?" I asked, my voice barely above a whisper, trying to mask the tremor of unease beneath my bravado. The dilapidated building before us sagged under the weight of its history, its cracked façade a testament to years of neglect. A flickering light from within suggested life, but not the kind that promised safety.

Jordan paused, his expression contemplative, the shadows casting angles across his chiseled features. "It's the only lead we have. If we want to uncover the truth, we have to dive in headfirst."

His words were resolute, yet beneath that confidence lay an undercurrent of concern, an acknowledgment of the danger we were stepping into. As we approached the entrance, I couldn't shake the feeling that we were walking into a trap, a meticulously laid snare designed to ensnare the unwary. The creaking door groaned as we pushed it open, revealing a dimly lit room filled with smoke and the muffled sound of laughter mingling with the clinking of glasses.

Inside, the atmosphere was thick with a sense of secrecy, the kind that wrapped around me like a fog, blurring the edges of reality. A few patrons lounged on worn leather sofas, their faces obscured by the haze. I recognized the look in their eyes—hardened, wary, the result of too many betrayals and too few lifelines. This was not my world, and yet, with Jordan by my side, I felt a flicker of courage igniting within me.

"Stay close," he murmured, brushing against my shoulder as he led me further into the room. His warmth seeped through my thin jacket, a silent promise that I wasn't alone in this chaotic dance. I found solace in his proximity, even as the atmosphere thickened with tension.

As we ventured deeper, our goal was clear: to find information about the unseen forces manipulating our lives, the ones who thrived on secrets and fear. My gaze darted around, searching for any hint of familiarity in this strange setting, but it was the laughter that caught my attention—high-pitched and unhinged, it echoed like a warning.

"Over there," Jordan pointed discreetly to a corner table where a group of three men leaned in, their whispers slicing through the din. One of them, a wiry figure with an unsettling grin, gestured wildly, his eyes darting around as if expecting someone to overhear.

"What's your plan?" I asked, my voice low but laced with urgency. The thought of confronting those who held the threads of our lives made my heart pound fiercely.

"Let's listen first," he replied, his intensity unwavering. "We need to know what we're up against."

As we moved closer, I could feel the heat of his body radiating against mine, a comfort amidst the uncertainty. I turned my head slightly, trying to catch snippets of their conversation while remaining inconspicuous. The tension in the air was palpable, wrapping around us like a living thing, and I could sense the danger simmering just beneath the surface.

"...they think they can play us for fools," the wiry man spat, leaning closer to his companions, his voice a sharp whisper. "But we hold the cards now. They won't know what hit them."

My stomach churned at the implications. Who were these people? What game were they playing? It felt as though I had stumbled upon a plot that ran deeper than I had ever imagined, a web woven with lies and manipulation that ensnared anyone foolish enough to cross their path.

Suddenly, Jordan stiffened beside me, his posture shifting into something more protective. I followed his gaze to the entrance where a figure loomed, tall and commanding, silhouetted against the neon glow of the street outside. The moment I caught sight of him, recognition sparked within me, igniting the fear I had hoped to keep at bay.

"Not him," I breathed, my heart racing. "We need to get out of here."

"Why?" Jordan's eyes narrowed, assessing the situation. "Do you know him?"

"Worse. He knows me."

Before I could elaborate, the figure stepped inside, and the smoky haze seemed to part around him, as if even the atmosphere feared his presence. As he surveyed the room, I felt the weight of his gaze land on me, a predatory gleam igniting in his eyes. Instinct kicked in, and I grabbed Jordan's wrist, tugging him toward the nearest exit.

"Now!" I urged, my pulse racing as the urge to flee overwhelmed me. The stakes had just risen higher, and with them came the urgency to uncover the truth before we became pawns in a game we never signed up for. With each hurried step, I could feel the barriers between Jordan and me dissolve further, not just through necessity, but through a burgeoning trust that whispered of deeper connections waiting to be explored.

In the heart of the chaos, where time felt suspended between heartbeats, our eyes locked for what felt like an eternity. The air crackled with electricity and the scent of smoke as the last of the skirmishers fell silent, their shadows retreating like wraiths into the depths of the night. The ground was littered with remnants of a struggle that felt both surreal and painfully real, as if the very earth beneath us had borne witness to the tumult of our hearts. In that instant, amidst the wreckage, I saw the man who had been my adversary, my ally, and now—though it felt reckless to admit it—something more.

His expression shifted, the steely determination that had always been present giving way to an unguarded vulnerability. "This isn't how I imagined our first date," he quipped, a wry smile ghosting across his lips, softening the sharp lines of tension etched into his features. I couldn't help but laugh, a sound that rang like music amidst the aftermath of battle, a melody of defiance and hope.

"Somehow, I think you owe me a proper dinner," I replied, my tone teasing but underpinned by a seriousness that echoed the sincerity of the moment. It was in the quiet between our words that I truly understood the depth of my feelings for him. We had danced around this truth long enough, letting fear and doubt dictate our steps. No more. The chaotic symphony of our surroundings paled in comparison to the urgent rhythm of my heart.

"Let's not get ahead of ourselves," he said, his voice low and serious, eyes scanning the periphery as if danger still lurked in the shadows. Yet, I caught a flicker of something—maybe a glimmer of shared understanding, or perhaps the dawning realization that we were not just survivors of this war but co-conspirators in our own saga. The tension of our pasts hung between us like a fragile thread, ready to snap at the slightest provocation. It was then, amidst the wreckage of our lives, that I felt a shift—an acknowledgment that love, like war, demanded courage, a willingness to confront the unknown.

Chapter 8: No Going Back

The horizon began to lighten, hinting at dawn's arrival, but my heart felt heavy with the weight of unsaid words and uncharted paths. "You know," I began, finding the courage to peel back layers of hurt and hope, "for a long time, I thought I'd be content keeping my heart locked away. I've built walls that even I couldn't breach."

His gaze softened, revealing the vulnerability beneath his hardened exterior. "And now?" he prompted, his voice a whisper that felt as intimate as a caress.

"And now," I continued, heart racing with the revelation, "I want to let you in, despite the risks." The admission hung between us, electrifying the air with its implications. I could see the flicker of surprise dance across his features, quickly replaced by a fierceness that ignited something deep within me.

"Risk is the price of admission," he replied, stepping closer, his presence a beacon amidst the uncertainty that threatened to engulf us. "But I need to know—are you truly ready for what that means? This isn't just about us anymore; it's about everything that brought us to this moment."

His words were a challenge, and I felt the weight of his gaze as it bore into my soul. "I am ready," I asserted, the conviction in my voice surprising even me. "I've faced worse than a broken heart." The truth of that statement resonated, echoing in the depths of my being.

As the first rays of sunlight broke over the horizon, illuminating the battlefield strewn with the remnants of our struggle, a sense of clarity washed over me. We were not defined by our pasts, but by our choices in this very moment. Together, we could forge a new path, a new narrative woven from the strands of our shared experiences and emerging feelings.

The atmosphere shifted, a palpable tension crackling in the air as we stepped into the light. "So, what now?" he asked, a mixture of hope and trepidation in his voice.

"Now we fight, but not just against the enemies that lurk in the shadows," I replied, resolve hardening within me. "We fight for each other, for our future."

His eyes gleamed with determination, and for the first time, I sensed an unwavering belief that we could face whatever came our way. "Together, then?" he asked, extending his hand—a simple gesture that felt monumental in its significance.

"Always," I affirmed, taking his hand, our fingers intertwining like vines seeking the sun. We stood united, ready to confront the trials that awaited us, not as individuals bound by the scars of our pasts, but as allies in a war of our own making.

As we moved forward, the first light of day cast a golden hue over the battlefield, illuminating not just the wreckage but also the promise of a new beginning. The road ahead would be fraught with challenges, but we faced it armed with love, resilience, and an unbreakable bond. It was in that moment of vulnerability and strength that I understood love was not merely a refuge from war, but the very reason to fight. And with that realization, I knew we would conquer whatever came next, together.

The world outside our bubble was still uncertain, but in this newfound alliance, we could weather any storm. And as the sun rose higher, bathing us in warmth, I felt the weight of my past lift, replaced by the exhilarating thrill of the journey ahead—unpredictable, messy, but undeniably ours.

As we stood there, our hands intertwined and our hearts racing from the adrenaline of battle, I felt an unspoken understanding settle between us. The air was thick with the remnants of conflict, but for the first time, the chaos seemed like a backdrop to our unfolding story rather than the center of it. "You know," he began, his voice a low murmur that seemed to wrap around us like a protective cloak, "if we survive this, I'm definitely taking you out for that dinner."

"Dinner? Please," I scoffed playfully, the tension in my shoulders easing slightly as I recalled the thrill of the fight. "After all this, we deserve a feast fit for kings. I'm thinking three courses, a bottle of wine, and a dessert that requires a fork and a spoon. No skimpy appetizers for us."

He chuckled, the sound rich and warm, breaking through the heavy weight of our circumstances. "Deal. But only if you promise to share that dessert. I refuse to let you take all the good stuff."

"Why? Afraid I'll eat your share?" I raised an eyebrow, a challenge simmering in my voice.

"Absolutely," he replied with a smirk, his eyes dancing with mischief. "You seem like the type who'd hoard all the chocolate mousse for yourself."

"Who can blame me? Chocolate is the only thing that has ever truly understood my struggles," I shot back, the playful banter acting as a salve to the rawness of our recent fight. The world around us began to fade, and for a fleeting moment, the past seemed manageable, as though our shared humor could carry us through anything.

Yet, as I glanced around at the debris of our battlefield—the scattered remnants of the life we'd fought to protect—a chill crept back in. "But in all seriousness, what if they come back? We can't let our guard down now."

His expression shifted, the laughter fading as reality crashed back in. "You're right. We have to regroup, figure out our next move. If they're still out there, we need to be ready."

"And this time, we should make it personal," I added, the fire in my belly igniting again. "I refuse to be a pawn in their game any longer."

He nodded, his resolve solidifying in the light of day. "Agreed. But we need intel, a plan. Let's see who else we can rally. If we're going to fight back, we'll need more than just us."

Our conversation steered into the logistics of what lay ahead, but underneath it all, a current of electricity flickered, sparking an awareness of the deeper connection we were forging. As we turned to leave the battlefield behind, I glanced back, a twinge of unease nagging at my conscience.

"We should check the perimeter before heading back," I suggested, eyeing the shadows that still danced at the edges of the clearing. The shadows were too quiet, too still, as if they were holding their breath, waiting for us to make a move.

"Right behind you," he replied, and together we ventured deeper into the wilderness of uncertainty.

The forest felt alive, each rustle of leaves and snap of twigs amplifying the tension coiling around us. "You think anyone else survived?" I asked, the weight of loss heavy in the air, echoing through the trees.

"I hope so. They need to know we're still fighting." He paused, his expression darkening. "We're stronger together."

"Or dead together," I quipped, but my heart wasn't in the jest. The specter of loss loomed large, threatening to overshadow the fragile bond we had begun to nurture.

As we pressed on, the dense foliage gave way to a small clearing. The ground was soft beneath our feet, and a strange silence settled, wrapping around us like a shroud. "This is odd," I whispered, glancing sideways at him. "It's too quiet."

"Maybe the universe is granting us a moment of peace?" he suggested, but even he sounded unconvinced.

A sudden rustle erupted from the thicket, and instinct kicked in. We both dropped into defensive stances, hearts pounding in sync.

The noise drew nearer, branches snapping and leaves crunching underfoot, and I held my breath, poised for whatever might emerge.

From the shadows, a figure broke free, stumbling into the clearing. My heart raced as I recognized the familiar face—one I had thought lost to the chaos. "Sam!" I gasped, disbelief washing over me. "You're alive!"

His disheveled appearance told a story of its own—dirt-streaked skin, torn clothing, eyes wide with panic. "They're coming! We don't have much time!"

"Who?" I demanded, stepping forward, adrenaline surging through my veins. "What do you mean?"

He hesitated, glancing back into the darkness as if the mere mention of the danger would summon it. "The enemy. They've regrouped. They're planning something... something big." His voice was hoarse, urgency dripping from every word. "We need to warn everyone. They're targeting us."

"Targeting us?" I echoed, incredulity mixing with the chill of dread that clawed at my insides. "What do you mean? Why us?"

"Because they know what we've discovered, what we're planning," Sam said, his eyes darting nervously. "You can't stay here; you have to get out. Now!"

The weight of his words settled like lead in my stomach. This wasn't just a fight for survival anymore—it was a battle against an unseen force determined to obliterate everything we stood for. "No, we can't just leave," I said, defiance igniting my voice. "We need to fight. We can't run anymore."

Sam's eyes widened, a mixture of fear and admiration swirling within them. "You don't understand. If you stay, you'll be walking into a trap."

"And what if it's a trap to keep us from fighting back?" I shot back, the resolve hardening in my chest. "We can't be cowed by fear any longer."

He took a deep breath, frustration evident in his expression. "Listen to me! This isn't just about you and him! There are lives at stake!"

Suddenly, a low rumble echoed from the direction of the trees, shaking the ground beneath us. I turned, my stomach dropping as the sound grew louder, more menacing. "What is that?" I asked, fear coursing through me.

From the shadows, a dark mass began to emerge—figures clad in armor, their faces obscured by menacing helmets, advancing with purpose. "Run!" I shouted instinctively, grabbing his arm and pulling him away from the advancing threat.

But as we turned to flee, the world exploded into chaos around us. The ground trembled beneath our feet, the enemy closing in, and in the split second before I lost sight of him, I felt the familiar warmth of his hand slip from mine.

"No!" I cried, panic surging through me as I reached back, desperate to grasp the connection we had forged in the fire of battle. But the shadows closed around him, and in an instant, he was swallowed whole.

My heart raced as I stood frozen, torn between the instinct to run and the urge to turn back. But before I could make a choice, a hand clamped down on my shoulder, yanking me backward into the safety of the underbrush. "We have to go!" Sam urged, pulling me away from the encroaching darkness, but the weight of the unknown loomed large behind us.

I stole one last glance over my shoulder, my breath catching in my throat as the shadows surged, and in that moment of despair, I knew the fight was far from over. With our future hanging in the balance, we plunged deeper into the forest, the echoes of the past and the shadows of the present merging into a singular, unrelenting force, and I couldn't shake the feeling that the worst was yet to come.

Chapter 9: The Crumbling Facade

The night air was thick with unspoken words, wrapping around us like a shroud as we stood in the dim light of my apartment. I could hear the soft hum of the city beyond the window—a chorus of life that seemed to mock the silence hanging between us. Jordan's gaze was locked on a point somewhere beyond my shoulder, his jaw set with a tension that felt almost palpable. I had thought that after our confession, a lightness would settle over us, but instead, the weight of uncharted territory pressed down like a heavy fog.

"What now?" I finally asked, my voice barely above a whisper, the fear of the answer curling around my heart. The words had been lodged in my throat, sticky and unwelcome, but I couldn't let the silence linger. It felt too ominous, as if the shadows were waiting for the chance to swallow us whole.

Jordan turned to me, his eyes dark pools reflecting an inner turmoil that mirrored my own. "I don't know. I thought maybe... maybe we'd figure it out together." His voice wavered, a slight crack breaking the facade of confidence he wore like armor. He was always so composed, the scion of a powerful family, exuding an air of certainty that made him irresistible. Yet, in that moment, he seemed achingly human, standing before me stripped of all pretenses.

The reality of his world was crashing in, a tempest of expectations and ancestral weight that threatened to drown us. My mind raced, recalling the lavish parties I had attended at his family's estate, the grand ballroom glittering with opulence, a stark contrast to the chaos swirling in our lives. Each person I had met there wore their masks expertly, their smiles plastered over secrets buried deep beneath layers of wealth and reputation. Would they accept our love, or would we become yet another scandal whispered about in the shadowed corners of those grand halls?

"What if they don't approve?" I ventured, my heart thrumming a frantic rhythm. "What if—"

"Stop," he interjected, stepping closer, a plea etched on his face. "I don't want to think about them right now. It's just... you and me." His hand found mine, warmth radiating through the cold air, anchoring me to this moment, this fragile sliver of hope.

But hope felt precarious, a fragile glass ornament dangling over a chasm. I couldn't shake the feeling that the threads of our lives, so intricately woven together in this newfound love, were being pulled apart by unseen hands.

"I can't help but think about it," I said, frustration bubbling to the surface. "Your family is everything. They have expectations—legacies, Jordan. They won't just let us waltz into their world like this."

Jordan exhaled sharply, his grip tightening around my fingers. "You make it sound like they're some kind of tyrants. They're just... complicated." The way he said "complicated" dripped with irony, as if the word was too polite for the reality we faced. The shadows of his family history loomed larger with each passing moment, and I could see the flicker of apprehension dancing behind his eyes.

"I get that you love them, but don't you ever wonder what's hidden behind the masks they wear?" My words felt bold, even reckless. In our vulnerability, it was easy to forget that our feelings were more than just romantic—there was an entire world of expectations and secrets swirling around us.

"Of course," he replied, his voice dropping to a whisper as if the walls might listen. "But it's not just me. It's my mother's ambitions, my father's expectations. They'll want to control every aspect of my life—who I date, where I work. They'll see you as a distraction, a liability."

My stomach twisted at the thought, the image of Jordan sitting across the table from his parents, the weight of their disdain heavy in the air. I imagined them dismissing me with a wave of their hands, as if I were an unworthy trinket, tarnished and unfit for their collection. "I can't just be a liability in your life, Jordan. I can't watch you suffer under their scrutiny."

He stepped back, frustration flaring in his expression. "You're not a liability. You're everything, and you know it. We'll find a way to make this work." The conviction in his voice was a fragile balm against my rising fear, but doubt gnawed at the edges of my optimism.

The night wore on, heavy with unspoken fears and lingering doubts. We navigated the conversation like two ships passing in a storm, desperately trying to find common ground. Our love felt as vibrant as the neon lights flickering outside, yet it was threatened by the storm clouds gathering on the horizon, looming larger with every hesitant word.

"Maybe we should take a step back," I suggested hesitantly, the thought weighing heavily on my heart. "Just until we figure things out."

The hurt in his eyes was like a knife twisting in my gut, but it felt necessary—a way to shield us from the world that threatened to tear us apart. "Are you serious? You want to push away what we have?" His voice cracked, the pain so raw it left a palpable silence hanging between us.

"I'm trying to protect you," I whispered, tears pricking at the corners of my eyes. "You deserve a chance to figure out what you want without the pressure of my feelings weighing you down."

He shook his head, frustration and longing battling for dominance on his face. "I don't want to lose you. You're the only thing that feels real in this mess."

In that moment, I felt the walls around my heart crack ever so slightly. The raw honesty in his eyes pierced through the fog of uncertainty, and I knew that despite the impending storm, our love was a force that could either be the anchor we needed or the tempest that swept us away. As I stared into his deep brown eyes, I felt a flicker of determination igniting within me. Perhaps love was messy, fraught with complications and familial legacies, but it was also powerful. And as long as we stood together, we could weather any storm.

The following days bled into one another, each marked by the same gnawing uncertainty that had settled into my bones. I awoke each morning with a sense of dread that nestled beside me like a reluctant companion, an uninvited guest that refused to leave. As the sun streamed through the thin curtains, it illuminated the small details of my life—the chipped mug I favored for my coffee, the stack of unfinished novels teetering precariously on the nightstand, the creeping plants that seemed to thrive against all odds. They reminded me that life outside my window continued to flourish, even as my heart felt trapped in a moment of suspended animation.

Jordan and I spent those days tiptoeing around the truth, our conversations swirling with half-finished thoughts and unspoken fears. Each touch was laden with tension, the warmth of his hand brushing against mine igniting sparks of hope that were quickly doused by the cold reality of our circumstances. I had never considered myself someone who would crumble under pressure, yet here I was, teetering on the brink of a nervous breakdown while pretending everything was fine.

Our moments together felt precious yet precarious, like walking on a tightrope strung high above a chasm. We found solace in shared laughter, but the specter of his family's disapproval loomed ever larger. One evening, we found ourselves on the rooftop of my apartment building, the city sprawled below us like a glittering sea of lights. The air was crisp, filled with the scent of fresh popcorn from a nearby vendor, and I could hear the distant sounds of laughter drifting up from the streets.

"This is nice," I said, pulling my sweater tighter around me, enjoying the feeling of the cool breeze on my skin. "Why don't we do this more often?"

Jordan leaned against the railing, a lazy grin spreading across his face that sent a flutter of warmth through me. "You mean escape our responsibilities? Sounds like a plan."

"Exactly! Why not live like we're not about to be crushed by family expectations?" I shot back, grinning as I nudged him playfully. "Or have you forgotten how to have fun?"

"Fun? I'm a member of the illustrious Dunlop family; I was practically raised to be serious." He feigned a stern expression that cracked into laughter, his eyes sparkling under the glow of the moonlight.

"Yeah, right," I said, rolling my eyes. "If you're serious, I must be a royal jester. You know, I think we should take a trip somewhere, just the two of us. A weekend getaway. We can pretend to be someone else, far from the prying eyes of your family."

He tilted his head, contemplating my words. "A getaway? Are you sure that's a good idea?" His tone shifted, a hint of caution creeping in.

"Why not?" I leaned forward, excitement bubbling in my chest. "A change of scenery could do us good. We could explore, breathe a little. Who knows, it might even help us figure things out."

"Or it could lead to more complications," he countered, the worry creasing his brow.

"True," I conceded, "but isn't that what life is all about? Embracing the chaos?"

He studied me for a moment, his gaze intense, and I could almost see the wheels turning in his mind. Then, with a resigned sigh, he said, "Alright. Let's do it. Just promise me you won't let the chaos scare you away."

I laughed, the sound bright and free, echoing into the night. "I'm not that easily frightened, Jordan. Besides, chaos is just another word for adventure."

As we leaned against the railing, our laughter mingling with the distant hum of the city, I felt a surge of hope, buoyed by the promise of escape. I knew that love didn't guarantee an easy path, but perhaps, amidst the complications and family legacies, we could carve out our own little world, even if just for a fleeting moment.

The following weekend arrived with a burst of sunshine and the scent of adventure in the air. We packed a small bag each, a haphazard collection of essentials that included far more snacks than clothing, and hit the road in Jordan's car. The city gave way to sprawling fields and winding roads, and I felt the weight of expectation begin to lift with every mile we traveled. The chatter of the world faded behind us, replaced by the soft hum of the engine and the gentle rustling of trees lining the highway.

As we drove, our conversation flowed easily, covering everything from our childhoods to our dreams. Jordan shared stories of his family's summer retreats—grandiose affairs filled with pressure and pretense. I listened, my heart aching for the boy behind the polished exterior, the one who longed for simplicity amidst the gilded cage of his life.

"Do you ever miss it?" I asked, glancing over at him. "The pressure? The expectations?"

He chuckled, a sound that was both nostalgic and bitter. "Not even a little. I'm far happier just being here with you, on this ridiculous adventure. I'll take popcorn and bad hotel coffee over a mansion full of people any day."

I smiled, feeling a warmth spread through my chest. "You're a rebel, Jordan Dunlop."

"Only because of you," he shot back, his eyes twinkling with mischief.

As we approached our destination—a cozy cabin nestled in the woods—excitement surged through me. The cabin was unassuming, a wooden structure surrounded by towering pines and the sound of a bubbling brook nearby. The air was crisp and fresh, a welcome contrast to the city's smog, and I inhaled deeply, letting the scents of pine and earth ground me.

Once inside, we tossed our bags onto the floor, laughter spilling out as we claimed the space as our own. The rustic charm of the cabin enveloped us, with its stone fireplace and plaid blankets. It felt like a sanctuary, far removed from the expectations that shadowed our every move back home.

"Let's make a fire," I suggested, my voice tinged with eagerness. "It'll set the mood."

Jordan grinned, his enthusiasm infectious as he gathered kindling and logs. As he worked, I arranged snacks on the coffee table, each item a testament to our shared sense of adventure.

"You know," I began, watching him with a smirk, "you really do look good with a bit of soot on your hands."

"Is that a compliment?" he shot back, pausing to raise an eyebrow, feigning indignation.

"Absolutely. It's like rugged meets refined. I can already see it on the cover of some romance novel." I couldn't help but laugh, the sound blending with the crackle of the fire as it began to catch.

His laughter echoed mine, a genuine sound that made my heart swell. "Just wait until you see me chop wood. Then you'll really be swooning."

"Don't tease," I replied, rolling my eyes playfully. "I'm easily impressed by a guy who can start a fire."

As the flames danced, the cozy glow filled the room, wrapping us in a warm embrace that felt both safe and exhilarating. I watched him, captivated by the way the light flickered across his features, revealing moments of vulnerability and strength that I was beginning to understand more deeply. The chaos of our lives melted away, replaced by the simple joy of being together.

"This," I said, settling into a chair, "is what I needed. Just you, me, and no one else."

Jordan sank into the couch across from me, his expression softening. "And no judgment, right? Just us against the world."

"Exactly. No family legacies or expectations. Just... us."

In that moment, I felt the walls around my heart crack open a little wider, allowing hope to seep through. Perhaps this weekend would be our turning point, a chance to redefine everything we thought we knew about love and each other. And as we settled into our own little universe, the world outside faded away, leaving only the glow of the fire and the promise of what was to come.

The cozy cabin wrapped around us like a warm blanket as the fire crackled, casting flickering shadows on the walls that danced to the rhythm of our laughter. Jordan leaned back on the couch, a devil-may-care grin stretching across his face as he tossed a marshmallow into the air and caught it with his mouth. I clapped, half in awe and half in amusement, and couldn't resist the urge to roll my eyes.

"Show-off," I teased, grabbing my own marshmallow and skewering it with a stick. "I'll have you know I was the queen of campfire snacks back in the day. Just watch."

"Is that so? A marshmallow warrior? I'm shaking in my boots," he said, his laughter ringing like a melody.

"Just wait until I whip out my graham crackers and chocolate," I replied, mimicking a stage magician as I revealed the hidden treasures from my bag. "Now, let's see who can make the best s'more."

The competition was fierce, with each of us putting our culinary skills to the test. Jordan insisted on toasting his marshmallows to perfection, the golden-brown color a testament to his patience. Meanwhile, I embraced my inner rebel, opting for the quick route that resulted in a gloriously charred marshmallow, oozing and blackened.

"This is culinary art," I said, taking a bite of my creation, my face lighting up as the chocolate melted against the warm marshmallow. "Perfection on a stick."

Jordan took a hesitant bite of his own meticulously crafted s'more, and his face contorted in exaggerated contemplation. "You know, I think yours is... interesting. Charred is definitely a flavor profile."

"Interesting? Is that your polite way of saying it's terrible?" I shot back, mock indignation spilling over into laughter.

"Not at all! It's just that the term 'delicately charred' has a nice ring to it. Like 'rare steak'—it's all in the marketing, really."

We fell into a comfortable rhythm, bantering back and forth as the sun dipped below the horizon, casting a golden glow over everything. The shadows outside lengthened, and the woods creaked gently in the wind, but here, in our little haven, nothing felt ominous. It was just us, lost in our cocoon of laughter and stolen moments.

As the fire crackled low, I leaned back into the cushions, a content sigh escaping my lips. "You know, if life could be like this all the time, I'd never complain."

"Agreed. No drama, just s'mores and bad jokes." He leaned closer, his tone shifting, curiosity flashing in his eyes. "But seriously, what's it going to be like when we go back? Do you think it'll all come crashing down?"

The question hung in the air, its weight settling like a stone in my stomach. The carefree moments were a welcome distraction, but the reality of our lives loomed ever closer. "I wish I could say it would be smooth sailing. Your family—"

"Is a whirlwind of chaos waiting to happen," he interjected, his voice tense. "But that chaos is part of me. I can't just... cut them off. They've always been there, for better or worse."

"Then how do we fit into that picture?" I asked, anxiety creeping into my voice. "If they see us as a problem..."

"They won't," he insisted, but the uncertainty in his eyes betrayed him. "Well, they might. But they don't know you like I do."

"What if that's not enough?" I pressed, a flutter of panic knotting my stomach. "What if they hate me?"

"Then I'll just have to convince them you're the best thing that's ever happened to me." His confidence was reassuring, yet my heart still raced with the thought of their judgment.

"Are you sure about that?" I asked, my voice softening. "What if they don't want you to be happy? What if they want to dictate your life? You said it yourself: your family is complicated."

He was silent for a moment, the fire crackling in the background like a heartbeat keeping time with our rising tensions. "I don't know," he admitted finally, his voice low. "But we have to find a way to navigate it together. Otherwise, what's the point?"

The sincerity in his words struck a chord deep within me. I knew he was right, but the thought of facing his family made my stomach twist painfully. "So, we go back, face the music, and hope for the best?"

"Exactly," he said, a determined glint in his eyes. "We're in this together, and I'll make sure they see you for who you really are. Not just some outsider, but someone who challenges me, who makes me better."

A shiver of warmth flooded through me at his words, but beneath it lay the undeniable fear of what awaited us. I took a deep breath, forcing myself to shake off the dread that threatened to anchor me down. "Alright, then. We'll face whatever comes next, head-on."

We shared a moment of silence, the air thick with unspoken fears and unyielding hope. Just then, the wind rustled the trees outside, causing a wave of unease to sweep through me. I shivered, despite the warmth of the fire.

"Did you hear that?" I asked, glancing toward the window.

"Hear what?" Jordan replied, frowning slightly. "Just the wind, I think."

"It sounded like—"

A loud crash interrupted me, echoing through the woods and sending a flock of birds into the night sky. My heart raced as I shot up, adrenaline coursing through me. "What was that?"

Jordan rose too, instinctively moving closer to me, the protectiveness in his posture undeniable. "I don't know, but let's check it out."

"No way!" I said, my pulse quickening. "We're not going out there."

"It could be nothing," he insisted, but there was a tension in his voice that suggested otherwise. "But we should at least look."

"Seriously? It could be a bear! Or a mountain lion!" The panic in my voice cracked through the calm of the moment.

"Okay, okay, no bears. I promise," he said, though the laughter in his eyes didn't quite match the seriousness of the situation.

As he reached for the door, I grabbed his arm. "Wait. We should take something—like a flashlight or... a spatula."

He chuckled, but there was urgency beneath it. "A spatula? That's the best you can come up with?"

"It's got a sharp edge!" I retorted, a mix of fear and humor swirling within me.

He rolled his eyes but grabbed the flashlight from the side table, illuminating the way as we stepped outside. The world was cloaked in darkness, the moon peeking through the trees, casting eerie shadows across the ground.

"Alright, what do we do if we see something?" I asked, gripping his arm tightly as we ventured closer to the source of the noise.

"Run," he said matter-of-factly, though I could hear the tension in his voice. "Or scream like a banshee."

"Charming," I replied, forcing a laugh to mask my fear. "I'll add that to my list of survival skills."

As we approached the edge of the clearing, the moonlight illuminated a fallen tree, its trunk split like a wishbone, the branches scattered across the ground like broken dreams. But just as I was about to breathe a sigh of relief, something caught my eye—a flash of movement deeper in the woods, a shadow shifting just beyond the reach of the flashlight.

"Jordan?" My voice trembled, and I felt his grip tighten around my arm.

"Did you see that?" he whispered, his eyes narrowing into the darkness.

Before I could respond, a figure emerged from the shadows, cloaked in the remnants of the night. My heart thundered in my chest, a wave of instinct pushing me to retreat. But before I could take a step back, the figure spoke, their voice cutting through the silence like a knife.

"Jordan... We need to talk."

Chapter 10: Beneath the Surface

The cabin nestled between towering pines exuded a rustic charm that almost felt like a sepia-toned memory—a place suspended in time, where the air was infused with the scent of pine needles and the distant echo of a babbling brook. As we pulled up the gravel driveway, I watched Jordan's shoulders relax, a subtle release of tension that I had grown accustomed to seeing during our whirlwind of a relationship. His typically sharp features softened in the warm glow of the setting sun, and I couldn't help but smile at the sight. We had come here to escape the cacophony of our everyday lives, but in truth, I was hoping for something much deeper: a chance to peel back the layers and discover the man hidden beneath the surface.

Inside the cabin, the fire crackled to life as I set about preparing our makeshift dinner—a mix of local cheeses and artisanal bread I had picked up from a charming market on the way. The flames danced in the stone hearth, casting flickering shadows across the walls, and I could feel the warmth seep into my bones, pushing back the chill that had settled there. Jordan leaned against the counter, watching me with a half-smile, a mixture of admiration and amusement painted across his face. "You know, I didn't peg you for the culinary type," he teased, his voice a smooth baritone that made my heart flutter.

"Surprise," I quipped back, tossing him a piece of cheese that he caught effortlessly. The air was thick with a playfulness that had been missing from our recent exchanges, and for the first time in what felt like ages, I dared to let my guard down. As we indulged in our impromptu feast, I began to notice the little things about him—the way his eyes crinkled at the corners when he laughed, the faintest dimple in his left cheek that appeared when he was genuinely amused. Each detail I absorbed felt like a piece of a puzzle falling into place, and I found myself eager to explore this newfound intimacy.

"Do you ever think about why we're so drawn to the chaos?" he asked, his tone suddenly serious, breaking the lightheartedness that had enveloped us moments before. The question hung in the air, and I felt the warmth of the fire recede as shadows crept into the corners of my mind. It was a raw, unguarded inquiry that demanded vulnerability, and I hesitated. "I mean, it's like we thrive on it. Maybe we're just scared of the quiet."

I took a breath, forcing the weight of my past to the surface. "Chaos feels familiar, doesn't it? It's like an old friend—predictable, even if it's painful." My fingers played with the edge of the tablecloth, suddenly feeling the weight of unspoken truths resting heavily on my chest. "But silence? That's where the real terror lies."

Jordan's gaze pierced through the flickering light, and I could see the gears in his mind turning. "You know," he started, his voice lower now, "I think we're both terrified of the same thing—losing ourselves in the quiet. But what if we could learn to embrace it? To find solace in each other without the chaos? Like here, now."

His words hung in the air like the fading echoes of our laughter, stirring something deep within me. I wanted to believe him, to grasp at the possibility of finding peace in the spaces between our conversations. But as quickly as hope flickered to life, the past surged forward, clawing at the edges of my mind. Memories of nights spent sleepless, lost in a cycle of self-doubt and regret, snaked their way into the forefront of my thoughts. The creaking floorboards whispered secrets of long-buried fears, and I felt a cold sweat bead at my temples.

"What if I can't?" I blurted, surprising myself with the confession. My heart raced as the truth spilled from my lips, raw and unfiltered. "What if I can't let go of the noise? What if I'm too broken to find that quiet?"

A long silence followed, heavy with unsaid words and emotions that felt like a fragile glass ball, ready to shatter at the slightest touch.

But instead of retreating or dismissing my fears, Jordan stepped closer, his presence radiating warmth and unwavering strength. "Then we'll learn together," he said, his voice steady and sincere. "One step at a time. You don't have to carry that weight alone."

His words wrapped around me like a blanket, a comforting embrace that momentarily staved off the chill of my insecurities. In that moment, I felt a flicker of trust ignite within me, a tiny spark of courage to face the shadows of my past. It was terrifying, the way he was stripping away my defenses, forcing me to confront the very fears I had kept at bay for so long. Yet there was something intoxicating about it, the raw honesty that tinged the air, almost as if we were dancing on the precipice of something profound.

Just as the flickering flames began to settle into a steady glow, a sudden noise outside shattered the fragile cocoon we had woven. A sharp crack echoed through the night, and my heart leaped into my throat. Instinctively, I looked at Jordan, his expression mirroring my own unease. "What was that?" I whispered, my pulse quickening. The sudden shift in atmosphere sent a shiver down my spine, reminding me that beneath the layers of warmth and connection, there were still fears lurking in the dark, ready to pounce.

The noise outside loomed larger than the mere crack of a branch; it resonated with the kind of unpredictability that stirs the heart and ignites the imagination. My gaze darted to the window, where the darkened forest seemed to pulse with life, shadows flickering like memories half-formed. "Probably just a raccoon," Jordan suggested, his voice laced with a casual bravado that barely masked the tension curling in the corners of his mouth. "Or maybe a deer. Those guys can be pretty rowdy after dark."

"A raccoon?" I echoed, incredulity woven into my tone. "In this ambiance? I was picturing more of a lurking predator, perhaps a disgruntled bear. They're the real party crashers in the woods."

Jordan chuckled softly, leaning against the doorframe, his silhouette sharp against the firelight. "I'm sure if there's a bear out there, it's just as scared of you as you are of it. Besides, you're the one who wanted to escape the chaos. A bear would definitely put a damper on the evening."

"Right, because nothing says peace and tranquility like the possibility of an unexpected wildlife encounter," I replied, trying to quell the fluttering anxiety that had taken root in my stomach. "I was aiming for hot cocoa and a novel, not a survival guide."

As if in agreement with my sentiments, the wind howled outside, and the cabin groaned in response, drawing a wary laugh from my lips. "So much for cozy vibes," I said, attempting to lighten the mood. "What's next? A thunderstorm? Lightning strikes? Maybe we should have stayed in the chaos."

"Chaos can be overrated," he countered, a glimmer of mischief dancing in his eyes. "But I like this chaos. It's... lively. Besides, nothing wrong with a little adventure."

His words hung in the air, and for a moment, I felt the warmth of our laughter envelop me, pushing back the encroaching shadows. "Adventure is great until someone loses a limb," I said playfully, though the shadows of my past loomed larger than ever. I could feel the familiar tendrils of anxiety creeping in again, a suffocating blanket reminding me of the struggles I had thought I could escape.

Before I could lose myself in that spiral of doubt, Jordan turned serious, his expression softening. "You okay?" he asked, his voice low and gentle. "You seem a little... distant."

"Just thinking about my plan for the rest of the evening," I replied, trying to deflect. "You know, practicing my bear-screaming technique."

He moved closer, invading the personal space I had just started to feel comfortable in. "No need for that. I promise to protect you from any and all bears," he said, a hint of a grin creeping back onto his lips. "I have my trusty pocket knife and my sheer manly charm."

I laughed, the tension breaking like a wave receding from the shore. "Ah, yes, I can see it now. You with your pocket knife, bravely facing the bear while I stand behind you, providing... moral support?"

"Exactly! That's the spirit." His eyes sparkled with mischief, and for a heartbeat, it felt as though we were simply two friends, lost in the woods and the world outside fading away. But just as quickly, the weight of the unresolved issues hung heavy in the air again, swirling around us like the leaves outside.

"Do you think we can really get away from all of it?" I asked, my voice quiet, almost swallowed by the crackling fire. "I mean, can we just... leave the chaos behind?"

Jordan's gaze turned contemplative, his brow furrowing slightly. "I think we can. But it takes work, you know? Like, real work. You can't just ignore it and expect it to disappear."

I considered his words, the raw honesty in them piercing through my defenses. "You're right. I'm just... I'm tired of fighting, Jordan. Tired of feeling like I'm on a hamster wheel, running but not getting anywhere."

He stepped closer, his presence grounding me. "What if we don't have to fight anymore?" he asked, his voice a soothing balm against my unease. "What if we learn how to navigate through it together? No more chaos—just you and me figuring it out."

For a fleeting moment, a flicker of hope ignited within me, and I felt the heaviness of my past lift just a little. But shadows lingered, gnawing at the edges of my newfound optimism, reminding me of the cracks that could so easily widen again. "It sounds easy when you say it like that," I murmured, a hint of doubt lacing my voice. "But what if we can't? What if the past just... catches up to us?"

"We deal with it as it comes," he replied firmly, his eyes locking onto mine with an intensity that made my heart race. "You have me, and I have you. We can face anything together."

As the words settled between us, a profound stillness enveloped the room, punctuated only by the crackle of the fire and the whisper of the wind outside. His promise hung in the air, a fragile yet powerful bond, like the thin strands of a spider's web glistening in the morning dew. In that moment, the enormity of my fears seemed less daunting, somehow manageable, as if the very act of sharing them with him diluted their power.

"Alright then," I said, a newfound resolve surging through me. "No more running. Let's confront whatever chaos is left—together."

His smile widened, revealing a depth of understanding that made my heart swell. "That's the spirit! Now, how about we make some hot cocoa and discuss our survival strategy? Just in case that bear shows up."

We both laughed, the sound rich and warm against the chilly backdrop of the forest. As we busied ourselves in the kitchen, the mundane task of preparing hot cocoa transformed into a shared ritual, punctuated by playful banter and the occasional brush of our arms. I could feel the layers of tension unwinding, and the flickering flames in the hearth reflected the promise of something new—a tentative partnership built on trust, laughter, and the willingness to embrace the unknown.

But as the cocoa simmered, the shadows outside crept closer, and an unsettling feeling settled deep within my gut, a reminder that while we could forge our path forward, the remnants of our past still lingered, waiting to be acknowledged.

The cocoa simmered, filling the air with rich, chocolatey sweetness that seemed to dance with the warm glow of the fire. As I stirred the pot, I couldn't shake the feeling that we were teetering on the edge of something extraordinary—or perhaps something perilous. Jordan moved around the small kitchen with an ease that belied his usual intensity, his presence anchoring me in a way that felt both reassuring and unsettling. I watched as he grabbed two mugs from the cupboard, their ceramic surfaces gleaming under the soft light, a stark contrast to the wildness brewing outside.

"Do you want marshmallows or should I go all gourmet and throw in some whipped cream?" he asked, his eyes sparkling with mischief.

"Marshmallows, obviously," I replied, the familiar warmth of banter sparking between us. "We're not trying to impress anyone here. It's about survival and comfort food."

"Ah, yes, survival. I should have known you were more into practical solutions than culinary masterpieces." He turned, brandishing the marshmallows like trophies, and I couldn't help but laugh.

As we settled down in the cozy nook of the living room, the fire crackled, and the warm light bathed us in a golden glow. I cradled my mug, letting the heat seep into my palms, savoring the moment. "You know," I began, peering over the rim of my mug, "this feels different. Good different."

"Good different? Is that the best you can muster?" He raised an eyebrow, teasing me in that charming way that made my heart flutter. "I was hoping for something more poetic."

"Fine," I retorted, a smile playing on my lips. "It feels like a turning point. A moment where the past fades, and we get to write a new story."

"Ah, the aspiring novelist speaks!" he exclaimed, a mock expression of awe crossing his face. "Tell me, what comes next in this riveting tale?"

I leaned forward, pretending to consider, but the weight of my thoughts began to seep back in, darkening the bright moment.

"Maybe it's about facing the ghosts we've been avoiding. You know, dealing with the mess we've created."

He sobered instantly, the banter giving way to a shared understanding. "You mean the ghosts we've both been running from?"

I nodded, the shadows creeping back in. "Exactly. I've spent so long trying to outrun them that I forgot what it felt like to stand still and face them."

Jordan set his mug down, leaning closer, the intensity in his gaze grounding me. "Then let's not run anymore. Let's confront whatever needs confronting. Together."

The resolve in his voice sent a jolt of warmth through me, but uncertainty still tugged at my thoughts, a persistent whisper urging caution. "What if I'm not ready? What if the past is too... messy?"

He reached out, his fingers brushing against mine, a simple gesture that sent electric sparks dancing up my arm. "Messy can be beautiful, too. Sometimes, you just need the right person by your side to see it."

The moment felt charged, and I leaned into his touch, allowing myself to believe in the warmth between us. But just as the flicker of hope took root, a sudden crash outside jolted me from my reverie. My heart raced as adrenaline surged, and I glanced toward the window, where the shadows in the woods seemed to deepen, the trees now appearing ominous and foreboding.

"What was that?" I asked, my voice rising with a mixture of fear and curiosity.

Jordan stood up, his demeanor shifting from relaxed to alert in a heartbeat. "I don't know, but let's check it out."

"Check it out?" I echoed, incredulity creeping into my tone. "Have you seen any horror movies? This is the part where people go outside and never return."

"Sure, but in those movies, they don't have the charming, courageous hero." He winked, but the lightheartedness of his words didn't quite reach his eyes. The playful banter felt heavy with unspoken tension, and I could see the determination hardening his features.

"Jordan..." I started, but he cut me off gently.

"Stay here. I'll take a quick look. It's probably just an animal or something."

"Or something?" I shot back, the flutter of dread in my stomach shifting to something more tangible. "You can't just leave me here!"

"Someone has to make sure the coast is clear," he insisted, his tone reassuring yet firm. "I'll be right back. Just—wait here."

Against my better judgment, I nodded, watching as he moved toward the door, the shadows stretching like fingers behind him. He hesitated, glancing back at me, the flicker of the flames casting a warm glow over his worried expression. "Lock the door behind me, okay?"

"Sure, because locking myself inside will definitely help if a bear attacks," I quipped, attempting to lighten the mood, but my heart pounded with uncertainty.

He chuckled softly, but the sound felt hollow. "Just do it, please."

With that, he slipped out into the night, and the door clicked shut behind him, sealing me within the cabin's walls. I was alone, the silence suddenly deafening. The shadows of the room danced ominously, and I wrapped my arms around myself, feeling the chill creep back in.

Minutes dragged on, each tick of the clock echoing ominously in the stillness. I busied myself with the mug in my hands, nervously tapping my fingers against the ceramic as I peered out the window. The forest loomed like a dark sentry, and I could see nothing but the faint outline of trees swaying gently in the wind.

"Jordan?" I called, the word slipping from my lips like a prayer. No response.

A gnawing unease settled in my stomach, and I forced myself to breathe steadily, even as doubt clawed at my mind. The shadows outside seemed to thicken, and a rush of cold air swept through the cracks around the window, sending a shiver down my spine.

"Jordan!" I called again, louder this time, panic lacing my voice. "Come back!"

Still nothing.

I moved to the door, hands trembling as I fumbled with the lock. The thought of opening it and stepping into the unknown filled me with dread, but the silence was unbearable. "I can't just sit here," I muttered to myself, the words a lifeline in the growing darkness.

With a deep breath, I unlocked the door and stepped outside, the cool air hitting me like a wave. The night enveloped me, and for a moment, I stood frozen, absorbing the wild sounds of the forest. Then I saw it—a flash of movement in the trees, a figure slipping through the shadows. My heart raced, and I called out once more, a desperate plea in the darkness.

"Jordan, is that you?"

The figure paused, and my heart sank as the wind shifted, carrying an unfamiliar scent that set off alarms in my head. The darkness shifted, and I felt the weight of something more than just the night pressing in around me—a presence lurking just beyond the light.

The hairs on the back of my neck stood on end as a low growl rumbled from the shadows, cutting through the stillness. I had crossed into a territory I didn't understand, and in that moment, I realized that the chaos I had tried so hard to escape might just have found me, creeping in with claws unsheathed and a darkness that threatened to consume us both.

Chapter 11: Unraveling Threads

The biting wind nipped at my cheeks, sharp as a betrayal, as I stood beneath the vast, indifferent sky. Stars twinkled above, each one a reminder of a universe that spun on, oblivious to the turmoil swirling within me. I shoved my hands deep into the pockets of my coat, hoping to warm the icy dread settling in my bones. The night wrapped around me like a shroud, thick with uncertainty and despair, while memories of the heated discussion with Jordan replayed in my mind. I could still hear his voice, filled with concern yet laced with frustration, as he tried to shield me from the truth I was desperately clawing at.

"Why can't you see? It's not just your past, it's ours!" he had insisted, his eyes darkening with worry. "I'm trying to protect you."

But his protectiveness felt like a chain, binding me to shadows I longed to escape. Each layer of his family's history I unearthed was like peeling an onion, revealing rot hidden beneath the surface. Jordan's lineage was entwined with the very fabric of my family's demise, a tapestry woven with threads of deceit and heartbreak. I took a deep breath, the frigid air filling my lungs like a chilling reminder that nothing was ever truly as it seemed.

With every revelation, my heart raced in a tumultuous rhythm, matching the pulse of the world around me. I had thought love was meant to liberate, yet I felt ensnared by a destiny written in secrets and half-truths. My fingers curled tightly around the fabric of my coat as if it could shield me from the icy tendrils of fate creeping closer. I stared up at the stars, my heart heavy with the weight of what I'd discovered. It felt as though the cosmos were mocking me, their twinkling light illuminating the darkness of my fears.

As I paced beneath the night sky, a distant sound broke through the silence—a muffled thud, the sound of footsteps crunching over the frosted ground. My heart leapt in my chest as I turned, half-hoping it would be Jordan, his face a mask of concern, ready to bridge the chasm that had grown between us. But the figure emerging from the shadows was unfamiliar, tall and cloaked in darkness. My instincts screamed at me to flee, to return to the warmth of my home and the safety of familiarity, but curiosity rooted me in place.

The figure approached slowly, the moonlight catching the sharp angles of their face—a man, eyes glinting with an intensity that sent another chill down my spine. I couldn't read him, and that unsettled me more than the cold. The air felt electric, crackling with tension as he stopped a few paces from me.

"Are you lost, or just running?" he asked, his voice low and smooth, like honey laced with a hint of danger.

I bristled, crossing my arms defensively. "Neither. Just enjoying the night."

"Enjoying, huh?" He took a step closer, hands shoved into the pockets of a leather jacket that looked as if it had seen its fair share of trouble. "You look like you've seen a ghost. Or maybe a memory you wish you could forget."

The way he pierced through my bravado made me wary. "What's it to you?" I shot back, my voice sharper than intended. "Are you a fortune teller or just a wandering philosopher?"

A smirk danced on his lips, and I felt a strange pull toward him despite the danger signs blaring in my head. "Just someone who knows a thing or two about running from shadows. I see them all around you."

His words struck a chord, and I felt an involuntary shiver race through me. "You don't know anything about me," I replied, my voice steadier than I felt. "Or the shadows I'm dealing with."

"Maybe not," he admitted, stepping even closer, his presence overpowering. "But I know when someone's trying to outrun their fate. What's haunting you, girl?"

That single word, 'girl,' stirred something rebellious in me. I was no girl; I was a woman battling ghosts from both my past and my present. "Why should I tell you? You're just a stranger."

"True," he said, a flash of something inscrutable passing through his gaze. "But sometimes, strangers can see the truth more clearly than those blinded by familiarity."

His words resonated, and I felt a strange connection, an urge to confide in him, even if just to unburden myself. I hesitated, the weight of my secrets heavy on my tongue. "Fine. I'm in love with someone whose family is tied to everything I've lost. Every revelation makes me question everything—my past, my present, even my future."

He studied me, his expression inscrutable. "Love can be a dangerous game, especially when it's woven into the fabric of your history. But perhaps it's also a thread you can pull on, unraveling the mess to find something pure underneath."

I snorted, the sound breaking the tension. "Or it can lead to more disaster. You know, like a bad romance novel."

"Or a beautiful one," he countered, his voice smooth as silk. "Sometimes, you need to embrace the chaos to find clarity. What if I told you there's a way to rewrite your story?"

Intrigued despite myself, I felt a flicker of hope igniting amidst the gloom. "And how would you propose I do that?"

"Meet me tomorrow," he said, taking a step back, the night swallowing him in shadows. "I might have the answers you're looking for."

And with that, he vanished into the dark, leaving me standing alone, heart racing, torn between caution and curiosity. The night stretched on, vast and unyielding, as I contemplated the strange encounter, each star flickering above like a question mark in the sky, daring me to seek answers buried in the shadows of love and betrayal.

The morning sun clawed its way through the curtains, painting the room in soft hues of gold and orange, but I lay awake, tangled in a cocoon of thoughts. The promise of the stranger's words echoed in my mind, a haunting melody of possibility and peril. I tossed and turned, trying to shake off the shadows of the night before. My heart thrummed with both anxiety and anticipation, like a metronome caught in a frenzy. The day stretched before me, each hour a ticking countdown to the unknown.

I finally slipped out of bed, the chill of the wooden floor sending a jolt through my system. Coffee—strong and black—was the first order of business. The aroma swirled through the air, comforting and invigorating, pushing away the remnants of last night's turmoil. I stood at the kitchen window, cradling my mug, staring out at the world awakening beyond. The neighborhood bustled with life: children in bright coats trudging through the frosty grass, neighbors chatting amiably over fences, their laughter drifting like a soft breeze. For a moment, I envied their uncomplicated lives, unmarred by the tangled threads of my own existence.

As I prepared for the day, I couldn't shake the thought of the man who had crossed my path. Who was he, really? There had been an air of mystery about him, something electric that pulled at my curiosity like a moth to flame. My mind buzzed with questions, but one loomed larger than the rest: What could he possibly know about my tangled history with Jordan that I didn't? I finished getting ready, each movement mechanical, my mind spinning in circles as I replayed the conversation in my head.

The meeting place was a small café on the corner of Maple and Second—a spot Jordan and I frequented, a place filled with the scent of fresh pastries and the sound of cheerful chatter. I arrived a few minutes early, my heart thrumming in my chest like a drum. The café was cozy, with mismatched furniture and soft lighting, a sanctuary from the harsh world outside. I found a table in the corner, the window casting a warm glow over me as I waited.

A few minutes ticked by, then five, and still no sign of him. I fidgeted, tapping my foot nervously against the floor. Was I being foolish for even considering this meeting? I took a sip of my coffee, the bitterness grounding me, reminding me why I was here: to unearth the truth that had eluded me for so long. The door chimed, pulling my gaze away from my swirling thoughts, and in he walked.

He looked different in the daylight—more approachable yet still enigmatic, like a book with a beautifully crafted cover hiding an unexpected plot twist. He caught my eye and gave a slight nod, a playful smirk tugging at his lips as he approached. "I was beginning to think you'd stand me up."

"I'd never miss a chance to talk about my existential crisis with a stranger," I shot back, a teasing lilt in my voice despite the butterflies dancing in my stomach.

He chuckled, sliding into the seat across from me. "Existential crises are my specialty. What are we unraveling today?"

I leaned forward, the air between us charged with an unspoken understanding. "Last night was… intense. I need to know what you meant about rewriting my story."

His gaze grew serious, the mirth replaced by a somber weight. "It's all about perspective. Your family's history doesn't have to dictate your future, especially if you're willing to confront it. There's a thread in your past that connects directly to Jordan's family, and it might be the key to understanding everything."

I took a deep breath, the gravity of his words settling over me. "How do you know about Jordan? And why do you care?"

"Because I've been where you are," he said, his tone earnest. "I grew up in a world shadowed by secrets. My family was tangled in a web of their own making, and it nearly cost me everything. I had to dig deep to uncover the truth, and in doing so, I learned how to rewrite my own narrative."

"Sounds dramatic," I replied, a hint of skepticism creeping in. "What's the twist? Are you going to tell me I'm destined to be the heroine of my own tragedy?"

"Or the hero," he countered, leaning back in his chair, an amused spark in his eyes. "What if I told you that the truth about Jordan's family could change everything you think you know?"

Intrigued, I leaned closer, the café fading into a blur around us. "Okay, I'm listening. Spill it."

"Jordan's family isn't just involved in shady dealings; they've been linked to something much darker. It's not just business—there's a reason why your families are intertwined, and it's not a coincidence. There's a danger there, and it's critical you understand what you're dealing with." His voice lowered, laced with urgency. "The truth is, love can be a powerful weapon. It can heal or destroy."

A knot formed in my stomach as I absorbed his words. "What do you mean?"

"There's a secret that runs deep. Something your families have tried to bury. If you really want to break free from the shadows, you'll need to face it head-on. But be warned, there are those who would do anything to keep that truth hidden."

I sat back, reeling, my mind racing. "So, what's the first step? Do we dig through family trees and old newspapers?"

He grinned, a flicker of mischief in his eyes. "Not quite. We need to gather information from sources that know the truth. It might take us to some unexpected places, and you might find allies—or enemies—in the process."

"Great, I've always wanted a scavenger hunt of familial dysfunction," I said, half-joking, though the weight of the task loomed large.

His laughter was genuine, breaking through the tension. "You might be surprised. Sometimes, the best revelations come from the most unusual sources."

I nodded, feeling the stirrings of hope mixed with trepidation. The thrill of the chase ignited something within me, a sense of purpose that I hadn't felt in ages. "Okay, then. Let's uncover whatever it is."

As the conversation flowed, a bond began to form between us, unexpected yet undeniable. Each word exchanged was charged with possibility, each laugh a shared secret, pulling us deeper into the tangled web of our lives. In that cozy café, amidst the scent of fresh coffee and the laughter of patrons, I felt the stirrings of a new chapter beginning to unfold—one that could either shatter the remnants of my past or lead me to the very answers I sought.

The plan began to take shape as we plotted over coffee, the warmth of the café providing a stark contrast to the chilly uncertainty nipping at my heels. We spent the next hour dissecting every detail, each piece of information acting as a thread in a tapestry I was desperate to unravel. The stranger, whose name I learned was Ethan, was sharp-witted and observant, unearthing insights about Jordan's family that sent shivers down my spine. He spoke with a fervor that made the air crackle with tension, as though the very walls of the café were eavesdropping on our conspiratorial whispers.

"Alright, let's say I'm on board," I said, fiddling with the sugar packets on the table, my mind racing with possibilities. "What's the first move?"

Ethan leaned back, a thoughtful expression crossing his face. "We start by digging into the past—your past, and Jordan's. You need to find the documents, any letters, anything that might give us clues. We might even have to talk to some old family friends or associates. The connections will lead us to the truth, I promise."

I nodded, feeling the weight of the task ahead. "It sounds exhausting. What if they refuse to talk?"

"Then we get creative," he said, a mischievous glint in his eye. "People talk when they think someone else has something to gain. We'll make it worth their while."

"You mean like blackmail?" I raised an eyebrow, half-joking but sensing the seriousness in his tone.

He laughed, a sound rich and warm, easing some of the tension coiling within me. "Not quite. Let's say we appeal to their nostalgia instead. Everyone loves a good story, especially if it involves a touch of scandal."

I couldn't help but smile, my apprehension easing slightly. "Alright, I'm in. But if this leads to trouble, I'm blaming you."

"Fair enough," he replied, his expression shifting to one of earnestness. "But just remember, knowing the truth can be dangerous. We're digging into things people would prefer to stay buried."

I felt a knot form in my stomach at his words, but there was also a thrill. With each moment spent with Ethan, I could feel my life shifting direction, the potential for something unexpected and transformative igniting a spark within me.

As we wrapped up our meeting, we made plans to meet again later in the week to continue our research. I left the café, the world outside buzzing with life, the crisp autumn air invigorating. My heart raced not just with the prospect of uncovering hidden truths, but also with an unfamiliar excitement that came from collaborating with someone who seemed to understand the weight of my burdens.

In the days that followed, I found myself diving headfirst into the investigation, flipping through old family albums and dusty boxes stored away in the attic. The scent of aged paper filled the air as I uncovered faded letters and grainy photographs of my family's past.

Each artifact felt like a piece of a puzzle, the picture growing clearer yet more complex with every new discovery.

But the deeper I dug, the more the shadows of Jordan's family loomed, dark and foreboding. The whispers of danger began to turn from murmurs to a chorus of warnings that echoed in the back of my mind. I unearthed documents that hinted at ties to dubious enterprises, a network that crossed paths with those who operated in the shadows of the law.

One evening, as I sifted through a particularly old box, I stumbled upon a letter that stopped me cold. The handwriting was familiar, and as I read the words, a chill slithered down my spine. It detailed a meeting, a covert discussion about something grander than I had ever imagined—an agreement forged between my family and Jordan's, one that hinted at a dark alliance rather than a mere connection.

I slammed the box shut, my heart pounding in my chest. This was not just family history; it was a blueprint for chaos. I felt the walls of my home closing in, the air thick with the scent of secrets too heavy to bear alone. I needed to talk to Jordan, but the thought of revealing what I had found made my stomach churn. How could I tell him that our love was entwined with shadows?

Later that night, I paced the living room, my phone clutched tightly in my hand. I glanced at the screen, weighing the decision to call Jordan. Each ring of the clock echoed my indecision, the tension winding tighter until I finally resolved to reach out. But before I could dial, a knock at the door startled me.

My heart raced as I glanced through the peephole. It was Jordan. He stood there, hands shoved deep into his coat pockets, his expression a mix of concern and frustration. I opened the door, a wave of emotions crashing over me as our eyes met.

"Hey," he said, stepping inside without waiting for an invitation. "We need to talk."

My breath caught in my throat, and the weight of the secrets I carried threatened to crush me. "Yeah, I was just about to call you," I replied, my voice barely a whisper.

He studied my face, his brow furrowing. "You look like you've seen a ghost. What's going on?"

I hesitated, caught between the desire to protect him and the need to confess. The words hung in the air, heavy and unyielding. Just as I opened my mouth to speak, my phone buzzed on the table, interrupting the moment. I glanced at the screen, and my heart dropped. A message from Ethan flashed before my eyes: We need to meet. It's urgent. I found something important.

Jordan noticed my change in expression, a shadow of worry crossing his face. "What is it?"

Before I could respond, another knock echoed through the house, more insistent this time. The sound reverberated in my chest, and I felt a chill crawl down my spine. "Wait here," I said, stepping toward the door, my heart racing as I reached for the handle.

As I opened it, a figure loomed in the doorway—an unfamiliar man, tall and imposing, with a piercing gaze that seemed to see right through me. "I need to speak with you," he said, his voice low and gravelly, filled with a sense of urgency that sent alarm bells ringing in my mind.

Before I could respond, Jordan stepped forward, tension radiating from him. "Who are you?"

The stranger's eyes flicked to Jordan, then back to me, a faint smirk tugging at his lips. "You're in deeper than you realize," he said, a hint of menace underlying his tone. "And I'm here to make sure you don't drown."

I felt the ground shift beneath me, the air thickening with the promise of danger as I stood there, caught in a web of secrets and uncertainty, the fate of my love—and perhaps my life—teetering on the edge of revelation.

Chapter 12: Ghosts of the Past

The air was thick with the scent of damp wood and something else—something musty that hinted at long-buried memories. I stepped into my apartment, the door creaking ominously behind me, a soft echo in the silence that filled the space. The flickering light bulb above cast erratic shadows, dancing like specters on the walls, reminding me that something was very wrong. My heart pounded as I surveyed the chaos. Furniture had been overturned, books lay strewn across the floor like casualties in a war I hadn't known I was fighting. The remnants of my life, my carefully curated sanctuary, had been violated.

As I moved deeper into the living room, my breath quickened. A single sheet of paper lay on the coffee table, the words scrawled across it in jagged letters that seemed to mock me. "Some secrets should stay buried." The words sent a chill down my spine, echoing in the silence of the empty room. I could almost hear the whispers of ghosts—memories of laughter and love intermingled with shadows of resentment and fear. I picked up the note, its edges curling slightly in my trembling grip. Who had done this? What secrets had I buried so deep that they were now clawing their way back to the surface?

My mind raced to Jordan. I could almost hear the cadence of his voice, the way he could calm the storm inside me with just a few words. I dialed his number, my fingers fumbling over the buttons as anxiety coursed through me like electricity. The phone rang only once before he answered, and the sound of his voice was a lifeline in the darkness. "Hey, what's wrong?"

"Jordan, my apartment... it's been ransacked." The words came out in a breathless rush, and I could hear the sudden shift in his tone. It was as if I had dropped a stone into still water, the ripples of concern spreading out between us, connecting us even over the phone lines.

"I'll be there in ten minutes," he said, his voice firm. "Lock the door and don't touch anything."

I did as he instructed, retreating to the safety of my kitchen, the only place that still felt familiar despite the turmoil. The aroma of the spices I had used for my latest culinary adventure lingered in the air, a strange contrast to the fear that gripped me. I fumbled for my favorite mug, fingers trembling as I poured myself a glass of water, hoping to quell the rising tide of panic.

As I waited for Jordan, my thoughts swirled like autumn leaves caught in a whirlwind. Our pasts were a tangle of heartache and unspoken truths, like threads woven into a tapestry that had started to fray at the edges. It hadn't been long since we had uncovered the first hints of our families' connections—a web of deceit that had tangled our lives together in ways we could barely comprehend. But this? This was new territory.

When the door swung open, Jordan stepped inside, his presence a grounding force against the chaos. He took in the scene with the practiced ease of someone who had faced danger before, but his eyes betrayed a flash of concern. "Are you okay?"

"Not exactly a welcome home," I quipped, attempting a light-hearted tone despite the heaviness that settled in my chest.

"Let's focus on what's important." He moved with purpose, checking the locks on the windows, ensuring we weren't followed. "Did you see anyone suspicious?"

"No, I was out all day," I replied, my voice barely above a whisper. "I thought I'd come home to a quiet evening, not... this."

Jordan turned to face me, his brow furrowing. "We need to figure out what they were looking for. Did you keep anything that might have drawn attention?"

The question hung in the air, heavy with implications. My mind flashed to the small box hidden in the back of my closet, filled with letters and photographs from a time I'd rather forget—secrets that could unravel everything I thought I knew about my family. "I have some old things," I confessed. "But I don't think they'd be interested in..."

He raised a hand, cutting me off gently. "Let's not make assumptions. What you think is insignificant might be a clue. We need to go through everything."

As we combed through the wreckage of my apartment, tension mounted, our movements laced with a sense of urgency. Every overturned chair and scattered book felt like a reminder that whatever had been lurking in the shadows was no longer dormant. I could feel the weight of my past pressing down, the secrets I thought I had buried stirring uneasily beneath the surface.

Jordan and I exchanged glances, unspoken understanding passing between us. The unravelling threads of our families' histories wove tighter, creating a tapestry of suspicion and dread that threatened to engulf us both. "If they're willing to go this far, it means they know something," he said, his voice steady despite the turmoil swirling around us.

A sudden thought struck me like lightning. "What if they're not just after my secrets? What if they're after yours too?"

Jordan's expression hardened, the lightness of our previous banter replaced by a seriousness that sent shivers down my spine. "Whatever it is, we're going to face it together," he vowed, his determination igniting a spark of hope in my chest.

In that moment, surrounded by the remnants of my shattered world, I knew that we were not just facing the ghosts of our past; we were about to confront a reality that would change everything. The stakes were higher than I could have ever imagined, and as we braced ourselves for what lay ahead, I could feel the tendrils of danger creeping closer, whispering promises of truths best left buried.

The broken glass crunched under my feet as I moved cautiously through the wreckage of my apartment, each step a reminder of how easily my sanctuary had been transformed into a nightmare. Jordan was already rummaging through what was left of my life, his brow furrowed in concentration. He picked up a book, flipping through the pages, and I couldn't help but notice how his expression shifted from concern to curiosity. "This is a classic. You really should consider leaving your taste in literature out of your secrets," he quipped, a faint smile tugging at his lips.

I shot him a look, half amused, half exasperated. "Right now, my taste in novels seems less relevant than why my living room looks like a tornado hit it." The smile faded from his face, replaced by the seriousness of our situation. I appreciated his attempt to lighten the mood, but the gravity of what had happened loomed over us like a storm cloud.

As we sifted through the remnants of my life, I couldn't shake the feeling that this was more than just a break-in. Someone had deliberately searched for something specific, and my instincts whispered that whatever they were looking for could change everything. I turned back to Jordan, who was now examining the overturned furniture with a methodical precision that revealed just how familiar he was with chaos.

"We need to think strategically," he said, running a hand through his hair, a gesture I had come to recognize as a sign of his determination. "What could they want? Is there anything—"

"The box in my closet," I interrupted, the words tumbling out before I could think them through. "I have old letters, family photos... things my parents thought were too painful to keep around."

His expression shifted, eyes narrowing as he considered my words. "You think it could be connected?"

"It's possible. My family had its share of secrets, and I've always felt they were tied to something bigger. What if this is the trigger?"

Jordan nodded, the gravity of the situation settling in. "Then we need to secure it. Let's get it before whoever did this comes back." He moved toward the hallway, his stride confident yet cautious, as if the very air around us crackled with potential danger.

I followed, the sound of my heartbeat echoing in my ears, drowning out the creaking floorboards beneath our feet. I opened the closet, revealing a jumble of clothes and forgotten items, and there, nestled in the back, was the small wooden box. Its surface was smooth, worn from years of being tucked away. I pulled it out, my fingers trembling as I felt the weight of what it contained—secrets, memories, and perhaps a connection to the chaos now enveloping us.

As I sat on the edge of my bed, the box resting in my lap, I hesitated. "Are you ready for this?" I asked, looking up at Jordan, whose expression remained stoic, masking whatever turmoil was brewing beneath the surface.

He met my gaze, unwavering. "Whatever it is, we'll face it together. Just open it." His voice was steady, laced with a warmth that soothed the frayed edges of my anxiety.

With a deep breath, I lifted the lid. The hinges creaked as it opened, revealing a trove of old letters and faded photographs. Memories came flooding back—of summer days spent in my grandmother's garden, the laughter echoing like a distant song. But alongside the nostalgia lay an unsettling reality.

"Look," I said, pulling out a letter that had yellowed with age. The handwriting was elegant, flowing with a grace that seemed to contrast sharply with the turmoil we faced now. "This is from my mother to her sister. It talks about a family rift... a falling out over something they never specified."

Jordan leaned closer, the tension palpable as we both read the words. "What if this is what they were looking for? If someone knows about your family's history, they might think it leads to something valuable."

"Valuable? Like money?" I asked, skepticism creeping into my voice.

"Or power. Sometimes the past holds more than just memories. It can unlock doors to a darker world." His eyes flicked to the window, as if he expected someone to come crashing through at any moment.

I took a moment to process his words. The thought sent a shiver down my spine. What if our families were intertwined in a way that meant more than just shared ancestry? What if they had been involved in something dangerous? "Do you think they're still out there, waiting for us to uncover the truth?"

"I don't think they've gone far." His voice was a whisper now, heavy with the weight of our shared fears. "We need to figure out what's at stake here, and fast."

As we rifled through the contents of the box, we uncovered more letters, each revealing snippets of conversations that hinted at secrets long buried. The tone shifted from innocuous to menacing, as if the very ink on the page was warning us of the trouble ahead. One letter in particular caught my eye, the words scrawled hastily, as if the writer had been racing against time. "They will never forgive us. We must protect what's ours."

"What could that mean?" I mused aloud, passing the letter to Jordan.

"Perhaps it refers to something that was stolen or hidden. If someone feels threatened enough to break into your home, it might mean they think you have something they want." He studied the letter, his brow furrowed in thought.

"Or something they believe I have." I felt a chill run down my spine as the implications sank in. What if I was the key to something much larger than myself, something that had ensnared both our families in its grip?

As we continued to dig through the box, I felt a growing sense of unease settle over me. Each revelation drew us deeper into the labyrinth of our pasts, intertwining our fates with a thread that was growing thinner with each discovery. The tension hung heavy in the air, and I couldn't shake the feeling that someone was watching us, waiting for the moment we uncovered the truth.

"Jordan," I said, glancing at the door, half-expecting it to burst open. "What if we're not just uncovering family secrets? What if we're stepping into something we can't control?"

He met my gaze, the seriousness of the situation reflected in his eyes. "Then we face it together. Whatever comes next, we'll tackle it as a team."

Just as the words left his lips, a loud crash echoed from the living room, the sound reverberating through the apartment like a thunderclap. My heart raced as I turned to Jordan, a silent question hanging in the air. What had we just unleashed?

The echo of the crash reverberated through the apartment, vibrating in my bones and raising the fine hairs on the back of my neck. Jordan and I exchanged panicked glances, the unspoken question hanging thick in the air. "That wasn't just the wind," I murmured, heart racing as I gripped the edges of the wooden box still resting in my lap, as if it could somehow shield me from whatever lay beyond the threshold of the living room.

"Stay here," he commanded, his voice steady despite the urgency of the situation. I wanted to protest, to argue that we were in this together, but I recognized the instinctual protective edge in his tone. He moved toward the sound, a determined silhouette framed by the dim light spilling into the hallway.

The shadows of the apartment grew longer, the flickering bulbs overhead casting eerie shapes on the walls. I held my breath, feeling a mix of dread and helplessness. My heart thumped wildly as I listened to Jordan's footsteps against the hardwood floor, each step echoing louder than the last.

Suddenly, a muffled voice broke the tense silence, sending a fresh wave of adrenaline coursing through me. "I know you're here!" It was a man's voice, low and threatening, reverberating through the air like a dark promise. My mind raced as I imagined the figure standing in my living room, the one who had so carelessly upended my world. What did he want? Why here?

I stood up, instinctively moving toward Jordan, but caught myself at the last moment. I needed to be smart, to not rush headlong into danger. Instead, I quietly moved to the doorway, peeking around the corner. There, illuminated by the remnants of sunlight filtering through the window, stood a man—tall and imposing, his back turned to me. He was rummaging through the debris, tossing aside my belongings as if they were nothing but discarded wrappers.

"Jordan?" I whispered, panic lacing my voice.

Jordan appeared beside me, his eyes scanning the room. "We need to get out of here. Now."

His calm demeanor was reassuring, but I could sense the tension radiating from him, a taut wire ready to snap. I nodded, and we edged back, trying to remain as silent as the grave.

The man turned slightly, catching a glimpse of something that sent a jolt through me. A glint of metal—was he armed? My mind reeled at the thought. "You think I don't know about you? I know all about the letters, the history," he called out, his voice dripping with derision. "You can't hide from the past forever."

My stomach churned as I realized he was aware of what lay in that wooden box—the very secrets I had hoped to protect. My fingers tightened around the edges of the box, and I suddenly understood the stakes. This wasn't just about my family; it was about a history that linked us all in ways we were still uncovering.

"Who are you?" Jordan demanded, his voice steady but low. "What do you want?"

"Your secrets," the man replied, a sinister grin spreading across his face as he turned fully to face us. I recognized his features now, sharp and angular, a haunting familiarity swimming just beneath the surface. "And I'm here to make sure you give them to me."

"Get back!" I shouted, surprising myself with the strength of my voice. The anger surged within me, fueled by fear and defiance. This was my home—my sanctuary—and I wouldn't let some stranger invade it without a fight.

The man laughed, a hollow sound that reverberated through the room. "You think you can fight me? You don't know what you're dealing with."

In that moment, a spark ignited between us, the tension like a live wire ready to snap. I glanced at Jordan, who was already formulating a plan. "We can't let him take anything," he murmured, urgency creeping into his tone. "If he wants the box, we can't let him have it."

We exchanged a knowing glance, a silent agreement passing between us. The past was no longer just history; it was a living entity that threatened to engulf us both.

With a sudden burst of adrenaline, I turned and ran back into the hallway, shoving the box into the bottom of my closet, hoping the darkness would keep it safe, if only for a moment. I could hear Jordan moving to block the entrance to the living room, positioning himself as a barrier between me and the unknown threat.

"Let's think this through," Jordan said, his voice steady. "What do you want? We can talk this out. There's no need for violence."

"Talk?" the man sneered. "I've had enough of talking. You've been playing games with forces you don't understand. You think I want to hurt you? I want the truth."

"Then tell us who you are!" I shouted, my voice trembling with a mixture of fear and fury. "What truth are you looking for?"

For a brief moment, his face flickered with uncertainty. "You don't even know, do you? You're standing in the shadows of something much larger than you can comprehend. You're playing with fire."

The words hung in the air, heavy and foreboding, and I could feel the walls of my apartment closing in around me. This was no ordinary confrontation; it was a clash of legacies, a battle that had been waged long before we were born.

Suddenly, without warning, the man lunged toward Jordan, who reacted instinctively, shoving him back with a strength I didn't know he possessed. "Get away from her!" he shouted, his voice a fierce roar.

I watched in horror as they struggled, the sound of fists hitting flesh echoing in the small space. My heart raced, a mix of fear for Jordan and a burning desire to protect my home. Grabbing the nearest object, a heavy lamp, I prepared to intervene, my mind racing with possibilities.

"Stop! Both of you!" I yelled, desperation rising in my chest. "We don't have to do this!"

The man glanced at me, and in that fleeting moment, I saw a flicker of recognition. "You don't understand what you're getting into," he warned, his voice low and dangerous. "There are forces at play that will destroy you if you're not careful."

"Is that a threat?" I shot back, unwilling to back down.

"Consider it a warning," he replied, a smirk creeping across his face. "You have no idea what the box contains. It's not just letters; it's a key."

"A key to what?" Jordan growled, pulling himself up from the floor, determination igniting a fire in his eyes.

The man hesitated, and for a brief moment, I thought we might gain the upper hand. But then he lunged again, this time breaking free from Jordan's grip.

In a split second, everything changed. The man surged forward, and before I could react, he reached for the box. I felt my breath catch in my throat as time seemed to slow, the world narrowing down to that single moment.

"No!" I screamed, but it was too late. He snatched it from the closet and held it aloft, a triumphant grin plastered on his face.

"Time to see what secrets are worth risking your lives for."

And with that, he tore the lid off the box, and the air around us crackled with the energy of forgotten truths, threatening to unravel everything we thought we knew.

Chapter 13: A Tangled Web

The room was thick with the smell of ink and old paper, the kind of scent that always seemed to whisper secrets if you leaned in close enough. Stacks of files loomed around us like towering monuments to every lie and half-truth we had unearthed, each one promising answers but holding their tongues. I found myself perched on the edge of the worn leather chair, biting my lower lip as I traced my fingers over a document that felt both mundane and monumental—a faded receipt from a long-abandoned law firm that seemed to hold the keys to a door I wasn't sure I wanted to open. Across the table, Jordan's eyes flickered over the papers with an intensity that made my heart race.

"I swear, this is like some twisted game of hide-and-seek," he muttered, running a hand through his tousled hair, which had grown a little too long during our late-night sleuthing sessions. His frustration mingled with determination, the lines on his forehead deepening with each passing hour. "Why would they keep this hidden? What were they afraid of?"

I leaned back, the chair creaking beneath me, trying to quell the unease churning in my stomach. "Maybe they were afraid of what we might find," I replied, my voice steadier than I felt. I could see it in his eyes—the mix of hope and fear that mirrored my own. Each discovery felt like a step deeper into a shadowy abyss, and I was torn between the thrill of uncovering the truth and the dread of what that truth might reveal.

The dim light of the desk lamp cast flickering shadows on the walls, illuminating the small, cluttered space that had become our makeshift headquarters. My gaze drifted to the window, where the night pressed against the glass like a dark secret waiting to be whispered. Outside, the sounds of the city pulsed softly, a distant hum of life that felt strangely comforting yet foreign. We were ensconced in our own little world, far removed from the ordinary hustle that swirled just beyond those walls.

Jordan's eyes landed on me, and for a moment, the weight of the papers and the threat of the unknown faded. "You know," he began, a playful smirk curving his lips, "I always pictured my life as an action movie. I didn't think I'd be stuck in a room with a mountain of paperwork instead of dodging bullets."

I laughed, the sound light and airy, an unexpected burst of levity amidst the tension. "You could always take the scenic route and join a bank heist. I hear the getaway cars have great legroom." My playful banter sparked a glimmer of mischief in his eyes, a brief respite from the gravity of our situation.

"Only if you're my partner in crime," he shot back, the warmth of his gaze sending a familiar flutter through me. There was something undeniably magnetic about him, the way he navigated between playful banter and earnest vulnerability, making it hard to remember that the stakes were so high.

Just then, Mia burst through the door, her presence brightening the dimly lit room. "You two look like you've been through a war zone," she remarked, a teasing lilt in her voice as she swept her gaze over the chaotic assortment of files and coffee cups. Her fiancé, a tall man with an easy smile and an air of authority, followed closely behind, his brow furrowed in thought.

"It feels more like a standoff," I replied, my expression softening at the sight of her. "But I think we might have hit a nerve with some of these documents."

Mia's eyes sparkled with intrigue. "What have you found?"

Jordan leaned forward, his fingers hovering over a particular file. "This receipt indicates a connection between our families—one that stretches back decades. It could explain everything."

Her fiancé, Derek, moved closer, his interest piqued. "If that's true, we may have a lot more to dig into. I can make a few calls, see what I can pull up in the legal archives."

As they strategized, I sat back, absorbing the warmth of their camaraderie. There was something powerful in our alliance, a collective determination that ignited a spark of hope. Yet beneath that spark was an undercurrent of fear—a fear of the darkness that loomed beyond our small circle, threatening to unravel everything we had worked to build.

The hours slipped away, filled with discussions that flared into heated debates and moments of unexpected silence. Each breakthrough ignited a rush of adrenaline, but it was the moments in between—those shared glances, the subtle brush of Jordan's hand against mine, the warmth of Mia's laughter—that truly tethered me to this chaotic whirlwind we found ourselves in.

It was late when I realized the shadows outside had deepened, the night now a thick velvet curtain. Jordan's voice broke through my thoughts, an easy command that sent my heart racing. "Let's take a break. We can't keep running on fumes."

His words echoed in my mind as we stepped out onto the balcony, the cool air wrapping around us like a welcome embrace. I leaned against the railing, inhaling the scent of the city—the mingled fragrances of street food, fresh rain, and something uniquely urban. The sky above was a tapestry of stars, twinkling with secrets and possibilities, and for a moment, I felt invincible.

"You okay?" Jordan's voice was low, laced with concern as he joined me at the railing, his shoulder brushing against mine.

I nodded, even as my heart raced with the weight of unspoken truths. "Just...taking it all in. It feels so surreal."

His gaze met mine, the connection palpable in the cool night air. "We'll figure this out. Together."

And as I stood there, wrapped in the comforting presence of someone who had become my ally—and more—an unexpected wave of courage washed over me. The path ahead was fraught with danger, but with each heartbeat, I felt more certain that whatever tangled web we were stepping into, I would face it head-on. After all, love and fear often walked hand in hand, and I was ready to unravel the mystery that bound us, no matter what darkness lay ahead.

The air crackled with an intensity that felt almost electric, as if the very atmosphere held its breath in anticipation. I leaned against the railing, my heart still racing from the moment we shared, that fleeting connection on the balcony that had ignited something deep within me. With each moment spent in Jordan's company, the complexities of our situation began to blur, the lines between fear and desire intertwining in a dance that left me dizzy.

"Do you think we'll find anything useful in the archives?" I asked, forcing myself to focus on the task ahead. It was easier to concentrate on the chase than to acknowledge the storm brewing in my heart.

Jordan chuckled softly, his breath warm against the cool night air. "With Derek involved? I'd say we've got a pretty good shot. The man's practically a walking encyclopedia when it comes to legal loopholes."

"Great. So we're counting on a human thesaurus to pull us out of this mess," I quipped, rolling my eyes playfully, trying to dispel the tension. "Should we just start calling him Google?"

His laughter rang out, cutting through the stillness. "If only it were that easy. Besides, I think 'Derek' is a bit more charming than 'Google.'" He shot me a sideways glance, his smile infectious, and for a moment, the looming dread melted away.

We descended from the balcony, the night shifting into something more palpable, more fraught with danger as we re-entered our cluttered sanctuary. Mia was poring over a fresh stack of papers, her brow furrowed in concentration. The flickering desk lamp cast long shadows that danced across her determined face. "I think I found something," she announced, breaking the heavy silence that hung in the air.

Both of us moved closer, curiosity piqued. "What have you got?" I asked, barely able to contain my excitement.

"Looks like our families were involved in a legal dispute decades ago, one that never quite made it to public records. It's all very hush-hush." She glanced at Jordan, her eyes alight with mischief. "It even mentions a secret meeting."

"Ah, the plot thickens," Jordan murmured, leaning in for a better look. "I hope this isn't leading us to some clandestine society. I didn't sign up for a secret handshake."

"Or a sacrificial ritual," I added, my tone dripping with sarcasm. "But I suppose we could always ask Derek to break out his inner Indiana Jones if it comes to that."

Mia shot me a look, her eyes narrowing. "Don't give him any ideas. If we end up in some creepy basement, I'm blaming you."

The playful banter between us felt like a lifeline, tethering us to some semblance of normalcy amid the chaos. But as we continued to sift through the documents, a feeling of unease settled into the pit of my stomach. Each piece we uncovered seemed to be pulling us deeper into a labyrinthine plot where trust was a luxury we could no longer afford.

Hours melted into one another as we worked, the glow of the desk lamp flickering like a beacon in the dark. Eventually, the silence grew heavy again, each of us lost in our thoughts, the weight of the past pressing down upon us like a shroud. I glanced at Jordan, who had fallen into a contemplative silence, his jaw clenched tightly.

"What are you thinking about?" I asked quietly, breaking the silence.

He looked up, his expression a mixture of determination and vulnerability. "Just wondering how far back this goes. What if it's more than just a legal dispute? What if it involves something... darker?"

The thought sent a shiver down my spine. "You think we're in danger?"

"Not danger, per se," he replied, his gaze steady. "But we're definitely stirring up a hornet's nest."

Just then, the phone buzzed on the table, a jarring reminder of the world outside our bubble. Mia reached for it, her expression shifting from curiosity to alarm as she read the message. "It's Derek. He says he's got some leads, but he's in a meeting with someone important, and it could take a while."

"Great. So we're left twiddling our thumbs," I said, the frustration bubbling to the surface.

Jordan's eyes met mine, a mischievous glint returning. "You know, we could always plan our escape if things go sideways. A covert operation, just the two of us."

I raised an eyebrow, suppressing a laugh. "And what would our code names be? You can't just go around calling yourself 'Jordan the Daring.'"

"Fair point. How about 'Caffeine Crusader' for you?" He paused dramatically. "And I'll be 'Mysterious Stranger.'"

I chuckled, the lighthearted moment a welcome distraction. "I can live with that. Just as long as we don't have to wear capes."

The banter danced between us, a sweet distraction from the reality we faced. But the laughter faded as the night deepened, replaced by an oppressive silence that wrapped around us like a thick fog. The unease settled in my chest again, and I glanced back at the papers strewn across the table, words blurring together as my mind raced.

A sudden thought struck me, and I turned back to Jordan. "What if this isn't just about our families? What if there are others involved? People who don't want us digging around?"

His expression shifted, concern flashing across his features. "You think someone is watching us?"

"Maybe not literally," I replied, my voice barely above a whisper. "But I can't shake the feeling that we're being led into something much bigger than we anticipated."

Jordan's expression hardened, his resolve palpable. "Then we need to be careful. We have to watch our backs."

Just as the words left his lips, a loud crash echoed from outside, followed by the unmistakable sound of tires screeching to a halt. Our banter faded, replaced by a shared, instinctual tension. We exchanged quick glances, a silent understanding passing between us as adrenaline surged through my veins.

"We should check that out," I suggested, my heart racing.

Jordan nodded, moving swiftly toward the door, the weight of uncertainty heavy in the air. Together, we stepped into the cool night, the world outside our bubble suddenly alive with possibilities—danger lurking just beyond our reach, secrets waiting to be uncovered. And as we ventured into the unknown, I realized that whatever tangled web we were caught in, we were no longer alone. We had each other, and together, we would face whatever awaited us in the shadows.

The night was thick with tension as we stepped out onto the street, the distant sound of sirens punctuating the air like a warning bell. Jordan's presence beside me was a steadying force, but even his calm demeanor couldn't dispel the prickling unease creeping along my spine. The noise we'd heard—metal on metal, a crash that echoed through the stillness—had shattered our momentary peace, pulling us into the chaos of the outside world.

"What was that?" I asked, my voice barely above a whisper as we moved cautiously toward the street corner where the sounds had emanated. Shadows danced in the streetlights, casting eerie shapes that made my heart race.

Jordan turned to me, his expression serious. "Could be an accident, or something more sinister. We should—"

Before he could finish, a figure darted past us, a blur of motion that sent my heart leaping into my throat. "Did you see that?" I gasped, instinctively clutching his arm.

"I did," he replied, eyes narrowing as he focused on the retreating silhouette. "Stay close."

We hurried down the street, the echoes of our footsteps mingling with the distant wail of sirens. The figure had turned a corner, and as we approached, the faint sound of muffled voices reached our ears, urgent and hushed. My instincts screamed at me to turn back, to retreat to the safety of our cluttered haven, but curiosity pulled me forward.

"We have to hear what they're saying," I urged, glancing at Jordan, whose expression was a mix of determination and concern.

He nodded, leading the way as we edged closer to the alleyway where the voices grew clearer. It was a risky move, but the promise of answers—of truth—drove us on. I felt a rush of adrenaline as we slipped into the shadows, the alley a narrow corridor between towering buildings that loomed over us like ancient sentinels.

As we pressed our backs against the cool, damp brick, I strained to catch the words filtering through the night. A low, gravelly voice rumbled, "You think they'll find out? If they do, we're done."

A second voice, sharp and agitated, replied, "We can't afford to let them get too close. Not now. We have to shut this down before it spirals out of control."

My pulse quickened, the implications of their conversation heavy with threat. "They're talking about us," I breathed, my heart thudding in my chest. "They know we're digging. We need to get out of here."

Jordan's grip tightened on my arm, grounding me as he whispered, "Wait. We need to know more. Just a little longer."

Just then, the tension of the moment shattered like glass. A shout erupted from deeper in the alley, a voice rising above the others, filled with anger and urgency. "You're making a mistake! You don't know what you're dealing with!"

The exchange morphed into chaos. I could see shadows shifting, and the clatter of something heavy hitting the ground echoed in the narrow space. The urgency of the moment propelled us forward, driven by the instinct to flee, but curiosity rooted us in place.

"What if they're part of the same network? The same people we've been researching?" I murmured, my mind racing with possibilities. "What if they know everything?"

"Then we need to be careful," Jordan said, his voice low and tense. "We have to get the evidence and get out. They can't see us."

As if summoned by our fear, the shadows of the alley began to converge. The figures I had glimpsed now loomed larger, and I caught sight of a familiar face in the melee—a woman, her features striking even in the half-light, pushing against a man who seemed to tower over her.

"Mia!" I gasped, my heart sinking as I realized she was caught in the middle of whatever storm was brewing.

"Go!" Jordan hissed, sensing the danger that crackled in the air. But before we could retreat, Mia's gaze met mine, and in that instant, I saw a mix of fear and defiance, a silent plea that ignited my resolve.

"Mia!" I shouted, drawing the attention of the figures around her.

Time seemed to freeze, and chaos erupted. The man shoved Mia aside, a flash of something metallic gleaming in his hand. "Get out of here! Now!" she yelled, her voice cutting through the confusion like a siren.

Jordan pulled me back, our instincts screaming that we needed to escape, but I couldn't just leave her. "We can't abandon her!" I protested, my heart racing as I struggled against his grip.

"Mia's a fighter; she'll hold her own," he replied, his tone urgent. "We need to find a way to get help. We can't get caught up in this."

The shadows danced closer, voices raised in anger, and my mind raced. We were in the eye of a storm, caught between a terrifying confrontation and the secrets we were desperate to uncover. But in that moment, I made a choice—a reckless, brave choice that felt like it had been carved into my bones.

"Not without her," I insisted, breaking free from Jordan's grasp and sprinting forward into the chaos.

"Mia!" I shouted, my voice cutting through the fray.

The scene unfolded like a nightmare, a whirlwind of motion as I barreled forward. The man, momentarily distracted by my shout, turned toward me, his expression shifting from surprise to something far darker.

"Mia, get out of here!" I urged again, desperation threading my voice as I pushed my way through the chaos, adrenaline surging through my veins.

"Mia!" The word escaped my lips again, but the shadows thickened, and before I could reach her, the man lunged, and in a flash, everything blurred into confusion and panic.

I felt a jolt as strong hands grabbed me, pulling me back, and I cried out, my heart pounding in a desperate rhythm. The world spun, the shouts of anger mixed with fear echoing off the brick walls, and as I struggled against the grip that held me, I caught a final glimpse of Mia, her face a mixture of determination and terror, before the shadows swallowed her whole.

In that moment, the ground beneath me felt unsteady, and an icy wave of dread washed over me. Whatever tangled web we were ensnared in was tightening, and with every beat of my heart, I realized we were no longer just witnesses to a secret. We were players in a game that had turned dangerously real, and I had just stepped onto the board, unaware of the stakes—or the impending fallout.

Chapter 14: Dark Omens

The evening air crackled with an energy I couldn't quite place, charged as if the city itself were holding its breath. With each step I took beside Jordan, the asphalt beneath our feet felt more like a living thing, pulsing in sync with the anxiety thrumming through my veins. The neon lights of the bars and cafés flickered overhead, casting colorful shadows that danced like phantoms around us. It was a typical Friday night in the city, yet everything felt off-kilter, like a record skipping at the worst possible moment.

"Why are we doing this again?" Jordan asked, glancing at me with a mix of concern and determination etched on his handsome face. His dark hair caught the glow of a streetlamp, framing his features in a way that always made my heart stutter. "We could just go home. We could—"

"Hide?" I interrupted, frustration bubbling beneath my surface. The warning had seeped into my bones, a chill that crept up my spine every time I recalled the message. It was too late for that. I was done letting shadows dictate my life. "We can't run away from this. Not anymore."

He sighed, a sound laced with both exasperation and admiration. "You're stubborn, you know that?"

"Stubborn or determined?" I shot back, a smirk tugging at my lips despite the anxiety gnawing at my insides. It was our usual banter, the kind of lightness that felt like a warm embrace against the dark reality pressing in around us.

We made our way through the crowded streets, the laughter and music spilling out from the bars creating a soundtrack to our own tension-filled narrative. I had a plan, though not a particularly well-thought-out one. I'd decided we'd visit the alley where I first spotted the man watching us—a dark figure lurking just outside the warmth of the streetlights. It felt ludicrous, the idea that I might find him there again, but I needed to confront this madness, to chase away the shadows whispering fears into my mind.

As we approached the alley, the atmosphere shifted. The laughter faded, replaced by an unsettling silence that enveloped us like a heavy fog. I turned to Jordan, his expression mirroring the trepidation bubbling in my chest. "Stay close," I murmured, the words barely escaping my lips as we stepped into the dimly lit passage.

The alley smelled of damp concrete and old trash, the kind of scent that lingered in the air long after the source had vanished. We moved slowly, the sound of our footsteps echoing against the brick walls, each step amplifying the tension wrapped around us like a vise. I felt Jordan's hand slip into mine, a grounding force in the creeping dread.

"I really don't like this," he muttered, scanning the darkness with wary eyes. "What if we're making a huge mistake?"

"Maybe," I admitted, a lump forming in my throat. "But I'd rather face whatever this is than cower in fear. We need to understand what's happening."

Just then, a noise echoed from the far end of the alley—a sharp scrape followed by a low, rumbling laugh that sent a shiver down my spine. My heart raced, and I squeezed Jordan's hand tighter, willing him to understand the urgency of the moment.

"We should go," he urged, his voice barely above a whisper.

"No," I breathed, my resolve hardening. "We need to see. We can't let fear win."

I pressed forward, driven by a force I couldn't name. The shadows ahead twisted and shifted, revealing an abandoned door that hung slightly ajar. My instincts screamed at me to turn back, yet curiosity propelled me forward. I pushed the door open, the rusty hinges protesting with a creak that echoed ominously in the stillness.

Inside, the space was a disheveled amalgamation of broken furniture and remnants of a life once lived. My senses heightened,

I surveyed the room, trying to catch a glimpse of something—anything—that would provide answers to the inexplicable tension that had gripped my life. I took a cautious step inside, and Jordan followed, his presence a steady anchor amidst the chaos.

"Maybe we should just call the police," he suggested, but even he could hear the doubt laced in his voice.

"Maybe we should just trust our instincts," I countered, letting go of his hand to take a few steps deeper into the room. The walls were covered in peeling paint, the air thick with dust that sparkled under the slivers of moonlight seeping through the cracks.

And then I saw it—scrawled on the far wall, in what looked like hurried strokes of dark paint or maybe even blood, were the words: "He's coming for you."

I froze, the reality of the message sinking into my bones like ice water. The letters seemed to pulse with a life of their own, each word a dark omen that echoed my own fears. "Jordan," I called, my voice shaking as I stumbled back to him, the room spinning slightly. "We need to go. Now."

"Wait!" he urged, reaching for my arm, but I shook him off, my instincts screaming at me to flee. The shadows danced around us, twisting and turning as if alive, and suddenly it felt as though the very walls were closing in.

As we turned to leave, I caught a glimpse of movement from the corner of my eye—a figure slipping through the shadows just outside the door. My heart stopped, a jolt of fear coursing through me as I realized that our confrontation had only just begun.

A figure stepped into the dim light of the alley, their face obscured by a hood, casting an elongated shadow that flickered like a specter against the wall. My breath caught in my throat as the reality of our situation crashed over me. Panic surged, threatening to overwhelm my senses. "Jordan," I whispered, urgency lacing my voice, "we have to move. Now."

Before he could respond, the figure advanced, shuffling slowly yet purposefully, as if savoring the moment. I felt my heart pound in my chest, each beat a warning drum echoing in my ears. "Run!" I urged, adrenaline propelling me forward even as fear tugged at my heels.

But instead of fleeing, Jordan stood his ground, a mixture of bravery and foolishness dancing in his eyes. "Wait! We need to find out who it is!" His grip tightened around my wrist, anchoring me just long enough for my courage to falter.

The figure paused, tilting their head slightly, and for a fleeting moment, I thought I caught a glint of recognition in the shadows. "You shouldn't have come here," they murmured, their voice low and gravelly, sending chills racing down my spine.

I tugged against Jordan's hold, a fresh wave of terror coursing through me. "Are you out of your mind? We're not here to make friends!"

"Just a little more," Jordan insisted, his determination igniting a flicker of hope in me, even as dread twisted in my stomach. "Let's see what they want."

In that moment, the figure stepped closer, revealing a familiar outline, and my heart sank as recognition washed over me. It was Max, an old acquaintance from a past I had hoped to leave behind. He had always been a bit of a shadow himself—troubled, enigmatic, someone who thrived in the underbelly of our city. "I didn't think you'd actually come," he said, his lips curling into a sardonic smile that didn't quite reach his eyes.

"Max," I managed, the name feeling foreign on my tongue, laden with memories of late-night escapades and reckless choices. "What are you doing here?"

"Just keeping an eye on things," he replied, his tone casual but laced with an undercurrent of something darker. "You're in over your head, you know. He's not the kind of guy you want to mess with."

I could feel Jordan's tension beside me, his posture shifting as he processed the implications of Max's words. "Who's 'he'?" Jordan asked, a protective edge creeping into his voice.

Max's gaze flicked between us, amusement dancing in his eyes. "You really don't know, do you? There's more to this than you think. There are forces at play that you can't begin to understand."

The shadows around us thickened as if the alley itself were eavesdropping on our exchange. I felt an urge to flee, but something about Max's presence held me captive. "Just tell us what you know," I pressed, trying to shake off the sense of vulnerability threatening to engulf me. "We're not afraid."

"Ah, the bravado of youth," he chuckled, but the humor didn't quite reach his gaze. "You should be. He's not just some random guy. He's connected. Dangerous. You've already piqued his interest, and trust me, that's not a good thing."

Jordan shifted, glancing at me, his brow furrowed. "What do you mean, piqued his interest? We haven't done anything—"

"Exactly," Max interrupted, his tone sharpening. "You don't realize the implications of what you've stumbled into. It's like stepping into a hornet's nest without a clue about the sting."

"What are you talking about?" I demanded, frustration boiling beneath my skin. "If you know something, just say it. We're done playing games."

Max stepped closer, lowering his voice conspiratorially. "There's a reason you got that message. Someone's been watching you. The guy you're curious about—he's not just a man. He's a player in something much bigger, something dangerous that you've unwittingly become a part of."

I swallowed hard, my throat suddenly dry. "What does that even mean?" The weight of his words pressed against me like a heavy blanket, suffocating and ominous.

"It means," he replied slowly, "that you need to watch your back. This isn't just about you anymore. You've caught someone's eye, and they won't let go easily."

Jordan shifted beside me, his body radiating tension, and I felt the weight of the world pressing down on us both. "We can handle ourselves," he said defiantly, but I could hear the uncertainty lurking beneath his bravado.

"Handle yourselves?" Max laughed, a sound devoid of real mirth. "You're in a realm where self-preservation is an illusion. This isn't about handling; it's about surviving."

With those words, he turned abruptly, retreating into the shadows. My heart raced, a cocktail of fear and adrenaline coursing through me. "What do we do?" I whispered, the words slipping from my lips as I felt the floor beneath me tilt dangerously.

"We need to figure this out," Jordan replied, gripping my arm, his resolve stronger than mine. "We can't let fear dictate our actions. We'll find out who he is and why he's watching."

But as we stepped out of the alley and back into the vibrant chaos of the city, I couldn't shake the feeling that we had just crossed an invisible line, one that would plunge us deeper into darkness. The warning had taken root in my mind, a bitter reminder that curiosity can be as treacherous as it is exhilarating. The night, once alive with possibility, now hung heavy with the weight of uncertainty, and I couldn't help but wonder if we were in way over our heads.

With every heartbeat, the city around us pulsed with a strange energy, a reminder that we were not alone in our quest for answers. Something—or someone—was watching, and the stakes were higher than we could have ever imagined.

The night air felt electric as we emerged from the alley, the city lights flickering like distant stars trying to pierce through the looming shadows. I could still hear Max's words echoing in my mind, a grim reminder of the invisible strings tugging at our lives. "You've caught someone's eye," he'd said, as if our existence had become a spectacle for a twisted audience. It sent shivers racing down my spine, igniting a flame of rebellion in my chest.

Jordan squeezed my hand tighter, grounding me in the chaotic swirl of the nightlife surrounding us. "Let's get out of here," he said, his eyes scanning the street, as if every passerby could be the ominous figure Max had alluded to. I could see the worry etched on his face, a blend of protectiveness and uncertainty, the same expression he wore when I suggested taking a leap of faith. It tugged at something deep within me, a longing to shield him from the storm I had inadvertently unleashed.

"I don't want to run," I replied, determination hardening my resolve. "We can't let fear control us. We need to find out what this is really about."

"Right," he replied, trying to mask his apprehension with a brave face. "And how exactly do you propose we do that? Should we put out an ad in the newspaper? 'Wanted: Information about shadowy figures and vague threats?'"

I shot him a playful glare, appreciating his attempt to lighten the mood, but the weight of the situation dampened my spirit. "Maybe we can start by retracing our steps. Let's go to the coffee shop where we first saw him."

Jordan raised an eyebrow, the tension easing slightly as he chuckled. "Oh sure, because nothing screams 'we're not afraid' like ordering a cappuccino while a potential stalker lurks nearby."

"Exactly!" I grinned, his humor a necessary balm against the rising tide of anxiety. "We'll be so caffeinated that even the shadows will think twice before approaching us."

We headed toward our favorite haunt, a cozy little café nestled between a bookstore and a quirky vintage shop. The aroma of freshly brewed coffee enveloped us as we pushed through the door, the comforting sound of espresso machines humming in the background blending with the low murmur of conversation. The warmth was almost palpable, wrapping around us like a blanket as we found a secluded corner table.

As I sat down, I caught sight of a barista with a bright blue mohawk, her laughter bubbling like the froth atop the cappuccinos she served. I momentarily lost myself in the vibrant atmosphere, but the reminder of our looming danger quickly snapped me back to reality. "What if he's watching us right now?" I whispered, casting a cautious glance toward the large window that offered a view of the bustling street outside.

Jordan leaned closer, his voice low and steady. "Then we're going to look him right in the eye and show him we're not afraid."

With each sip of our drinks, the energy in the café infused me with a sense of normalcy, however fleeting. The laughter and chatter buzzed around us like a comforting symphony, grounding me in a reality that felt increasingly surreal. We discussed everything from favorite books to the latest indie films, slipping into a rhythm that almost made me forget the shadows lurking outside. But the conversation always found its way back to the figure in the alley, the message that haunted us both.

Just as I began to relax, the bell above the café door jingled, drawing my attention to a new arrival. My stomach twisted in knots as I recognized the man from my nightmares—dark hair, sharp features, an unmistakable presence that felt like a storm cloud rolling in. He entered casually, scanning the room, and I felt my heart leap into my throat. "Jordan," I hissed, gripping the table's edge as my pulse quickened. "He's here."

"Who?" Jordan turned, but by the time he looked back, the man had already blended into the crowd. My imagination flared with panic as I pictured him closing the distance between us. I fought the urge to bolt but knew fleeing would only confirm my fear.

"I don't know," I replied, my voice trembling. "But we need to get out of here. Now."

"Okay, but how?" he asked, urgency creeping into his tone. "He could be anywhere."

I took a deep breath, trying to quell the tide of panic. "We'll slip out the back. Stay low and keep quiet."

Jordan nodded, his expression a mix of apprehension and resolve. We pushed our chairs back, attempting to be discreet as we slid through the throng of patrons, the clinking of cups and laughter a stark contrast to the tension thrumming in my veins. My heart raced as we navigated the narrow aisles, my senses on high alert, scanning for any sign of him.

Just as we reached the door to the rear exit, the unmistakable sound of a chair scraping against the floor halted us in our tracks. I turned, dread pooling in my stomach as I locked eyes with him. The man stood by the front counter, a sly smile curling his lips as if he had been waiting for this moment, this very second.

"Leaving so soon?" he called out, his voice smooth yet laced with a dark undercurrent that sent chills cascading down my spine. The café seemed to fade around me, the laughter and chatter dissolving into a haunting silence.

"Let's go," I whispered urgently, my instincts screaming for us to move, but Jordan hesitated, the weight of our predicament pressing down on him.

"Who are you?" Jordan demanded, his voice steadier than I felt, but I could see the uncertainty flicker in his eyes.

The man took a step forward, his posture relaxed, yet there was a predatory glint in his gaze. "Let's just say I'm someone with a vested interest in your little escapade. You really shouldn't have poked your nose where it doesn't belong."

A chill gripped me, the gravity of his words crashing down like a tidal wave. "What do you want from us?" I managed, my voice trembling despite my best efforts to sound composed.

"Ah, it's not what I want," he replied, his smile widening, "but rather what you're about to uncover. The world you're about to step into is far more dangerous than you realize."

With every word, the walls of the café seemed to constrict, the air thickening with the weight of his threat. I took a cautious step back, instinctively drawing Jordan closer to me as I searched for an escape. But the man's presence loomed larger than life, filling the space with an air of impending doom.

"Don't run," he warned, his voice low, almost playful. "You wouldn't want to make things worse. You're in this now, whether you like it or not."

Before I could respond, the door swung open with a crash, revealing a group of suited men, their expressions hardened and purpose-driven. My heart raced as I realized the stakes had just escalated. The café, once a haven, now felt like a trap closing in around us.

"What do you want?" Jordan shouted, adrenaline surging as he squared his shoulders, ready to defend me against the unknown.

But the man merely chuckled, a sound devoid of any real humor. "You'll find out soon enough," he said, his gaze shifting past us, as if he were the puppeteer orchestrating our impending doom.

I felt the world tilt beneath my feet, and as I turned to flee, a hand gripped my arm, pulling me back into the darkness that seemed to loom just beyond the chaos.

Chapter 15: The Final Confrontation

In the dim light of the warehouse, the air hung thick with the scent of rust and old secrets, wrapping around me like a second skin. Shadows clung to the walls, swaying as if they too were drawn into the tension crackling in the air. I could hear my heartbeat echoing in my ears, a staccato rhythm that felt too loud, too insistent. Jordan stood beside me, his profile a mix of determination and vulnerability. His presence anchored me, yet the weight of our discovery bore down on us like the heavy steel beams overhead, creaking with age and the burden of history.

We had unspooled a thread that led us here, to this forsaken place where old wounds threatened to reopen. Each step forward felt like we were trespassing into a realm of darkness, a domain where trust had long been extinguished, and betrayal whispered from every corner. I glanced at Jordan, his brow furrowed, eyes sharp with an intensity that made my stomach twist. It was the look of someone who had seen too much and yet was resolute in facing what lay ahead. "We have to be careful," he murmured, his voice barely above a whisper.

"Careful?" I shot back, a smirk tugging at my lips despite the gravity of the situation. "You mean we shouldn't stroll in like we own the place? Because I was really looking forward to that."

A flicker of surprise danced in his eyes, a brief moment of levity in this storm of dread. "Right. I'll keep that in mind," he replied, shaking his head, a hint of a smile breaking through his tense facade.

We moved cautiously, my footsteps echoing ominously against the concrete floor, while the air thickened with the unspoken truths that had woven our families' lives together in a tangled web of deceit. Each twist and turn unveiled another layer of the dark legacy we had inherited—one that didn't just implicate strangers, but those we loved.

The chill of realization settled in the pit of my stomach as I recalled the names my mother had whispered during late-night phone calls, the hushed tones filled with fear and fury. This place was the nexus of all those conversations, the crucible where our fates had been forged. The lights flickered above us, casting eerie shapes on the walls, mirroring the chaos swirling in my mind.

"Jordan," I started, feeling the words stick in my throat. "What if it's not just the organization we need to worry about? What if our families are tangled in this mess too?"

He turned to face me, his gaze piercing through the gloom. "I've been thinking the same thing. It would explain why we couldn't get any answers before. They're hiding something... or someone."

Just then, the sound of footsteps echoed from deeper within the warehouse, halting us in our tracks. My heart raced as we exchanged a look, the unspoken fear reflecting in our eyes. "Hide," I whispered, pulling Jordan into the shadows just as a group of figures emerged from the darkness.

They moved with a predatory grace, each step deliberate and menacing. I strained to hear their conversation, the gravelly voice of a man rising above the rest. "We need to make an example out of them. They're getting too close. If they think they can uncover the truth—"

"Then we'll show them what happens to those who pry into matters beyond their understanding," another voice cut in, sharper than the rest.

I felt a shiver run down my spine, the weight of their words hanging heavy in the air. Jordan's hand tightened around mine, a silent promise that we wouldn't back down. The flicker of defiance ignited within me, mixing with the adrenaline coursing through my veins. We couldn't let fear dictate our actions; we had come too far to retreat now.

The figures shifted, and I caught a glimpse of one of them—a man with a distinctive scar running down his cheek. My breath hitched; it was someone from my past, a shadow that had lingered long before I had realized the truth. "No," I breathed, recognition dawning.

"Do you know him?" Jordan asked, concern etched across his features.

"Yes, he's... he's connected to my family." The revelation hit me like a jolt, a rush of memories flooding back, twisting into a knot of confusion and dread. "He knows what we've discovered. We have to warn—"

Before I could finish, the man glanced in our direction, a sinister smile creeping across his face. "Well, well, what do we have here?" he drawled, his voice dripping with mockery. "Playing detective, are we? How adorable."

Panic surged within me, but it was quickly replaced by a fierce determination. "We're not afraid of you," I declared, surprising even myself with the steadiness of my voice.

Jordan stepped forward, his posture resolute beside me. "You think you can intimidate us? We know about the organization, and we won't let you silence us."

The man's smile widened, revealing a glint of malice. "Brave words, but you're stepping into a world you don't understand. You're in way over your heads."

In that moment, I understood the depths of the danger we faced—not just from him, but from everything we had uncovered. The lines between ally and enemy blurred, and with every breath, the weight of our families' legacies threatened to crush us beneath their expectations and sins.

"Then let's find out just how deep this rabbit hole goes," I replied, a defiant spark igniting within me. I glanced at Jordan, and in his eyes, I saw my reflection—a determination that mirrored my own. We were ready to face whatever darkness lay ahead, our hearts intertwined in a fight that had become more than just about our families. It was about us, our choices, and the future we dared to seize.

The man's laughter echoed through the warehouse, a sound so cold it could have frozen the flickering lights above us. My heart raced, but it wasn't fear alone that fueled my adrenaline; it was the sudden, electrifying realization that this confrontation was not merely a clash with a criminal—it was a collision with my own history, an unraveling of the truths my family had buried deep beneath layers of denial and deception. I could feel the weight of my lineage pressing down on me, like an anchor dragging me into the depths of a murky sea.

"What's the matter? Cat got your tongue?" he taunted, stepping closer, the dim light casting long shadows that flickered like the tales of family secrets I had been told all my life. His confidence was unnerving, a smugness that felt like a betrayal in its own right.

I swallowed hard, the need to stand my ground overwhelming. "We're not afraid of you," I said, though the tremor in my voice hinted at the uncertainty clawing at the edges of my resolve. "We know what you've done."

"Ah, ignorance is such bliss," he replied, his eyes glinting with a mixture of amusement and malice. "You have no idea what you're stepping into."

Jordan shifted beside me, and I could sense the tension radiating from him, a silent promise that we wouldn't back down. He stepped forward, his voice steady. "We've come too far to back off now. You think you can intimidate us with your threats? We won't be silenced."

The man's smile faded slightly, replaced by an icy glare. "Bravery without knowledge is reckless. You should know, there are forces at play here that even you can't comprehend."

"Is that a threat?" I shot back, emboldened by Jordan's unwavering presence. "Because if it is, I'm afraid you're going to have to try harder than that."

"Enough games," he growled, his patience wearing thin. "You're just children playing with fire, and I will make sure you get burned."

With that, he gestured behind him, and the shadows shifted, revealing figures emerging from the darkened corners of the warehouse. Each face was unfamiliar, yet a shared air of menace hung around them like a thick fog, a palpable aura that suggested they had all taken part in the same sinister ballet of deception.

I felt my pulse quicken as I scanned the room, searching for an escape route. "Jordan, we need to—"

But before I could finish, one of the newcomers lunged forward, charging at us with the agility of a predator. Instinct kicked in; I sidestepped just in time, but Jordan wasn't so lucky. The assailant tackled him to the ground, sending a jolt of panic through me. "Jordan!"

"Get back!" he shouted, grappling with the man, their bodies colliding in a frenzy of flailing limbs. My heart dropped into my stomach as I watched the struggle unfold, the chaos spinning around us like a wild cyclone.

Without thinking, I grabbed a nearby metal pipe, its cold weight reassuring against my palm. "Hey!" I yelled, brandishing it as a makeshift weapon. "You want a fight? I can play that game too!"

The men surrounding us paused, surprise flickering in their eyes. The sudden shift of focus was all I needed; I rushed forward, swinging the pipe with all the strength I could muster. It connected with the assailant's shoulder, sending him stumbling back and allowing Jordan to break free.

"Nice shot!" he grinned, breathing heavily as he regained his footing. "Maybe we should consider a career change."

"I'd rather be anywhere else," I replied, my voice strained as I glanced at the others closing in. The situation was spiraling, but we had momentarily gained the upper hand.

"Let's push back!" Jordan shouted, rallying his strength as we prepared to face our attackers together.

With adrenaline coursing through me, we charged forward, my heart pounding like a drum. The chaos erupted into a whirlwind of shouts and frantic movements, our bodies colliding with those of our foes in a dance of desperation. I ducked and weaved, every instinct screaming at me to survive.

But as we fought, a nagging thought lingered in the back of my mind. This was just a distraction, a ploy to keep us occupied while the real battle unfolded elsewhere—perhaps a greater scheme that we couldn't see yet.

"Jordan!" I yelled amid the din. "We need to find out who's really pulling the strings! This isn't just about them!"

"I know!" he shouted back, throwing a punch that landed squarely against one man's jaw, sending him reeling. "But right now, we have to survive!"

With a surge of determination, I pressed on, dodging another attacker and swinging the pipe again. The clanging metal echoed around us, a soundtrack to our struggle, each hit a reminder of the fight we were forced into. But with every moment, the reality of our situation became clearer: the real enemy lurked in the shadows, behind the faces of these pawns.

Just as I began to feel the tide turning in our favor, the flickering lights overhead sputtered and died, plunging the warehouse into darkness. Panic surged within me as the sounds of our scuffle morphed into an overwhelming cacophony. I could barely see Jordan, only the faint outline of his figure moving through the dark, his form melding into the shadows.

"Jordan!" I called out, the void around me swallowing my voice, fear creeping into my chest.

"Right here!" he replied, his voice a beacon in the blackness. I felt my way toward him, my heart hammering as I fought to keep my composure.

"Stay close," I urged, gripping his arm tightly. "We have to find a way out."

Suddenly, a bright beam sliced through the darkness, illuminating the chaos around us. A flashlight had been turned on, revealing the men regrouping, their expressions a mix of surprise and annoyance.

"Don't let them escape!" one shouted, and I felt a surge of dread wash over me.

We were being hunted, the stakes higher than ever. But just as I began to panic, I caught a glimpse of something out of the corner of my eye—a door, slightly ajar at the far end of the warehouse. It beckoned to me like a lifeline thrown into turbulent waters.

"Jordan, the door!" I pointed, urgency sharpening my voice.

"Let's go!" he replied, and we bolted toward it, weaving through the chaos as our pursuers rallied to intercept us.

Every step felt like a gamble, the darkness wrapping around us like a shroud as we raced toward what felt like our only chance at escape. The air crackled with the weight of our urgency, but my resolve strengthened with each passing moment. Whatever awaited us beyond that door, we were ready to face it together, hand in hand, against whatever darkness lay ahead.

With the door barely ajar, I could feel the cool rush of air spilling into the darkness like a promise of freedom. Jordan and I exchanged glances, the unspoken urgency coursing between us like electricity. The clamor of our pursuers surged behind us, the shouts and footsteps merging into a cacophony of chaos. There was no time for hesitation; this was our moment to escape the suffocating grip of the warehouse and whatever dark secrets awaited us beyond its walls.

"Ready?" Jordan asked, his voice low and steady despite the storm of anxiety brewing in his chest.

"Not really, but let's do it anyway," I replied, a nervous laugh bubbling up as I pushed the door open wider.

The light outside spilled in, illuminating the pathway ahead like an invitation. I could see the night sky stretching infinitely above us, stars twinkling like distant promises. The concrete ground felt rough beneath my feet, a sharp contrast to the oppressive atmosphere we had just left behind.

As we stepped outside, the sound of the door slamming shut echoed behind us, a final barrier between us and the shadows of our past. We sprinted down a narrow alley, my heart pounding in sync with the rapid beats of our escape. Every breath I took was filled with the taste of freedom mixed with fear—fear of what lay behind us and uncertainty about what lay ahead.

"Where to now?" Jordan gasped, glancing over his shoulder as we rounded a corner. The alley opened up into a larger street, the headlights of cars slicing through the darkness.

"Let's head for the park. It's secluded, and we can figure out our next move there," I suggested, my mind racing to process everything that had just transpired. The shadows we had left behind might still be lurking, waiting for us to let our guard down.

We bolted into the park, the trees looming like ancient sentinels, their branches swaying gently in the breeze. The moon bathed everything in silver light, casting long shadows that danced in rhythm with our racing hearts. I felt the weight of adrenaline ebb slightly, replaced by a sense of clarity as the night air filled my lungs.

"Okay, we need to regroup," I said, finally slowing down. I leaned against a tree, trying to catch my breath, my heart still racing. "What do we know? What are we up against?"

Jordan ran a hand through his hair, frustration flickering in his eyes. "We know that our families are somehow involved in this mess, and they've been lying to us our whole lives. But why?"

"Maybe they're afraid of what we'll uncover," I mused aloud, the pieces of the puzzle swirling in my mind. "If this organization is as dangerous as they make it out to be, maybe they think we'll be safer if we don't know the truth."

"And yet, here we are, in the thick of it," he replied, a wry smile breaking through the tension. "Safer than ever."

I couldn't help but laugh, the absurdity of our situation settling in. "Right? All those family dinners, and not once did anyone mention the possibility of a criminal syndicate lurking in our backgrounds. They could have just said, 'Oh, by the way, watch out for the mob.'"

We shared a brief moment of levity, but it quickly dissipated as reality crashed back in. "What do we do next?" Jordan asked, his voice dropping to a serious tone. "We can't just walk away from this. They'll come after us again."

"First, we need to find out what we're truly up against. I want to know how deep this goes," I said, steeling myself for what lay ahead. "If our families are involved, then we have to confront them. We need to get answers."

"Confront them?" he echoed, his brows knitting together. "Are you sure you're ready for that?"

"Not really. But running isn't an option anymore. We have to take charge of this situation before it consumes us."

Jordan nodded, his resolve firming. "Okay, then we need to get our hands on any information we can. I might have a lead on someone who can help."

"Who?" I asked, curiosity piquing as I tried to envision who would be able to navigate the tangled web of our families' dark histories.

"My uncle. He's always been on the fringes of this world, you know? He knows things—things that might connect the dots."

"Isn't he the one who went missing a few years back?"

"Yeah, but that was all part of the family cover-up. No one really knows what happened to him. He could still be in touch with people who know what's going on."

"Do you trust him?" I asked, skepticism creeping in.

"Trust him? No. But we need information, and he's the best lead we have."

"Great, let's call him. What's his number?"

"Um, well..." he hesitated, an awkward laugh escaping him. "I might not have it on me. But I think I can find it if we get back to my place."

"Alright, then let's get moving. The longer we linger here, the more time they have to catch up with us."

We turned to leave the park, and just as we stepped onto the main road, a loud crash echoed through the night, a sound so jarring it froze us in our tracks.

"What was that?" I whispered, my heart plummeting as I scanned the darkness around us.

"Let's check it out," Jordan urged, and despite my instinct to flee, I nodded. Curiosity warred with fear, pulling me toward the source of the sound.

We moved cautiously, creeping toward the edge of the park where the noise had originated. The flicker of headlights from a nearby street illuminated the scene before us—a car had careened off the road and into a row of bushes, metal crumpling like paper.

As we approached, I noticed the figure stumbling away from the wreck, their silhouette barely visible against the night. "Hey!" I called, my voice breaking the stillness. "Are you okay?"

The figure froze, then turned slowly to face us. The moment their face was lit by the headlights, a rush of recognition flooded over me. "No way," I gasped, the shock stealing my breath.

The person was someone I hadn't seen in years, someone whose existence had been carefully tucked away in the recesses of my memory, a ghost from my childhood that I never expected to confront again. "What are you doing here?" I demanded, a mix of disbelief and dread churning in my gut.

They opened their mouth to speak, but before they could utter a word, the ominous sound of approaching sirens filled the air, slicing through the night like a knife. My heart raced as I glanced at Jordan, fear mirrored in his eyes.

"We have to go!" he urged, but as we turned to flee, the figure called out, their voice tinged with desperation. "Wait! I know what happened to your families! You don't understand—"

But before they could finish, the blare of sirens grew closer, drowning out their words as we sprinted into the shadows, uncertainty trailing us like a shadow of its own. The path ahead twisted into darkness, and as I glanced back one last time, a single thought gripped me: Was this encounter a lifeline, or the harbinger of something far more sinister?

Chapter 16: Shattered Illusions

I could still hear the echoes of our argument as I stood on the cracked pavement, sunlight filtering through the gnarled branches overhead, casting a dappled pattern on the ground. The warmth of the day was in stark contrast to the chill that wrapped itself around my heart. Jordan's face was a storm of emotions, his dark hair tousled by the wind, framing eyes that once sparkled with mischief and affection. Now, those same eyes were clouded with confusion and hurt, mirroring my own turmoil. How had we arrived at this point, teetering on the precipice of something that felt both impossibly fragile and weighty?

"Are you even listening?" Jordan snapped, the sharpness of his voice slicing through the air. I flinched, the accusation stinging more than the guilt I had been grappling with.

"Of course I am," I replied, forcing a steadiness into my voice that I didn't feel. "But what do you want me to say? That I understand why your brother would—"

"Don't you dare!" His anger erupted, a tempest of feelings spilling forth. "You can't just excuse his actions. You don't know what it's like to be in my shoes."

I had never wanted to wear his shoes, not when they came with the weight of family loyalty twisting into betrayal. I felt the sting of tears behind my eyes, and I blinked them away furiously. I refused to be that girl—the one who crumpled under pressure, the one who let vulnerability become her downfall.

As I turned away, the late afternoon sun hung low in the sky, its golden hue illuminating the fragments of our shattered trust, glinting off the shards of our once-promising future. I inhaled deeply, the scent of pine mingling with the faint aroma of smoke from distant barbecues—a reminder of simpler times when our lives felt uncomplicated and blissfully naive.

"Can't you see?" Jordan's voice softened, the anger giving way to desperation. "I'm fighting for us. For everything we built. But how can I do that when my brother—"

"—when your brother is a monster?" I interjected, the words spilling out before I could stop them. "Jordan, what he did—"

"He's still family!" The urgency in his tone made my heart ache. "And I can't just write him off. We've got history—blood ties that are hard to sever, even when the heart wants to."

"Sometimes family is a poison, Jordan," I said, my voice barely above a whisper. "And the hardest thing to do is admit it. To let go."

He stepped closer, the tension between us crackling like static electricity. The warmth radiating from him was intoxicating, but I couldn't let it distract me from the reality of our situation. "You think I want to stand here arguing with you?" he said, exasperation lacing his words. "I want to believe in you. In us."

"I want to believe too," I admitted, my resolve faltering. "But every time I think about what he did, it's like a knife twisting in my gut. How can we move forward when there's this—this shadow hanging over us?"

The weight of his silence filled the space between us. I could see the struggle etched into his features, the way his jaw clenched as he battled his inner demons. In that moment, I wanted nothing more than to reach out, to close the gap and wrap my arms around him, to banish the darkness lurking behind his eyes. But I hesitated, unsure if the comfort I craved would bring us together or drive us further apart.

"Tell me something," he finally said, breaking the tension with a question that hung heavy in the air. "If we're to move on, what does that look like for you? What do you want?"

It was a question I hadn't dared to consider fully. My dreams had become tangled with the reality of our circumstances, and now, every thread felt frayed, threatening to unravel completely. I took a moment, gathering my thoughts like scattered leaves caught in the wind. "I want a future where we're not defined by our families' mistakes," I began slowly. "I want us to be strong enough to overcome all of this."

"Then let's be strong together," he urged, stepping forward, his intensity drawing me in like a moth to a flame. "We can't let this destroy us, Em."

The way he said my name, with that deep timbre that sent shivers down my spine, ignited something inside me. "But how? It feels like we're fighting against the tide, and it's pulling us under."

"I don't know," he admitted, vulnerability threading through his bravado. "But I do know that I love you, and that's got to mean something. Even amidst all this chaos."

The truth hung between us, a fragile yet undeniable force. In that moment, the world around us faded, and it was just us—our hearts beating in sync, each pulse a testament to the love that remained despite the wreckage. I stepped closer, letting the warmth of his presence wash over me. "I love you too," I said, the admission freeing me from the chains of doubt that had bound my heart.

Yet, as the words slipped from my lips, a nagging thought whispered in the back of my mind—what if love wasn't enough? What if the shadows of our past consumed us whole, leaving nothing but ashes in their wake? Would our devotion withstand the trials yet to come? And as I searched his gaze for answers, I knew we had only just begun to unravel the tangled web of our lives, a journey fraught with peril, passion, and the haunting echoes of choices made long before we'd even met.

The sun dipped lower in the sky, casting a golden hue that shimmered on the cracked pavement as we lingered in our own private storm. I could hear the distant laughter of children, their carefree shouts a stark contrast to the turmoil swirling in my heart. Jordan's presence beside me felt like a lifeline, yet the weight of our shared history pressed down harder than the humidity of the summer evening. The world continued to turn, oblivious to the shattered pieces of us that lay strewn across the ground like autumn leaves in a tempest.

"Why is it so easy for them to make choices for us?" I murmured, half to myself and half to him. The words spilled out, a mixture of frustration and longing. I had always believed that our choices defined us, that we could forge our own paths, but in that moment, it felt like our families had written our stories in ink before we'd even had a chance to pick up a pen.

Jordan let out a humorless chuckle, shaking his head as if to shake off the gravity of our situation. "Maybe because they've never had to face the consequences of their actions." His voice carried a bite, laced with bitterness that cut through the air. "They just keep dancing around their messes, expecting us to sweep it under the rug."

I stepped back, a rush of emotions flooding my senses. "What are we supposed to do, then? Keep pretending that it doesn't hurt? That their mistakes don't hang over us like a dark cloud, threatening to drown us?"

"Pretending feels a lot safer than accepting reality," he replied, his tone softening. The hint of vulnerability made my heart ache in ways I hadn't anticipated. "But I don't want to pretend anymore. Not with you. I want to fight for something real."

Those words hung in the air, a promise mingled with hope. But the flicker of optimism was tempered by doubt. "What does that even look like, Jordan? What do we have to fight against?"

His eyes locked onto mine, intense and piercing, as if searching for the answer buried deep within the chaos of our emotions. "We fight against the expectations, the guilt, the history that's been thrust upon us. We forge our own path, even if it means confronting the demons lurking in our families."

"Demons, huh?" I let out a half-laugh, trying to lighten the atmosphere. "I'm not sure my demon-hunting skills are up to par." The momentary levity faded as the truth settled back in. "What if confronting them only pulls us apart? What if it reveals more wounds than it heals?"

"That's a risk I'm willing to take." He stepped closer, the proximity sending warmth spiraling through me. "I want to face whatever comes our way, but I need you by my side. I can't do this alone."

My heart thundered in my chest as I considered his words. The idea of stepping into the fray, of facing the ghosts of our pasts, was terrifying, yet the thought of retreating felt like surrendering to fate. "So, what's the plan? Do we have a battle strategy?" I asked, half-teasing, half-serious.

"We start with honesty," he said, a glimmer of determination lighting his features. "We share what we've been holding back. We confront our families, tell them how their choices have impacted us. No more hiding."

"Just like that? We'll sit down at Sunday dinner and spill our guts?" I raised an eyebrow, skepticism lacing my words. "I can already picture the stunned silence."

"Exactly. Let them be stunned. Let them realize we're not children anymore." He crossed his arms, an air of defiance surrounding him. "It's time they understand the consequences of their actions."

I bit my lip, the idea swirling in my mind like a storm. "And what if they don't understand? What if they lash out?"

"Then we'll deal with it," he replied, his conviction unwavering. "Together. We can't let fear dictate our lives. Not anymore."

His words ignited a flicker of courage within me, and I found myself nodding. "Okay, together it is. But let's make sure we have an escape route, just in case. I can't handle the drama without a safety net."

"Deal." He grinned, that familiar spark returning to his eyes, and for a moment, the world outside our bubble faded away.

We stood there, lost in each other's gaze, the weight of our burdens lightened by the possibility of shared resolve. The tension that had hung between us like a drawn bowstring began to relax, replaced by an unspoken understanding that perhaps love could be the bridge across the chasm of our family's chaos.

As the sun dipped below the horizon, painting the sky in hues of orange and pink, I felt a renewed sense of hope—a fragile, flickering flame igniting in the depths of uncertainty. Perhaps this was the turning point, the moment when we chose to rewrite our narratives instead of letting the past define us.

"Just promise me one thing," I said, the words spilling out before I could second-guess myself. "Promise that no matter how messy this gets, we won't turn against each other. We'll keep communicating, even when it's hard."

"I promise," he said earnestly, reaching for my hand and squeezing it gently. "I'm not going anywhere, Em. Not this time."

His warmth seeped into my skin, and I clung to that promise like a lifeline as we stood there, hand in hand, ready to face whatever storm brewed on the horizon. The path ahead was uncertain, but the strength of our bond felt like a fortress against the chaos that threatened to engulf us.

In that moment, I realized that while the ghosts of our families might never fully fade, we had the power to carve out a space for our love amidst the shadows, a sanctuary where trust could slowly be rebuilt. As we turned to leave the remnants of our old lives behind, I felt a surge of determination coursing through me, propelling me forward into the unknown. Together, we would navigate the labyrinth of our intertwined destinies, armed with honesty and an unyielding resolve.

The warmth of the summer evening faded as we made our way back toward my apartment, the air thick with the scent of blooming jasmine. Each step felt heavier than the last, a reminder of the emotional weight we carried. I could see the streetlights flickering to life, casting pools of golden light that danced like fireflies on the pavement. It should have felt comforting, but instead, it amplified the tension crackling between us, a palpable reminder of the shadows we were determined to confront.

"What if we're making a huge mistake?" I asked suddenly, the words slipping out before I could suppress them. The uncertainty gnawed at my insides like an unwelcome guest, refusing to be ignored. "What if confronting our families just drives us apart instead of bringing us together?"

Jordan stopped short, turning to face me, his expression a mix of determination and something softer—fear, perhaps. "I'd rather try and fail than keep pretending everything's fine. I want to be real with you, Em. I don't want our love to be built on a foundation of lies or secrets. It's too fragile for that."

His honesty cut through my doubts, leaving a raw ache in its wake. "But honesty can be brutal. It can break things that should stay whole." I gestured vaguely to the world around us, to the laughter echoing from a nearby café, where couples shared drinks and stories without a care in the world. "Look at them. They don't know what we're going through. They're blissfully ignorant."

"Or they're just better at hiding it," he countered, a small smile breaking through his seriousness. "Maybe they've faced their demons and come out stronger for it."

"Maybe," I conceded, crossing my arms as a cool breeze ruffled my hair. "But it still feels like we're standing on a tightrope with no safety net beneath us. One wrong step and we could fall into the abyss."

"Then let's take that step together," he said, his voice steady and reassuring. "We can't let fear of falling keep us from walking the line."

With those words, a spark of courage ignited within me. I nodded slowly, feeling the tension in my shoulders ease just a bit. "Okay, together. But if we're doing this, we need a plan. I can't just charge in blindly, or I might end up saying something I'll regret."

"Agreed." He glanced around as if gauging our surroundings before leaning in closer, lowering his voice conspiratorially. "We'll set a time to talk with our families. And we'll outline what we want to say. No surprises. Just honesty."

I couldn't help but laugh a little at the seriousness in his tone. "So, a family meeting with an agenda? Should we prepare an executive summary too?"

"Why not? If we're going to do this, we might as well do it right." He smirked, the playful banter lighting a flicker of warmth in my chest. "Plus, it might take some of the edge off if we can laugh a little."

"Fine, but you're in charge of the PowerPoint presentation." I returned his grin, grateful for the lightness that had begun to settle over us like a cozy blanket. "And I get to add the pie chart showing how many times your brother has ruined my life."

Jordan chuckled, the sound a balm against the heaviness we'd been feeling. "Deal. Just promise me you won't include any embarrassing pictures."

"Only if you promise to wear a suit," I shot back, my heart buoyed by our newfound resolve. "I mean, we're addressing the family here. It's a big deal."

As we continued down the street, a sense of anticipation tinged the air, wrapping around us like a warm embrace. I couldn't shake the feeling that something significant was on the horizon, a shift that would either bind us closer together or tear us apart entirely.

The moment we reached my apartment, the cozy familiarity of the space washed over me. It was a sanctuary filled with memories—the walls adorned with photos capturing laughter and love. Yet, as I opened the door, a chill ran down my spine. The atmosphere felt different, charged with an energy I couldn't quite place.

"What is it?" Jordan asked, sensing my hesitation as I paused on the threshold.

"I don't know," I replied, glancing around the dimly lit room. "It just feels... off."

"Maybe it's just the nerves," he suggested, stepping inside and nudging the door shut behind him. "You know, the anticipation of what's to come."

I nodded but couldn't shake the feeling of unease settling in my stomach like a stone. "Yeah, maybe."

As we moved further into the apartment, the silence deepened, amplifying the sounds of our footsteps on the hardwood floor. I headed to the kitchen, needing to distract myself with something familiar—a cup of tea, perhaps. But as I reached for the kettle, a flicker of movement caught my eye.

On the kitchen table lay a letter, stark against the floral tablecloth, the envelope unsealed. My heart raced as I approached it, my name scrawled across the front in an unmistakable hand.

"Who's it from?" Jordan asked, his curiosity piqued.

I tore open the envelope, my fingers trembling as I pulled out the contents. The words swirled on the page, a dark ink that seemed to pulse with a life of its own: "You need to know the truth about your families. Before it's too late."

"What does it say?" Jordan leaned closer, his breath warm against my neck.

I barely registered his question, my mind racing with implications. "It's... I think it's from my mother." My voice trembled, uncertainty creeping in. "She must have sent this while we were out. But why now? What truth?"

"Em, read it," he urged, his intensity sharpening.

I glanced down again, my heart pounding as the words sank in deeper. "It says she has information that could change everything. About us. About our families."

"Change everything how?" Jordan's tone was tight with concern, his eyes narrowing.

Before I could respond, my phone buzzed sharply on the counter, cutting through the tension. I snatched it up, my breath hitching as I saw the name flashing across the screen. My stomach dropped.

"It's my mother."

Jordan's expression hardened, his body tensing as he regarded me. "You should answer it."

Taking a deep breath, I swiped to accept the call, the weight of anticipation heavy in the air. As I pressed the phone to my ear, a chill ran down my spine, my heart racing with both fear and curiosity.

"Hello?" I managed, my voice barely above a whisper.

"Emily," my mother's voice came through, laced with urgency. "We need to talk. Now."

A sudden crash outside made me jump, the sound reverberating through the walls. I glanced at Jordan, his eyes wide with alarm.

"What was that?" he whispered.

"I don't know," I replied, my heart racing. But even as I spoke, I sensed that whatever was about to unfold would rip through the fragile fabric of our lives, pulling the strings tighter until something had to give.

"Emily, listen to me. It's about your father," my mother continued, her voice trembling with a fear that was unmistakable.

"There are things you don't know—things I should have told you long ago."

The world outside fell silent, the air thick with anticipation as I exchanged a glance with Jordan, uncertainty mirrored in his expression. I could feel the gravity of the moment, the realization that our lives were about to change in ways we couldn't yet comprehend.

"Mom, what do you mean?" I pressed, gripping the phone tighter.

"Just get to the café by the corner—"

Her voice cut off abruptly, replaced by a crackling silence that sent ice coursing through my veins.

"Mom? Mom!" I shouted, panic rising as the line went dead.

Jordan's hand gripped my arm, grounding me. "What just happened?"

"I don't know!" I cried, the weight of the moment crashing down around us. "She was about to tell me something important, and then she just—"

Before I could finish my thought, the door burst open, slamming against the wall with a deafening bang. A shadowy figure stood in the doorway, and my breath caught in my throat as the reality of the situation hit me like a freight train.

"Emily!" the figure called, their voice filled with a frantic urgency that echoed in the stillness.

The chill that washed over me was unlike anything I'd ever felt, a premonition of the storm that was about to descend. As I stood there, heart racing, every instinct screamed that our world was on the brink of unraveling in ways we could never have anticipated.

Chapter 17: The Fractured Path

The streets pulsed with life as I navigated through the throng of tourists and locals, each person wrapped in their own narrative, oblivious to the storm brewing within me. The air was thick with the scent of pretzels and roasted nuts, a sweet distraction that momentarily lifted my spirits. I ducked into a nearby café, its inviting aroma of freshly brewed coffee and baked goods beckoning me like a long-lost friend. The sound of laughter and the clatter of cups felt foreign yet comforting, a reminder of simpler moments spent with Jordan, where the world faded away, leaving only us.

I ordered a slice of cheesecake, the decadent layers of cream and graham cracker crust offering a bittersweet escape from my turmoil. As I settled into a corner table, I pulled out my phone, half-hoping for a message from him—some word, any word—that might bridge the chasm that had opened between us. But the screen remained stubbornly silent, reflecting only my own desolation. I pushed the phone away, unwilling to give the device any more power over my emotions.

Moments ticked by like the slow drip of the coffee I absentmindedly sipped. I stared out the window, watching the city's heart beat with relentless vigor. Couples strolled hand in hand, sharing laughter that echoed through the air, while families snapped pictures against the backdrop of towering skyscrapers. My chest ached at the sight, each laugh a reminder of what I had lost and the bonds that had frayed under the weight of our families' expectations.

Just as I was about to drown in my own thoughts, the door swung open, ushering in a gust of brisk air that carried the chatter of the streets. My gaze flickered to the entrance, and there he stood, framed in the doorway like a lost soul seeking refuge. Jordan's dark hair tousled in the breeze, his eyes scanning the room until they found me, wide with surprise. I didn't know if I wanted to leap up and run to him or sink deeper into my seat, hiding from the tumult of emotions that roiled within me.

"Hey," he said, the word caught between hope and hesitation as he approached my table. "I didn't expect to find you here."

"Looks like we both have a talent for wandering." I forced a smile, though it felt more like a mask than an expression of joy. He looked so good, dressed casually in a fitted shirt that accentuated his frame, but the warmth in his eyes was dimmed, shadowed by our recent confrontation.

"I've been thinking..." he began, the uncertainty in his voice wrapping around my heart like a vine tightening its grip. "About everything. About us."

The words hung heavy in the air, each syllable dripping with potential and peril. I set my fork down, my appetite lost to the weight of our unresolved tension. "Is it really everything, or is it just our families that you're worried about?" I couldn't help but prod, my tone sharper than intended.

Jordan's jaw tightened, a familiar flicker of frustration passing over his features. "You know it's not that simple. My father... he's not just a man with opinions. He's a force."

"And what about my family?" I countered, feeling the heat of my own frustration bubble to the surface. "They have a stake in this too. It's not just about your father; it's about my mother and her dreams for me. I can't just ignore that."

He raked a hand through his hair, a gesture I had come to recognize as a sign of his growing agitation. "So what do we do? Just let them dictate our lives? Let them tear us apart?"

The fight in his voice ignited a spark of defiance within me, igniting a small flame against the coldness that had settled in my heart. "I don't know, Jordan! I don't have all the answers. I just know that I can't pretend everything is fine when it's not."

He leaned closer, his voice dropping to a whisper that felt intimate yet laden with tension. "What if I told you I'm willing to fight for us? To stand up against my father, against everything? Would that change anything?"

His words were a lifeline thrown into turbulent waters, but I couldn't shake the doubt that clung to me like a shroud. "And what if it doesn't work? What if it just makes things worse?"

Jordan's eyes bore into mine, a mix of desperation and hope swirling within them. "Then at least we'll know we tried. I refuse to let our love become collateral damage in a war fought by others. We're worth fighting for, aren't we?"

In that moment, I felt the air around us shift, charged with an energy that pulsed like the city outside. His words stirred something deep within me—a yearning for connection, a desire to reclaim what had been fractured. Yet the fear of potential heartbreak loomed large, a shadow that threatened to smother any glimmer of hope.

"I want to believe that," I admitted, my voice barely above a whisper. "But what if it's just wishful thinking?"

Jordan's hand brushed against mine, a tentative yet electric touch that sent a shiver up my spine. "Then let's take that leap together. If we fall, we'll do it side by side. But if we fly... think of what we could become."

His words hung in the air, filled with the promise of possibility. My heart raced, the pulse of a thousand conflicting emotions warring within me. I could feel the allure of his proposal, the intoxicating thrill of hope mingled with the bitter taste of fear. Would I dare to chase after what felt impossible, to fight for a love that had been tested in the fires of doubt and familial expectations?

The warmth of Jordan's hand lingered on mine, a tether to the world I longed to reclaim. My heart thudded with the weight of his words, each syllable a challenge wrapped in desire. I could feel the bustling energy of the café fading into the background, the clinking of cups and murmur of conversation melting away as his gaze anchored me in a moment that felt both electrifying and terrifying.

"Look, I didn't come here to argue," he said, breaking the silence that had settled like dust. "I came here to talk. Really talk." His earnestness drew me in, making it hard to resist the pull of his conviction.

I bit my lip, torn between the instinct to protect myself and the urge to dive headfirst into the turbulent waters of our relationship. "Talk about what? How we're caught in a tangled web of family expectations? How everything feels like a ticking time bomb?"

"Exactly," he replied, a spark igniting in his eyes. "But instead of letting it blow us apart, why don't we figure out how to defuse it? Together."

His determination was infectious, yet the scars of our recent battle were still fresh in my mind. I inhaled deeply, letting the comforting aroma of coffee and cheesecake wrap around me like a warm embrace. "And how do you propose we do that? Just wave a magic wand and make our families see reason?"

Jordan leaned in closer, his voice dropping to a conspiratorial whisper. "What if we staged a little coup? We could present our relationship on our terms. If we can show our families that we're serious, they might back off. Or at least give us a chance to prove them wrong."

"Are you suggesting a dramatic showdown?" I couldn't help but chuckle, though the absurdity of his idea was laced with a hint of thrill. "Because that sounds like something straight out of a rom-com."

"Hey, if it ends with us victorious and holding hands in the sunset, I'll take it," he replied, a playful grin breaking through his earlier intensity. "But seriously, we can't just sit back and let them dictate our future. We have to fight for what we want."

His words, simple yet profound, tugged at something deep within me. I had spent so long conforming to everyone else's expectations that the thought of actively fighting for my desires felt almost foreign. But what was I truly afraid of? Losing Jordan? Or losing the chance to carve out my own path?

"What if they don't understand?" I asked, skepticism creeping back in. "What if this only makes things worse?"

"Then we handle it," he said, confidence radiating from him like the sun breaking through clouds. "We're stronger together. I've seen how passionate you are about what you want, and I don't want to live in a world where we don't even try."

I studied him, the man who had once been my safe harbor, now standing before me as an unpredictable storm. The tenderness I felt for him mingled with a fierce longing to reclaim my own voice. Perhaps it was time to step out of the shadows and into the light of my own desires.

"Okay," I said finally, determination coating my words like sugar on a donut. "Let's do it. Let's show them that we're not going to be pushed around."

His eyes lit up with excitement, and for a moment, the weight of doubt was lifted, replaced by a rush of adrenaline. "Great! So how do we start?"

A plan began to form, sketching itself in my mind like the bold outlines of a painting waiting for color. "First, we need to gather intel on our families. Figure out their concerns and objections. Understanding where they're coming from might give us a leg up in this battle."

"Mission: Family Intel. I like it," he said, his playful tone cutting through the tension. "I can start with my dad. He loves to bluster about his opinions over dinner. It's like having a live commentary on my life choices."

I laughed, feeling the tension ease. "And I can corner my mom during her weekly brunch with the ladies. Nothing like a group of mothers to spill the family secrets."

"Sounds like a plan. We'll take their fears, dissect them, and use that knowledge to build our case," he said, the spark of a rebellion lighting his eyes. "This is going to be epic."

We left the café, stepping back into the fray of the city, where life pulsed around us like a vivid tapestry. The sun hung low in the sky, casting long shadows that danced at our feet, mirroring the path ahead. With each step, a flicker of excitement built within me, a sense of purpose propelling me forward.

"Where to next, fearless leader?" Jordan teased, his hand brushing against mine, a casual gesture that ignited warmth in my chest.

"Let's go to Central Park. We can brainstorm and plot our master plan," I replied, feeling a thrill course through me at the thought of a secret meeting in the heart of the city.

As we strolled through the park, the vibrant colors of fall painted the trees in hues of amber and crimson, leaves crunching underfoot like whispered secrets. The laughter of children echoed nearby, weaving a symphony of innocence and joy that contrasted sharply with the storm brewing in our lives. I watched a group of kids chase after a soccer ball, their shouts of glee reminding me of simpler times when life revolved around dreams rather than expectations.

We found a quiet bench nestled beneath a sprawling oak, its branches like protective arms overhead. As we sat, I turned to Jordan, my heart racing with a mix of fear and exhilaration. "So, how do we start?"

Jordan leaned back, contemplating. "First, let's lay out what we know about our families. What are their concerns? What do they want for us?"

"Okay, for my mom, it's all about stability and security," I said, racking my brain. "She's always talked about how important it is for me to find someone who can provide for me, someone 'suitable.'"

"Suitability," Jordan scoffed, rolling his eyes. "What even is that? A degree? A trust fund? A penchant for plaid?"

I laughed, grateful for his ability to lighten the mood. "You know, a bit of all that. And she wants me to have the traditional career path. You know, marry well, have kids, and settle down. The usual."

Jordan's brow furrowed as he listened. "And your dad?"

"He's a bit more laid back, but he worries about my happiness. He just wants me to be successful, but he's also a romantic at heart. He wants me to find love, but on his terms."

Jordan nodded, understanding the intricate dance of familial expectations that twisted and turned like the paths in the park. "For my dad, it's all about legacy. He wants me to uphold the family name, to follow in his footsteps. But I can't breathe when I think about being just another cog in his machine."

I felt a surge of solidarity as we shared our burdens, our families' expectations weaving a common thread between us. "So, we're both trapped in our own gilded cages," I mused.

"Yeah, but cages can be broken," he replied, a fierce glint in his eye. "Let's break them together."

In that moment, surrounded by the rustling leaves and the fading warmth of the sun, I realized that for the first time, I was ready to fight.

The air in Central Park was alive with the rustling of leaves, each whisper a reminder of the plans we had just laid out. The sun dipped lower, casting golden hues over the grass and illuminating Jordan's face, highlighting the intensity of his gaze as he leaned closer, elbows resting on his knees. "So, what's next?" he asked, a spark of mischief dancing in his eyes.

I leaned back, feeling the weight of possibility settle comfortably in my chest. "We need to gather intel first, right? We can play it cool—like we're just having regular family time while we figure out how to navigate this."

"Right," he said, nodding with enthusiasm. "We'll blend in like chameleons. We'll be so nonchalant they'll never suspect a thing." He grinned, his boyish charm shining through, and I couldn't help but smile back, my heart warming at the thought of embarking on this absurdly bold adventure together.

"Exactly. We need to keep our heads down," I said, mimicking a spy in a bad thriller, my voice taking on a dramatic tone. "Infiltrate the family gatherings, gather intelligence, and report back to headquarters—aka this bench."

Jordan burst out laughing, the sound vibrant and carefree, cutting through the tension like a hot knife through butter. "Perfect. And who knows? Maybe by the end of this, we'll discover some hidden treasure—like a secret stash of their true feelings!"

"Or at least find out what they think of us dating." I turned serious for a moment, the gravity of our situation washing over me. "I'm just worried that if we push too hard, they might push back harder. I don't want to lose you over this."

He reached for my hand, intertwining his fingers with mine, grounding me in this whirlwind of emotions. "You're not going to lose me. We're in this together, remember? No matter how much they might try to pull us apart."

With newfound determination, we strategized through the golden hour, mapping out our next moves with the seriousness of generals preparing for battle. We parted ways, promising to reconvene for a debriefing after each family meeting. As I walked home, I felt a mix of exhilaration and dread. This was a risky game we were playing, one that could easily blow up in our faces.

The following week unfolded with a flurry of activity. Jordan's father had invited him for dinner, and I braced myself for my own family's Sunday brunch, a ritual that involved a parade of my mother's finest dishes, all accompanied by her relentless pursuit of the perfect match for me. As I set the table that morning, I could almost hear my mother's gentle nagging echoing in my head.

"Just remember to play it cool," I muttered to myself, pouring coffee into my favorite mug—a chipped relic of my college days. I took a sip, letting the warmth seep through me, preparing for the inevitable onslaught of questions about my love life.

When the doorbell rang, my heart raced. I opened the door to find my mother, her expression one of curious anticipation as she swept into the living room with a flair that could rival any Broadway star. "Darling, I hope you're ready for today. I've invited the Johnsons. You remember their son, Kyle, right? He's a rising star in finance!"

Of course, I remembered Kyle—the epitome of the "suitable" bachelor, with a perfect smile and a family tree that could be traced back to royalty. "Mom, I really don't think—"

"Nonsense! He's just back from a business trip, and I thought you might like to catch up. You two always hit it off!" she interrupted, her excitement unfurling like a peacock displaying its feathers.

I sighed, feeling the weight of expectation settle heavily on my shoulders. "Mom, I've been busy with work. And you know, Kyle and I... we're just not—"

"Just give him a chance, sweetheart," she said, cutting me off again. "I just want you to be happy."

As she fussed around the kitchen, prepping the brunch spread, I mentally prepared myself for the interrogation that would follow our meal. I could almost hear the wheels turning in her mind as she plotted the perfect moment to plant the seed of "suitability" into the conversation.

When Kyle arrived, he was everything I expected—charming, well-spoken, and overly eager to impress my mother. The brunch unfolded with all the usual pleasantries, and as we settled into a comfortable rhythm of small talk, I felt my resolve begin to waver. Perhaps I could make this work. Maybe I could convince myself that this was the right path, the sensible path.

But then, as my mother launched into a story about her latest garden club escapade, my thoughts drifted back to Jordan—his laughter, his fire, the way he challenged me to be bold. The realization hit me like a splash of cold water: I was not ready to settle for a life defined by someone else's expectations. I wanted more than safety; I wanted passion, unpredictability, and someone who saw me as I truly was, not just a reflection of their desires.

I excused myself under the pretense of checking on dessert, my heart racing as I stepped outside for a breath of fresh air. The world felt bright and vibrant, filled with possibility. I pulled out my phone, hesitating before tapping Jordan's name. I needed to talk to him, to share my resolve.

"Hey, how did it go?" he answered, his voice instantly calming me.

"It was... interesting," I replied, glancing back at the door, half-expecting my mother to follow me outside. "Kyle was charming, just like always, but I couldn't shake the feeling that I was wearing a mask. I can't do this anymore."

"Are you okay?" Jordan's concern was palpable through the phone.

"I'm not just okay, I'm done pretending." I took a deep breath, feeling a rush of clarity. "I need to tell my mom I'm not going to settle for 'suitable.' I want to be with you."

"Are you sure?" he asked, his voice low and steady. "That's a big step."

"I'm tired of living someone else's life. I want to fight for what makes me happy, and that's you," I affirmed, a newfound strength blossoming within me.

"Then let's do it. Let's face them together."

The words ignited a flame of courage in my chest, but just as I was about to respond, I heard the crunch of footsteps behind me. I turned sharply, my heart leaping into my throat as I came face to face with my mother, her expression a mix of surprise and understanding.

"Who are you talking to?" she asked, her eyes narrowing slightly.

Panic coursed through me, and the weight of the moment settled like lead in my stomach. I had been ready to embrace my truth, to stand tall beside Jordan, but now, standing here caught in the act, the words stuck in my throat.

"I—" I began, but before I could formulate a response, the door behind her swung open, revealing Kyle, who had evidently decided to join the conversation.

"Everything okay out here?" he asked, his eyes flicking between my mother and me, curiosity etched on his face.

In that instant, I felt the ground shift beneath me, the carefully constructed walls of my plans crumbling like a house of cards. My heart raced as I stood on the precipice of revelation, the weight of the truth pressing heavily on my chest, threatening to spill out at any moment.

I realized then that I had a choice to make, and the air crackled with the electricity of unspoken words. This could be the moment that defined everything—the moment I either stepped back into the shadows of expectation or seized the opportunity to embrace my own desires.

Chapter 18: The Gathering Storm

The scent of turpentine mingled with the faint echoes of laughter from past gatherings, wrapping around me like an old, cherished blanket. The art center, my haven amid the chaos that had become my life, buzzed with an energy only the night could awaken. Each stroke of my brush was a rebellion against the shadows that threatened to engulf me. I painted not just to create but to assert my presence in a world that often felt intent on stripping it away.

The canvas before me transformed under the weight of my emotions, each color a testament to my resolve. Crimson swirled with deep cerulean, the conflict of joy and sorrow bleeding into one another. With every flick of my wrist, I poured myself into the work, my heart racing not from fear but from a fervent desire to reclaim my agency. The art center, a mosaic of dreams and aspirations, was my sanctuary where the outside world faded, allowing me to escape into a realm of creativity and catharsis.

Yet, that night, as the clock chimed the witching hour, a chill snaked its way up my spine. I felt it before I saw it—a prickle of awareness that something was off. I glanced towards the large windows, the jagged outlines of the trees casting eerie silhouettes against the moonlit sky. My brush hesitated mid-stroke, the vibrant paint pooling at the edge of the canvas. Just beyond the glass, a shadow flitted past, swift and silent. I blinked, and it was gone. My heart thundered in my chest, the rhythmic thump echoing the fears I'd been trying so hard to suppress.

I grabbed my phone, my fingers trembling as I dialed Jordan's number. The seconds stretched interminably until he answered, his voice a comforting balm amid my rising panic. "What's wrong?" he asked, instantly alert.

"Something...someone was outside," I managed, my voice barely a whisper. "I don't know what I saw, but it felt wrong, Jordan."

"Stay inside. I'm on my way," he replied, the steel in his tone leaving no room for argument.

I hung up, my heart still racing as I pressed my back against the cool wall, my mind racing through possibilities. Was it just my imagination playing tricks, or had I really seen someone lurking in the shadows? I could still feel the weight of the gaze, the sense that I was being watched. I shook my head, trying to banish the creeping dread that threatened to settle over me like a fog. Art had always been my escape; now it felt like a cage.

Moments later, the sound of footsteps echoed in the corridor outside, each step a promise of safety. The door swung open, and there stood Jordan, his silhouette outlined by the harsh overhead lights. He looked every bit the protector, his brow furrowed with concern, the tension in his shoulders palpable.

"Where did you see him?" His voice was low, a murmur of urgency that snapped me out of my reverie.

"I don't know. It was just a flash. I thought it was someone, but..." I trailed off, feeling foolish. "It could have been nothing."

Jordan stepped closer, his presence steadying me. "Nothing doesn't make you feel this way. Let's check it out together."

I hesitated but nodded, the weight of his gaze pushing me to confront the fear that gnawed at my insides. Together, we stepped into the corridor, my heartbeat thumping in my ears, a drumroll heralding the unknown. Jordan moved ahead, scanning the darkened corners as if he could wrestle the shadows into submission.

"Stay close," he instructed, glancing back at me, a flicker of vulnerability beneath his bravado. I appreciated his concern, but I also sensed his own turmoil simmering just beneath the surface.

We approached the windows, and I peered outside, my breath hitching as I took in the stillness of the night. The moon bathed the courtyard in a ghostly glow, casting long shadows that danced like phantoms. "See anything?" he asked, leaning in beside me.

"No." My voice came out softer than intended, barely breaking the heavy silence that enveloped us.

But then, just as I turned away, I caught a flicker of movement—a figure darting behind the trees. My pulse quickened again, a primal instinct kicking in. "There! Someone's out there!" I pointed, adrenaline flooding my veins.

Jordan's expression hardened, determination crystallizing in his eyes. "Stay here."

"Are you serious? I'm not hiding while you confront a stranger!" I stepped forward, defiance coursing through me.

He shot me a look, one that clearly said I had no choice. "You'll be safer inside. I'll check it out."

"Like hell you will!" I felt the heat rise in my cheeks, a mixture of fear and indignation. "We're in this together."

With a resigned sigh, he nodded. "Alright, but stay behind me."

We crept toward the door, the weight of our unspoken fears lingering in the air. The night outside seemed to hold its breath, the world wrapped in an ominous stillness that promised nothing good.

As we stepped outside, the crisp air bit at my skin, heightening my senses. Every rustle of leaves, every distant sound, echoed like a threat. Jordan led the way, but I kept pace, refusing to be the damsel waiting for rescue.

Suddenly, a branch snapped underfoot, and we froze, hearts pounding in synchrony. "Who's there?" Jordan called out, his voice steady, betraying none of the fear I felt.

"Show yourself!" I added, my voice stronger than I felt.

We stood poised in the darkness, an island of bravery amidst a sea of uncertainty, ready to face whatever awaited us in the shadows.

The chill of the night wrapped around us like a shroud, making the air feel thicker, more pressing. Jordan's presence was a solid anchor, a rock against the tempest of uncertainty swirling in my chest. Each rustle of leaves seemed to mock our bravado, taunting us with reminders of the unknown lurking just beyond the flickering streetlights. I glanced sideways at him, noticing how his jaw tightened as he focused on the darkness, his expression a mix of determination and something deeper—an anxiety I didn't want to name.

"Okay, you're the brave knight," I whispered, half-heartedly trying to inject some levity into our grim surroundings. "Just don't go all gallant and get yourself slayed, alright?"

His lips quirked slightly, a flash of warmth in an otherwise tense moment. "I'll do my best to keep my armor intact," he replied, and I could hear the underlying current of humor despite the situation. The bravado, however, was a fragile thing, barely holding back the weight of fear that loomed over us like the night sky.

We stepped further into the courtyard, my heart thrumming with each tentative movement. The world felt suspended, as if we had stumbled into a moment frozen in time, the night concealing secrets it was unwilling to share. My mind raced through every conceivable horror story, conjuring images of what could lie in wait—each scenario more outlandish than the last. A lost soul? A petty thief? Or perhaps a ghost longing for a bit of mischief?

"Focus, Juliet," I murmured under my breath, shaking my head to dispel the shadows dancing in my imagination. "No need to be overly dramatic."

Jordan cast me a sideways glance, a ghost of a smile teasing the corner of his mouth. "Dramatic? Never. You're practically Shakespeare out here."

"Ah, but Shakespeare didn't have to face the looming specter of doom, now did he?" I shot back, matching his humor with an exaggerated sigh. "He had a knack for tragedy, but I'm more into bright colors and abstract thoughts."

"Just keep your bright colors on standby," he replied, his eyes scanning the edges of the courtyard, a hawk on the hunt. "If we're lucky, we won't need them."

We continued forward, inching closer to the line of trees that bordered the edge of the property. The moon cast ghostly shadows that danced across the ground, creating an unsettling ambiance that made my skin crawl. I could almost hear the trees whispering, their branches swaying as if confiding their secrets to the wind.

"Do you think whatever it was will come back?" I asked, my voice barely above a whisper.

Jordan stopped, his gaze piercing through the gloom. "If it does, we'll be ready."

"Right, because that's reassuring," I quipped, the edge of anxiety sharpening my tone. "I mean, we're definitely not out here hoping to be the stars of our own horror movie."

He turned to me, a mix of amusement and seriousness in his eyes. "We can make a run for it if it gets too scary. I'm sure you'd win an Oscar for your performance."

I laughed, the sound breaking the tension like a sharp knife through silk. "I can see it now: Best Dramatic Exit," I mused, imagining my frantic dash back to the safety of the center, flailing like a windmill in a storm.

But before he could respond, a sudden rustle behind us made us freeze. Jordan's hand shot out, gripping my wrist with a firm yet gentle touch. The grip was both protective and a tether to reality as we turned toward the sound.

"Who's there?" he called, his voice steady, though I sensed the edge of urgency creeping in.

Silence answered us, stretching on like a taut string ready to snap. The only sound was the whisper of the wind, playing tricks on our senses.

"Maybe it was just the wind," I suggested, forcing a casual note into my voice. But deep down, I felt the anticipation thrumming through the air, electric and thick.

"Or it could be the person we're looking for," he replied, his eyes narrowing as he stepped forward, his body tensing as he prepared for confrontation. I found myself stepping in line with him, a surge of courage igniting in my chest.

"Together?" I asked, the word hanging between us like a promise.

"Always."

With a nod, we moved cautiously toward the source of the sound, the moonlight guiding our way. The underbrush crunched beneath our feet, each step an echo of our determination. We reached the edge of the trees, where shadows melded into the darkness, and I squinted into the abyss.

Suddenly, a figure emerged—a disheveled man, his clothes tattered, and wild eyes reflecting the moonlight. My heart dropped as a rush of instinct told me he wasn't a benign presence.

"Please, I don't want any trouble," he stammered, holding up his hands, palms outward in a gesture of peace. "I just... I need help."

The moment hung suspended, a fragile balance between fear and compassion. Jordan stepped slightly in front of me, instinctively protective. "Help with what?" he demanded, his voice a low rumble.

"I swear, I'm not here to cause any issues," the man implored, his voice shaky. "I just need to get out of town for a while. There are... things happening."

"Things?" I echoed, skepticism tinged with curiosity.

He glanced over his shoulder, as if the shadows themselves were creeping closer, and then leaned in, his voice dropping to a whisper. "You don't understand. I saw something I shouldn't have. They know I'm here."

A shiver ran down my spine at the urgency in his voice, a resonance of the very fear that had driven me to call Jordan in the first place.

Jordan exchanged a quick look with me, a silent conversation filled with questions and possibilities. "What did you see?"

"They're coming for me. You can't let them take me," the man said, desperation etched in his features.

The storm that had been gathering in my mind broke into a downpour of thoughts, each one more chaotic than the last. I could feel the weight of the world closing in again, but the ember of defiance flickered brightly. "Who is 'they'?"

"People who don't want the truth to get out," he said, glancing nervously at the treeline. "And if they find me here... it won't just be me they come for."

The tension hung heavy between us, a tangible force that could tip either way. In the depths of my uncertainty, one thing became clear: the night was far from over, and the true danger had only just begun to reveal itself.

Fear wrapped around me like a fog, heavy and suffocating as I processed the man's words. I could feel my heart thudding in my chest, a frantic rhythm mirroring the tension building between us. "You're saying there's a secret? Something people don't want us to know?" My voice trembled slightly, the question hanging in the air like an unwelcome ghost.

"Yes!" he insisted, his eyes wide with urgency. "I saw something—something big—and now I'm being hunted. You don't understand how dangerous this is!" His plea hung between us, a desperate attempt to convey the gravity of his situation.

Jordan stepped forward, his protective instincts flaring to life. "And what exactly did you see?"

The man hesitated, glancing around as if the very shadows were eavesdropping. "I can't say here," he murmured, the words slipping through his lips like a timid confession. "Not where they could hear."

"Then where?" I pressed, my curiosity igniting alongside my fear. "Because standing out here in the dark isn't exactly safe either."

"Meet me at the old train station," he urged, desperation coloring his tone. "I know it's risky, but it's the only place I can talk without looking over my shoulder. I swear I'll explain everything."

My instincts screamed at me to say no, to retreat back to the safety of the art center where paint and canvas offered solace from the world's madness. But something about his fervor pulled me in, an invisible thread weaving its way through the fabric of my apprehension. I shared a look with Jordan, and his brow furrowed as he weighed our options.

"Fine," Jordan finally said, though I could see the reluctance etched on his face. "We'll go, but if this is a trap—"

"It's not a trap!" the man interrupted, raising his hands as if to deflect the accusation. "I just need your help. Trust me."

The request hung in the air, delicate yet heavy, the weight of our choices pressing down upon us. I nodded slowly, swallowing the knot in my throat. "Alright. The train station. But if this is a wild goose chase—"

"It's not," he insisted, and with that, we turned and headed toward the street, leaving the safety of the art center behind.

As we walked, the night seemed to thicken, the shadows shifting and elongating as if they were alive. My mind raced, a whirlpool of thoughts and fears, each one darker than the last. I glanced sideways at Jordan, whose jaw was set in a grim line. "You think we're making a mistake?" I asked, trying to lighten the mood despite the tension crackling between us.

"Not unless you're into secrets and possible conspiracy theories," he replied, his voice low and sardonic, though the flicker of humor in his eyes reassured me.

"Hey, I've always wanted to be the leading lady in a thriller," I shot back, trying to inject some levity into the suffocating atmosphere. "I just didn't think it would involve running from shady figures in the middle of the night."

"Welcome to my life," he joked, but there was no mistaking the steel behind his words.

We soon approached the old train station, its dilapidated structure looming against the night sky like a forgotten relic of the past. The iron gates creaked ominously as we pushed them open, the sound echoing into the vast emptiness. Vines crawled up the walls, nature reclaiming what humanity had abandoned. A shiver raced down my spine, but I steeled myself against the creeping dread.

"Stay close," Jordan murmured as we stepped inside, the air thick with the scent of rust and mildew. The once-bustling platform was now a ghost of its former self, crumbling bricks and faded posters whispering stories of journeys long forgotten.

"Nice ambiance," I quipped, attempting to mask my unease. "Perfect for a horror film."

"Just wait for the creepy music to start playing," he replied dryly. "Then we'll really be in trouble."

We moved deeper into the station, the silence amplifying the soft echoes of our footsteps. I glanced at Jordan, his expression focused, his eyes scanning the shadows for any sign of movement. The uncertainty settled heavily in my gut, the fear of the unknown rising like bile in my throat.

Then, from the far corner, I heard it—a soft sound, like the rustling of fabric. My heart quickened, a pulse of adrenaline flooding my system as I turned toward the source. "Did you hear that?" I whispered, my voice barely a breath.

"Yeah," Jordan replied, his body coiling like a spring, ready for action.

The man we'd followed appeared at the edge of the platform, his face pale and drawn. "You made it," he said, relief flooding his voice. "I was worried you wouldn't come."

"Why wouldn't we?" I shot back, my nerves frayed. "You think we'd just let you dangle in the wind?"

He stepped closer, his eyes darting nervously as if checking for unseen threats. "I'm glad you did. There's a lot at stake here."

"Spill it," Jordan demanded, his patience wearing thin.

"I saw them—some sort of meeting. They're planning something big," the man said, urgency clawing at his throat. "People I thought I could trust turned on me. I had to get away."

"Who are they?" I pressed, feeling the weight of the moment pressing down on us.

"Those who want to keep the truth hidden," he replied, glancing over his shoulder again, panic creeping into his tone. "They don't want anyone finding out."

"Finding out what?" Jordan asked, the tension coiling tighter around us.

"About the art center," he said, his words rushing forth like a dam bursting. "It's not just a place for creativity. It's a cover for something much larger—a hub for information they want to control."

A chill raced through me, the implications settling heavily in the air. "What do you mean?"

"Art isn't just paint and canvas," he explained, his eyes wild. "It's a language. A way to communicate ideas without detection. They've been using it to pass information."

"Wait, you're saying our little art haven is some kind of secret network?" I asked incredulously, trying to wrap my head around the enormity of his claim.

"Yes! And I stumbled onto it."

Before I could respond, a distant sound echoed through the station—footsteps, heavy and deliberate, growing closer with each passing second. My heart raced as I exchanged a glance with Jordan, whose expression had turned steely and determined.

"We need to go," he said urgently.

But just as we turned to flee, the lights above flickered ominously, plunging us into darkness for a heartbeat before the emergency lights blinked to life, casting an eerie glow across the station.

In that moment, a figure stepped from the shadows, a smirk curling on their lips. "Did you really think you could escape that easily?"

The air crackled with tension, the night closing in around us like a noose. The atmosphere pulsed with danger, and as my heart pounded against my ribs, I realized the true depth of the peril we faced had only just begun to unfold.

Chapter 19: Eclipsed by Fear

The chill of twilight settled over the town, draping it in a cloak of unease. I could almost taste the tension in the air, a bitter aftertaste mingling with the sweet, earthy scent of damp autumn leaves. It was during these unsettling evenings that Jordan and I found refuge in our shared moments, clinging to the warmth of whispered secrets and tentative smiles. In the flickering glow of the fireplace, we created our own little universe, one where laughter could drown out the silence creeping in from the outside world.

"Do you think ghosts can haunt your family tree?" Jordan asked one evening, the light dancing in his eyes as he leaned closer. The flames cast playful shadows on his face, making him look both boyish and dangerously handsome. He always had this way of challenging me, pushing me just enough to keep the spark alive, yet with a sincerity that pulled at the tender threads of my heart.

"Only if you've got a particularly juicy scandal lurking in the branches," I replied, trying to mask the anxiety gnawing at my insides. The weight of our families' histories pressed down like a heavy blanket, suffocating yet familiar. "I mean, what's a little ghosting between relatives, right?"

He laughed, the sound rich and warm, but I caught the edge of concern lurking beneath it. "You think we'll find something scandalous?" His smile faltered as he swept his gaze over the dimly lit room, as if searching for answers among the shadows. "Or just more skeletons?"

"Skeletons, I'm afraid," I said, my voice trailing off as the reality settled in like an unwelcome visitor. Each night spent unraveling our parents' secrets felt like peeling back layers of an onion—only to reveal the tears hidden just beneath the surface. "I can't shake the feeling that someone's watching us, you know?"

His brow furrowed slightly, the playful banter slipping away like the fading daylight. "It's probably just the paranoia creeping in. This whole situation..." He gestured vaguely to the walls, the bookshelves lined with dusty tomes that felt more like tombstones to old grievances than sources of knowledge. "It's enough to make anyone jumpy."

I nodded, but the unease lingered, a persistent echo of anxiety that resonated in the pit of my stomach. The world outside felt alive, almost sentient, as though it were holding its breath, waiting for the next piece of our puzzle to fall into place. It was then that I caught a flicker of movement beyond the window, just a shadow flitting across the yard. My heart raced, pounding like a drum echoing in the silence, but when I turned back to Jordan, he was oblivious, lost in thought.

"Maybe we need to dig deeper," I said, shaking off the feeling of being watched, the sudden chill that had crept down my spine. "If we uncover the truth, perhaps we can break this cycle of fear."

Jordan leaned back, considering me with that serious expression that made my heart twist. "Or it could just put a bigger target on our backs." His voice was steady, but I could hear the underlying current of worry that threatened to break through. "The more we find out, the more dangerous it gets."

"Dangerous? Or enlightening?" I challenged, leaning forward. "Maybe we're meant to face this together. I can't do it alone, Jordan. I need you." The vulnerability slipped out before I could stop it, my heart racing as I waited for his response.

He met my gaze, those deep eyes filled with something that made my breath hitch—a mixture of determination and uncertainty. "You're right. We're in this together." His words settled over me like a balm, soothing the raw edges of my fear. "But we need a plan."

The conversation shifted then, the tension breaking like a fragile thread. We plotted our next steps, the thrill of discovery momentarily pushing aside the shadows that loomed over us. Yet, as we spoke, a sense of foreboding clung to the edges of my thoughts, the fear that every moment we spent digging deeper could lead us to a truth neither of us was prepared to face.

The following days were a blur of half-hearted attempts at normalcy overshadowed by the weight of our findings. Each new revelation felt like a puzzle piece that didn't quite fit, leaving us grappling with questions that hung in the air, heavy and unyielding. The sense of being hunted grew more pronounced, as if the very walls of our homes had ears, whispering secrets to unseen watchers.

One afternoon, I stumbled upon an old photograph tucked away in a dusty box of family heirlooms. It showed my mother and Jordan's father, young and carefree, their faces alight with laughter—a stark contrast to the tangled web of secrecy that now seemed to envelop us. I clutched the photo, my heart pounding as I felt the ghosts of their past collide with our present.

"Jordan," I called, unable to contain the urgency in my voice. He came rushing into the room, concern etched on his features as he leaned over to see what I had discovered. "Look at this."

He took the photo, his eyes scanning it with an intensity that sent shivers down my spine. "What does this mean?" His voice was low, almost reverent, as if we were holding a sacred artifact rather than a faded picture.

"I don't know, but it feels important," I admitted, the weight of the moment pressing down on us. "We have to find out why they were together. It could be the key to everything."

As we stared at the image, the tension between us crackled with a new intensity, a mixture of fear and unspoken promise. I could feel the walls closing in, the shadows whispering their secrets, but within that darkness, there was also a glimmer of hope—a chance for redemption buried beneath the layers of deception that had entangled our families for far too long.

The days blurred into nights as we spiraled deeper into our investigation, each revelation drawing us closer together yet pushing us toward an unsettling precipice. The once-comforting corners of my home felt transformed, every creak of the floorboards now a reminder of the secrets lurking just out of sight. I found myself questioning every shadow, every whisper of the wind that rustled the leaves outside. Jordan was my anchor in the storm, a steady presence that provided a sense of normalcy amidst the growing chaos.

One evening, as the sun dipped below the horizon, we sprawled on the floor of my living room, surrounded by piles of old newspaper clippings and family records. The golden glow of the desk lamp flickered, casting elongated shadows that danced across the walls, creating an intimate yet eerie atmosphere. "What's our next move, detective?" I quipped, nudging him with my shoulder, trying to lighten the mood. "Should we don our trench coats and hunt down the family villains?"

He chuckled, the sound resonating warmly in the otherwise quiet room. "Only if you promise to wear a fedora. I think it would suit you," he teased, his eyes sparkling with mischief. I couldn't help but laugh, the tension dissipating momentarily, reminding me that laughter was still possible, even in the midst of unraveling the past.

"Fine, but only if you agree to sport some ridiculous mustache," I shot back, raising an eyebrow in mock seriousness. "We'd be the most stylish sleuths in town."

But beneath our banter lay an unspoken understanding. Each joke, each playful jibe, was a thin veneer over the dread that had settled in our hearts. I turned back to the stack of papers, scanning the faded headlines for anything that might shed light on our families' entwined destinies. My fingers brushed over an article detailing a decades-old feud that had torn our parents apart—two families once united, now enemies locked in a battle of secrets and betrayal.

"What if we're not just uncovering the past?" Jordan said suddenly, breaking the silence. His voice was low, almost reverent, as if acknowledging a truth that was too heavy to bear. "What if we're digging up something that should stay buried?"

The air thickened with his words, wrapping around us like a cold fog. "We have to find out," I insisted, a rush of determination coursing through me. "If we don't confront whatever is out there, it'll always linger, a ghost haunting us."

"Or it could blow up in our faces," he replied, his brow furrowed in thought. "What if someone doesn't want us to find out?"

The thought sent a shiver down my spine. I had already felt the weight of unseen eyes, the sensation that we were being followed, our movements tracked like pieces on a chessboard. "Then we outsmart them," I declared, trying to summon the courage I wasn't sure I felt. "We can't let fear dictate our actions."

The next morning brought an air of resolve with it, a newfound clarity that settled in the pit of my stomach. I dressed in a fitted sweater that clung to my frame, hoping it would bolster my confidence, then made my way to the local library. It was a place of dusty tomes and forgotten tales, the perfect sanctuary for our search. Jordan met me there, his brow slightly damp with the promise of rain, but his expression was unwavering.

"Ready to dive into the rabbit hole?" he asked, a smile playing at the corners of his lips.

"More like ready to unearth a whole warren," I shot back, feeling a flicker of excitement surge through me. Together, we navigated the labyrinth of shelves, hunting for any records that could connect the dots between our families. As we sifted through yellowed pages and bound volumes, I couldn't shake the sense that every detail was vital—a missing piece that could lead us closer to the truth or plunge us into further danger.

After hours of digging, we stumbled upon a dusty ledger tucked away in a forgotten corner. The leather cover was cracked and worn, the pages yellowed with age. "What do you think?" I murmured, running my fingers along the spine as if coaxing it to reveal its secrets. "Do we dare?"

"Absolutely," he replied, his excitement infectious as he opened the book. The musty scent of old paper wafted up, and we leaned closer, eager to uncover its contents. As we read through the names and events chronicled within, a familiar name jumped out at me—a name that sent a jolt of recognition through my veins.

"Jordan, look!" I exclaimed, pointing to a name that felt like a dagger to my heart. "This mentions my grandfather. He was involved in some sort of deal with your family. It's all right here."

His eyes widened, the realization dawning upon him as he scanned the entries. "What kind of deal?" he asked, a thread of urgency threading through his voice.

"Something about land and... a betrayal," I stammered, the implications wrapping around my thoughts like a noose. "This could be the key to understanding the feud."

Before he could respond, the heavy wooden door swung open, a gust of wind following in like an unwelcome visitor. An older woman stepped inside, her presence commanding yet oddly unsettling. She carried a stack of books, her gaze piercing as it swept over us. "What are you two up to?" she inquired, a knowing smile playing on her lips.

I glanced at Jordan, sensing the tension rise between us. "Just doing some research," I replied, trying to keep my tone light despite the warning bells ringing in my head.

"Ah, research can lead you to unexpected places," she said cryptically, her eyes glinting with something that made my skin crawl. "Be careful what you dig for. Some truths are better left buried."

Her words hung in the air like a fog, wrapping around us and tightening its grip. As she turned and walked away, I exchanged a glance with Jordan, the unease between us palpable. "What was that about?" he whispered, his brow furrowed.

"I don't know, but I have a feeling we've just scratched the surface," I murmured, a chill racing down my spine. The shadows felt closer now, whispering secrets only we could hear, and as we turned back to the ledger, I knew we were on the precipice of uncovering something profound, something that could either liberate us or plunge us into darkness.

The following week unfolded like a tightly wound coil, each day adding pressure to the uncertainty that wrapped around us. We became nearly nocturnal creatures, our research conducted in hushed whispers under the watchful gaze of the library's flickering overhead lights. The dusty ledger, with its tantalizing hints of betrayal and secrecy, felt both like a treasure map and a warning, leading us toward truths we could barely comprehend.

Jordan and I slipped into our routine like seasoned detectives, fueled by takeout and cold coffee. The lingering scent of lo mein mingled with the musty aroma of old books as we spread our findings across the large oak table. The shadows of our past loomed larger, each detail like a ghost emerging from the depths of time. It was on one such evening, our eyes bleary from reading, that I made a startling connection.

"Jordan," I said, the name slipping from my lips like a breath of wind. "What if this isn't just about our parents? What if there's something more at stake?" I gestured at a series of names that had been mentioned repeatedly in the ledger—names tied to both our families, intricately woven into the fabric of our shared history. "What if there are others involved? People who might still be alive and have their own agendas?"

His brow furrowed, eyes narrowing as he scanned the notes strewn about. "You mean like a secret society?" He leaned back, the chair creaking under the shift of his weight, a playful spark lighting up his gaze. "Should we grab our cloaks and join the ranks of the mysteriously clad?"

"Very funny," I replied, rolling my eyes but unable to suppress a smile. "But seriously, look at this—these names appear alongside deals, partnerships, and even some suspicious-looking transactions. It's like a web of secrets, and I have a feeling it leads back to why our families are at odds."

"Great, now we're delving into financial conspiracies," he teased, but the edge of concern crept back into his voice. "And what happens when we find them? Are we prepared for the fallout?"

"Prepared?" I echoed, a thrill of defiance sparking within me. "I'd rather face a conspiracy than let it fester like an untreated wound. The truth is, I'd rather know if someone out there wants to silence us than live in fear of shadows."

As if to punctuate my determination, the library door swung open once more, letting in a gust of wind that rattled the pages of our research. A chill ran through me, but this time it wasn't just the cold air. There was something disconcerting about the way the wind seemed to whisper, carrying with it a sense of foreboding.

"I think we need to get out of here for a bit," Jordan suggested, glancing toward the door as though sensing the same unease. "How about we take a walk? Clear our heads?"

"Good idea," I agreed, eager to escape the suffocating atmosphere of secrets and shadows. We gathered our things and stepped out into the fading light, the crisp autumn air wrapping around us like a refreshing embrace.

As we walked through the park, the last remnants of daylight painted the sky in hues of lavender and gold, creating a picturesque scene that belied the tension simmering beneath the surface. The leaves crunched underfoot, each step echoing the weight of our discoveries. Jordan and I strolled in silence for a moment, lost in our thoughts.

"Do you think we're in over our heads?" he asked suddenly, breaking the silence. His voice was low, almost hesitant, and I could hear the weight of uncertainty there.

"Maybe," I admitted, biting my lip as I considered the gravity of our situation. "But we can't let fear dictate our choices. We've come this far, and it feels like we're on the verge of something big."

"Or on the verge of getting ourselves into something we can't handle," he countered, his gaze fixed on the ground as if searching for answers among the fallen leaves.

I paused, turning to face him. "Are you scared, Jordan?" I asked, my heart pounding with the sudden seriousness of the moment.

"Honestly? Yeah, I am," he replied, his honesty a breath of fresh air. "But I'm more scared of losing you to this. If something were to happen..."

He didn't finish, and the unspoken words hung heavy between us, thick with the gravity of our shared fears. The bond we had forged in our quest for truth felt both exhilarating and terrifying, a fragile thread woven through the dark tapestry of our families' pasts.

We continued walking, our steps syncopated to the rhythm of our thoughts, when I caught sight of something out of the corner of my eye. A figure stood a distance away, partially obscured by the trees. My breath hitched as I recognized the silhouette, my pulse quickening.

"Jordan, do you see that?" I whispered, pointing toward the figure.

He turned, squinting against the setting sun. "Yeah. Who is that?"

"I don't know," I replied, the hairs on the back of my neck standing on end. "But they've been following us."

Before I could react, the figure stepped into the light, revealing a familiar face, one I had not expected to see. It was my older brother, Ryan, looking disheveled and urgent, his eyes wide with a mix of fear and something else—determination, perhaps.

"Get away from her!" he shouted, his voice piercing through the tranquility of the park, shattering the moment into chaos. "You don't know what you're getting into!"

"Ryan?" I exclaimed, confusion mixing with the mounting dread in my stomach. "What are you talking about?"

But before he could answer, the ground beneath us seemed to shift, a tremor running through the earth that echoed the tumult in my heart. The wind picked up, swirling around us, carrying with it an unsettling energy. And then, as if the very shadows had teeth, I felt a presence behind me, looming and dark.

My breath caught in my throat as I turned, the world blurring into a swirl of confusion and fear. The air thickened with tension, the sky above darkening as a storm brewed on the horizon. In that moment, I realized we were not just uncovering family secrets; we were standing on the edge of a precipice, about to be thrust into a darkness that could swallow us whole.

And just as the first drops of rain began to fall, cold and heavy, I heard a voice—low, sinister, cutting through the chaos like a knife. "You've gone too far, and now it's time to pay the price."

Chapter 20: Tangled Loyalties

The room hummed with a heavy silence, punctuated only by the distant clinking of glassware from the neighboring restaurant. The dim glow of the overhead lights cast long shadows on the walls, creating a sense of intimacy that felt dangerously deceptive. I could feel the tension curling around us, thick as fog, as I sat across from Jordan, our eyes locked in a fierce battle of wills.

"Did you ever think it would come to this?" he asked, his voice a low rumble, tinged with disbelief. He rubbed the back of his neck, a gesture I knew too well. It was his way of masking frustration, a telltale sign that he was on the verge of something monumental, yet unsure of how to express it.

"Honestly?" I replied, leaning forward, my hands gripping the edge of the table. "I thought we were just chasing shadows. But look at what we found." I slid the files across the table, the papers crinkling slightly as they came to rest between us like a fragile bridge spanning an ever-deepening chasm.

Mia, his fiancé, perched nervously on the edge of her chair, her fingers tapping rhythmically against her leg, as if willing her own thoughts to settle. She had been our steadfast ally through this unraveling mystery, but the look on her face suggested that even she was beginning to question everything she thought she knew. "I mean, this is just... monumental," she breathed, her wide eyes darting between Jordan and the documents. "These connections, they change everything."

Jordan's gaze narrowed, and I could see the wheels turning in his mind, racing through the implications. "We can't just sit here and pretend like this doesn't matter. My father and yours—" he hesitated, the weight of those words hanging heavily in the air. "They've been tied together in ways we never understood. It's like they've built a web around us, and now we're trapped in it."

The words echoed like an incantation, the truth wrapping around us like a snake ready to strike. I took a deep breath, my chest tightening. "What do we do now?" I asked, the question hanging between us like a cliff's edge.

Mia leaned back, her brow furrowed in thought, and I could see the spark of determination igniting in her eyes. "We need to confront them. This isn't just about us anymore; it's about breaking free from whatever chains they've forged between our families."

Jordan shook his head, a flicker of uncertainty crossing his face. "Confronting them could lead to even more chaos. We need to be strategic about this."

"Strategic?" I echoed, incredulity bubbling up within me. "You mean sit back and let them dictate the terms? We can't just let this go." My voice rose, betraying the anger simmering beneath the surface. The idea of being puppets in a game I didn't even know I was a part of sent a shiver of indignation racing down my spine.

As the tension thickened, the door swung open, ushering in a rush of cool air and the scent of damp earth—a reminder that the world outside continued to turn, oblivious to our turmoil. A figure stepped inside, shaking off the rain that had clung to their coat, and my heart stuttered for an instant as I recognized the newcomer.

"Jules?" The voice was warm yet laced with an edge I couldn't quite place. My brother, Oliver, sauntered in, a casualness in stark contrast to the chaos enveloping us. He surveyed the scene, his smile faltering as he took in the gravity of our discussion. "What's going on?"

"Oliver, this isn't a good time," I replied, attempting to keep my tone even, but the tension cracked like glass.

He shrugged, oblivious or uncaring. "I've heard things, Jules. About the two of you digging into the past. I figured it must be important." He dropped into a chair, crossing his arms.

"Things are complicated," Jordan interjected, casting a wary glance at Mia. "We're trying to piece together our families' histories, and it turns out... well, it's a lot."

"What do you mean?" Oliver leaned forward, his interest piqued. "What have you found?"

I took a moment, weighing the implications of sharing our discoveries with him. "It's not just some old family feud. It goes deeper than that. Our parents—" I hesitated, unsure of how much I should reveal. "They've been involved in something that's been kept from us."

"Kept from you, you mean," Oliver shot back, an edge of defensiveness creeping into his tone. "Why didn't you tell me sooner?"

"This isn't about you," I snapped, frustration bubbling over. "You think I wanted to drag you into this? It's bigger than any of us. I don't even know how deep the rabbit hole goes."

"Then let me help," he insisted, a glimmer of earnestness breaking through his earlier bravado. "If we're tangled up in this, I deserve to know."

The pressure in the room intensified, suffocating me as I weighed the burden of truth against the potential for further unraveling our fragile alliances. I could feel the walls closing in, the air heavy with the weight of unspoken words and hidden loyalties. Would sharing everything strengthen our resolve, or would it serve to deepen the divides that had begun to form between us?

"I just want to understand," he added softly, the tone disarming. "What is it you found?"

Before I could answer, the sound of a chair scraping against the floor caught my attention. Mia stood abruptly, her expression a mixture of defiance and concern. "You know what? Maybe we need to confront them—together. No more secrets, no more shadows. If our families have been hiding the truth, then we owe it to ourselves to uncover it."

Jordan's eyes met mine, and in that fleeting moment, a shared understanding ignited between us. The path ahead might be fraught with peril, but perhaps this was the spark we needed to forge a new path. One that didn't just unravel our families' pasts, but also charted a course toward a future we could claim for ourselves.

Jordan shifted in his seat, his fingers tapping against the table in a rhythm that matched the erratic beating of my heart. The air was charged, thick with the weight of our revelations and the potential fallout. I could almost hear the silent conversations raging inside his mind, fighting against the desire to protect our families while grappling with the undeniable truth that our lives were now irrevocably intertwined.

Mia paced the small space between the tables, her heels clicking sharply against the wooden floor, punctuating her agitation. "We need to dig deeper," she declared, her voice firm but slightly unsteady, like a tightrope walker one wobble away from a fall. "We can't just stop here. If our parents have been hiding something, there's no telling what else is out there."

"What else could there possibly be?" I shot back, my frustration bubbling over. "What, are we supposed to uncover a family treasure map next? Or maybe a hidden journal filled with sordid details of family betrayals?"

Mia stopped abruptly, turning to face me, her expression a mix of surprise and admiration. "Well, you might be onto something there. I mean, wouldn't it be just like our families to have a secret diary? You know, detailing all their misdeeds and, oh, possibly a warning about the impending doom of their children?"

Jordan chuckled, breaking the tension for a brief moment. "Right? An ominous prophecy about how we're all cursed to repeat their mistakes."

But the laughter felt fleeting, like a delicate soap bubble that could pop at any moment. I leaned back, crossing my arms, the weight of everything bearing down on me. "Joking aside, what if this goes deeper than we think? What if there's something... more dangerous lurking beneath the surface?"

Jordan's brow furrowed, the lightness in his eyes dimming as he considered my words. "Dangerous how?"

"Think about it," I said, my voice dropping to a whisper, the shadows of the restaurant creeping closer. "What if they were involved in something illegal? Something that could ruin not just their reputations but ours too?"

Mia nodded, the color draining from her face as she caught the implications of my words. "I... I hadn't thought about it that way. But you're right. If that's the case, we could be stepping into something that's far beyond our control."

The door swung open once again, and the sound of laughter erupted into our serious atmosphere. A group of people entered, their energy spilling over the threshold like confetti. I glanced over, momentarily distracted by the rush of normalcy. The scene felt almost jarring—a stark contrast to the gravity of our discussion.

"See? There's still joy in the world," Jordan said, his eyes flickering toward the lively group. "We should find a way to inject a little of that into our lives."

"Maybe a dance party will solve all our problems?" I suggested wryly, the absurdity of the idea bringing a smile to my lips despite the tension.

"I can see it now," Mia chimed in, mimicking a dramatic announcer. "And here we have the valiant trio, dancing their worries away while family secrets loom over them like a dark cloud. Truly a sight to behold."

Just then, a sharp voice cut through our banter. "What are you three doing in here? Planning a revolution?"

I turned to see Oliver leaning against the doorframe, arms crossed, an amused grin plastered across his face. "You look like you're plotting something nefarious. Should I be concerned?"

"Only if you're on the wrong side of history, Oliver," I shot back, the words slipping out before I could rein them in. "But no, we're just talking about the possibility of familial treachery and the potential end of our sanity. Same old, same old."

Oliver's smile faded, replaced by a look of genuine concern. "Look, if there's something going on, you need to let me in on it. You're not alone in this. Whatever it is, we can face it together."

"Together," I echoed, the word wrapping around me like a lifeline. But the thought of dragging him deeper into our tangled mess left me uneasy. "I don't want you to get hurt. It's complicated."

"Complicated is my middle name," he retorted with a hint of bravado, and for a moment, I could see the younger brother I had always protected from the world's harsher realities. "And besides, you're stuck with me. So spill it. What did you find?"

Jordan exchanged a glance with me, the tension between us palpable as we considered how much to reveal. Finally, he spoke up, his voice steady. "We found evidence linking our families—financial dealings, old business ties... things that could seriously complicate our lives if they come to light."

"Financial dealings?" Oliver raised an eyebrow, intrigued yet wary. "You think they're involved in something shady?"

"Shady is putting it lightly," I said, my heart racing. "But it could be more than just bad business. We're talking about possible illegal activities that could change everything for all of us. This isn't just about family feuds anymore; it's about survival."

The gravity of the situation settled heavily in the air. Oliver straightened, his casual demeanor replaced by the weight of responsibility. "Then we need to take action. We can't let this slide. Whatever they've done, we need to confront them."

"Confrontation seems to be the theme of the evening," I muttered, trying to keep my voice light, though anxiety twisted in my gut. "But how do we even begin to approach that?"

"First, we gather more information," Mia said, determination flooding her voice. "We can't go in blind. If there's a storm brewing, we need to be prepared. Knowledge is our best weapon."

Oliver nodded, his usual humor subdued. "And if it means digging deeper, then we're in this together, right? All for one and one for all?"

"Exactly," Jordan agreed, his voice a steady anchor amidst the swirling chaos. "We'll dig until we find the truth, and then we'll confront them. Together."

As we exchanged glances, a newfound sense of camaraderie sparked between us, igniting a flame of hope in the darkness. Whatever lay ahead, we would face it as a unit. But as the weight of our shared burden pressed down on my shoulders, I couldn't shake the feeling that we were standing on the precipice of something that could irrevocably alter the course of our lives.

The tension in the room had transformed into a tangible force, as if we were all trapped inside a pressure cooker about to blow. I could feel the uncertainty creeping along my spine, prickling the back of my neck. With every beat of my heart, the stakes seemed to rise higher, as if our decisions now carried the weight of entire legacies.

"Let's think about this logically," I said, forcing my voice to remain steady. "If we're going to confront our families, we need a solid plan. We can't just storm in there with accusations and half-formed ideas."

Jordan leaned back, crossing his arms. "What do you suggest? We prepare a PowerPoint presentation?"

Mia couldn't suppress a chuckle, the sound breaking the tension like a bubble bursting. "I'd pay to see that! 'Ladies and gentlemen, esteemed parents, today we shall discuss your intricate web of deception.'"

"Very funny," I shot back, trying to ignore the way my stomach flipped at the thought of facing my mother, her icy gaze cutting through me like a knife. "But seriously, we need to know what we're dealing with. Are we talking about simple lies, or is there something darker at play?"

Oliver, who had remained quietly contemplative, finally spoke up. "We need to uncover the truth about the financial ties first. If we can expose that, it might give us leverage. But we'll have to be careful—if they catch wind of what we're doing, we'll be walking into a trap."

"Exactly," Jordan said, his gaze sharpening. "We have to be strategic, like spies in a very melodramatic spy movie. I'm not sure I'm cut out for that, but it's our only option."

I nodded, absorbing their ideas, my mind racing. "We'll start by going through any old correspondence or documents we can find. Maybe there are letters, contracts... something that can provide clarity."

Mia's eyes lit up with an idea. "My parents have a small safe in the study. I could sneak in and check it out when they're not around. I've seen them place some old files in there. If there's anything incriminating, we could find it."

"Great plan," Jordan encouraged, a hint of admiration in his voice. "But we need to make sure you're not caught. This is a delicate operation. It could backfire spectacularly."

"Welcome to my life," Mia replied with a grin, but I could see the flicker of nervousness beneath her bravado. "I'll handle it. Just tell me what to look for."

Oliver chimed in, "We can cover for you. Just give us a signal if you need us to back you up. But we should also think about how we want to confront our parents afterward. Should we go in pairs? That way, if things escalate, we can keep each other in check."

The strategic planning had started to energize me, but a nagging feeling tugged at my insides, a lingering doubt that reminded me just how fragile our situation was. "Okay, so we've got the infiltration plan, but what happens when we uncover the truth? How do we handle the fallout?"

"We tackle it head-on," Jordan stated with unexpected confidence. "We can't let fear dictate our actions. The truth may hurt, but it's our only way forward. Besides, we're in this together."

I felt a rush of warmth at his words, but deep down, I still feared the potential consequences. "Let's just hope our families don't react like they've just been cornered by a pack of wild dogs," I muttered, half-joking, but the seriousness of our predicament hung heavily in the air.

Mia shrugged, her face a mix of determination and trepidation. "What's the worst that can happen? A family feud that's already been brewing for years? I mean, at least we know what we're dealing with now."

Her words lingered in the air, a desperate rallying cry against the looming shadow of our familial legacies.

With a nod of agreement, we finalized our plan for the night: we would regroup in two days, allowing Mia the time to gather whatever information she could unearth. Until then, I was left with a restless mind, a cacophony of thoughts echoing through my skull, each one more insistent than the last.

The following day, I found myself in a whirlwind of anticipation and anxiety, pacing my small apartment while the clock ticked down to our next meeting. With every tick, the weight of our plan pressed on my chest, an iron band tightening around my heart.

When the evening finally arrived, I was a bundle of nerves. I made my way to our usual meeting spot—a quaint café tucked away in a quiet corner of the city. The flickering candlelight inside offered a warm glow that stood in stark contrast to my anxious energy. As I entered, the familiar sound of laughter and clinking cups greeted me, momentarily soothing my frayed nerves.

Mia was already seated at our usual table, her hair a tousled mess from the wind outside, but her eyes sparkled with mischief. "Guess what?" she announced as I approached. "I found something. And it's a doozy."

The excitement in her voice pulled me in, and I felt my pulse quicken as I sat down. "What did you find? Please tell me it's not another family recipe for disaster."

"Oh, it's much worse than that." She leaned in, lowering her voice conspiratorially. "I went through my parents' safe, and I found some old ledgers. They're dated from years ago, and they contain transactions that don't make any sense. Large amounts of money moving between accounts with no clear purpose."

"Are you serious?" I gasped, my heart racing. "That could mean—"

"Exactly," Mia interrupted, her eyes wide. "There's a connection to Jordan's family. It's all in there—mysterious payments, possibly linked to whatever shady business they've been involved in. And then..." She hesitated, her breath hitching as if she were preparing to unleash a storm.

"What?" I urged, leaning closer.

"There's a name." Her voice dropped to a whisper, and I could feel the tension coiling between us, tightening like a noose. "A name that could change everything: your father's."

The weight of her words crashed over me, an avalanche of realization that left me breathless. "My father? But he's... he's always been the pillar of our community. What are you saying?"

"I don't know yet, but if this ledger is correct, it suggests he's been involved in something bigger. Something that could shatter everything we believe about our families."

Before I could respond, a shadow loomed over our table. I looked up, my breath catching as I met the gaze of a figure I never expected to see. "Well, well, what do we have here?" Oliver's voice dripped with sarcasm, but there was an edge of something darker beneath it. "You two seem awfully chummy. What are you plotting now?"

Mia's expression turned to panic, and I could feel the ground shift beneath me. In an instant, everything we had planned teetered on the edge of exposure, and with it came the harrowing realization that we might not be alone in this treacherous game.

Chapter 21: Through the Darkness

The air hung thick with tension, a weight that pressed down on my chest and quickened my heart rate. Each tick of the clock echoed like a countdown to an unknown fate. The room felt smaller, the shadows creeping in from the corners, eager to envelop us in their cold embrace. Jordan stood beside me, his hand firmly clasped around mine, a lifeline amidst the encroaching darkness. The warmth of his touch grounded me, reminding me that I was not alone in this. He met my gaze, his eyes reflecting a mix of determination and fear, a silent agreement passing between us—we would face whatever came next together.

It was a week since we uncovered the first layer of deceit—a seemingly innocuous piece of information that had unraveled into a tangled mess of betrayal and manipulation. Every lead we chased seemed to sprout a dozen more, each one leading us deeper into a labyrinth of secrets that twisted and turned in ways I could never have anticipated. I had never envisioned my life would devolve into such chaos, where whispers turned to shouts and safety felt like a distant memory.

We had set up a makeshift command center in my apartment, which now resembled a cross between a detective's office and a war room. Papers littered the coffee table, some marked with hastily scrawled notes, others sporting colorful highlighter lines that connected names and dates like a manic spider's web. The once-cozy space had transformed into a battleground of our minds, where we waged war against an unseen enemy. The vibrant colors of my throw pillows stood in stark contrast to the gray pallor of anxiety that clung to the air, a reminder of the normal life I once had.

I rifled through the papers again, frustration bubbling beneath my skin. "How can something so simple spiral into such a mess?" I murmured, tossing a sheaf of documents aside. Jordan watched me, his brow furrowed in thought, before speaking.

"Maybe that's the point. Whoever is pulling the strings wants us to feel overwhelmed. If we can't see clearly, we can't fight back." His voice was steady, a rock against my storm.

I looked at him, a flicker of appreciation for his clarity cutting through the chaos. "You make it sound so simple. Just unravel the layers, find the truth. But each layer seems to reveal something even darker." I sighed, feeling the burden of uncertainty settle in again.

He squeezed my hand tighter. "And we will. But we have to be smart about it. We need allies who can help us navigate this mess, who can offer us protection."

I nodded, my mind racing with thoughts of our friends and contacts who could offer a lifeline. There was Lila, who had a knack for digital sleuthing, her skills honed in the tech trenches where she thrived. Then there was Ben, an old college buddy who had connections in law enforcement. Together, they could help us piece together the puzzle, but it meant reaching out, exposing ourselves to the very people we were trying to trust. I felt a twinge of hesitation. "What if it backfires? What if we expose ourselves even more?"

"Or what if they can help us turn the tables?" Jordan countered, his resolve unwavering. "We can't do this alone, not anymore. We need to take the fight to them."

The determination in his voice ignited a spark within me. "Okay, let's do it. Let's reach out to Lila first. She'll have insights we haven't even considered." I grabbed my phone, my fingers dancing across the screen as I texted her, the rhythmic clicks a promise of action.

As I hit send, the momentary rush of adrenaline faded, leaving a residue of anxiety. The truth was, I felt exposed, like I was standing on the edge of a precipice, staring into an abyss where unseen dangers lurked, waiting for the slightest misstep. Jordan leaned closer, his breath warm against my ear, grounding me again. "No matter what happens, we'll figure it out. I promise."

Before I could respond, my phone chimed with a reply. Lila was game to meet, eager to help untangle the web we'd stumbled into. Relief washed over me, but it was short-lived, replaced by an unsettling sensation that clung to my gut. What if this was a trap?

The evening air was cool when we stepped outside, a welcome relief from the stifling atmosphere of my apartment. The city buzzed around us, alive with its usual symphony of honking cars and distant laughter. I took a deep breath, inhaling the scents of grilled street food mingling with the faint aroma of blooming jasmine. It was a bizarre juxtaposition to the chaos swirling in my mind, reminding me that life continued beyond our immediate crisis.

We headed to a quaint café a few blocks away, its charming outdoor seating filled with a mix of patrons lost in their own worlds. Lila was already there, her dark curls bouncing as she waved enthusiastically from a table nestled beneath the twinkling fairy lights. She exuded an infectious energy that was impossible to resist. I felt a flicker of hope as I and Jordan approached her, and her face brightened at the sight of us.

"Hey, you two! You look like you've seen a ghost!" Lila exclaimed, her eyes sparkling with curiosity.

"More like a ghost story that refuses to end," I replied with a wry smile, settling into the chair across from her.

Jordan leaned forward, his expression serious. "We need your help, Lila. Things are getting out of hand."

Her playful demeanor shifted instantly, the gravity of our situation dawning on her. "Tell me everything."

And just like that, as I began to unravel the tale that had ensnared us, the words spilled out in a rush, the shadows that had clung to me starting to dissipate, if only for a moment. I could feel Jordan's hand inch closer to mine beneath the table, a silent reminder that even in the darkest moments, we could lean on each other. As the evening deepened, the connections we forged would be the very threads that pulled us from the brink, weaving a tapestry of resilience against the encroaching darkness.

The café buzzed with life, the clatter of cups and low hum of conversation blending into a comforting background noise. Lila leaned forward, her fingers tapping a rapid rhythm on the table, the gleam in her eye suggesting she was already plotting our next move. "So, let's get to it. You've got me curious, and you know I can't resist a good mystery," she quipped, her voice low but laced with excitement.

I took a deep breath, channeling the swirling energy around us into words that would peel back the layers of our unfolding story. "Okay, so we found this connection between the missing files and a string of suspicious transactions. It's like someone is pulling the strings behind the scenes, and every time we think we're close to the truth, another layer gets added, making it harder to see what's real."

Lila nodded, her eyes narrowing in thought. "So, you're saying you've got a corporate spy situation on your hands? Intrigue, deception... I love it! This could be one hell of a ride. Do you have any leads?"

Jordan chimed in, his voice steady. "We have some names, but every time we dig deeper, we run into dead ends. It's almost as if someone is watching us."

Lila raised an eyebrow, a grin spreading across her face. "Are we in a thriller movie? Because I'm here for it! The drama, the suspense... it's practically begging for a popcorn moment. But seriously, if you're being watched, we need to tread carefully. This isn't a game."

I felt a pang of anxiety at her words, a reminder of just how deep we were wading into murky waters. "We can't let fear paralyze us, though. We need to keep moving, to keep digging. But maybe we should consider how we share information from now on."

"Agreed," Jordan said, his tone serious. "If they're monitoring us, we need to be smarter about our communication. Lila, do you have any secure channels we could use?"

Lila leaned back, considering. "I can set you up with a secure messaging app. You know, the kind that self-destructs after reading. It'll make things more difficult for anyone trying to eavesdrop." She winked, her enthusiasm infectious, and I felt the knot in my stomach loosen a fraction.

"Perfect. Let's do it," I replied, a renewed sense of determination flooding through me. The notion that we could take back some control, even a little, invigorated me.

After brainstorming for a while, we settled on a plan. Lila would contact some of her tech-savvy friends to help us access more hidden information about our lead suspects, while Jordan and I would revisit the sites connected to the transactions, hoping to unearth something that could point us in the right direction.

As we wrapped up our meeting, the café began to empty, the patrons filtering out into the night. Lila stood to leave, her chair scraping against the floor, and for a moment, I felt a flash of uncertainty. "You'll be careful, right?" I asked, concern creeping into my voice.

"Me? I'm always careful," she replied with a mischievous grin. "But I promise, I'll be in touch. And if you two find anything juicy, you better share! I want all the details."

Once Lila disappeared into the night, Jordan and I lingered at the table, our conversation shifting to lighter topics. We joked about our disastrous cooking attempts and the ridiculous amount of takeout we had ordered since starting this investigation. Laughter felt like a sweet reprieve, a brief escape from the shadows pressing in around us.

But as the evening waned and the glow of the café's lights dimmed, the weight of our reality returned, settling over us like a heavy blanket. The moment of levity passed, replaced by a silent agreement that we were stepping into uncharted territory.

"Ready?" Jordan asked, breaking the tension. I could hear the unspoken question in his voice: Are you ready to face whatever is coming?

I nodded, though my heart raced with apprehension. "Let's go."

We stepped out into the crisp night air, the chill brushing against my skin like a warning. The city lights twinkled around us, casting a surreal glow that felt both comforting and disorienting. As we walked, the streetlamps flickered above, and I couldn't shake the feeling that we were being watched. My instincts prickled, and I glanced over my shoulder more than once, half-expecting to see a shadow lurking in the darkness.

Jordan caught my gaze, his brow furrowing in concern. "What is it? You look like you just saw a ghost again."

"Just... a feeling," I admitted, my voice barely above a whisper. "I can't shake the sense that we're being followed."

He stepped closer, his presence a protective barrier against my spiraling thoughts. "We're in this together, remember? Whatever happens, we face it side by side."

I swallowed hard, nodding. The comfort of his reassurance was a lifeline in the tempest brewing around us. As we made our way toward the first location on our list, a seemingly innocuous office building that had been connected to one of the suspicious transactions, the tension simmered just beneath the surface.

The building loomed ahead, its glass façade reflecting the moonlight, creating an almost ethereal glow. I felt a rush of adrenaline as we approached, an inexplicable mix of dread and anticipation coursing through my veins. "This is it," I breathed, peering through the glass doors.

"Let's go in," Jordan replied, his determination palpable.

As we crossed the threshold, the sterile scent of cleaning supplies hit me like a wall, the faint buzz of fluorescent lights humming overhead. The receptionist looked up, surprise flickering across her face as we walked in. "Can I help you?" she asked, her voice devoid of warmth.

"Just visiting a colleague," Jordan replied smoothly, his demeanor casual as if we weren't standing at the precipice of chaos.

The receptionist raised an eyebrow, clearly skeptical, but waved us through. My heart pounded as we navigated the empty corridors, the fluorescent lights casting a stark glow that did little to soothe my frayed nerves.

Every step echoed in the silence, heightening my awareness of the delicate line we were treading. Jordan's hand brushed against mine, a quiet reminder that we were in this together. As we approached the door labeled with the name of our target, I hesitated, my breath catching in my throat.

"Ready?" he asked, a reassuring smile on his lips that made me feel a little braver.

I nodded, steeling myself for whatever awaited us on the other side. With a deep breath, I pushed the door open, the hinges creaking ominously as we stepped into the unknown.

Inside, the room was dark, the curtains drawn tight as if hiding the secrets within. A desk sat in the center, littered with papers, and the air was thick with an unsettling stillness. Jordan and I exchanged a glance, our hearts racing as we ventured further inside.

As we began to sift through the documents, the reality of our precarious situation settled in. The shadows deepened around us, whispers of the unknown creeping closer, but with each paper we turned, I felt a flicker of hope. Maybe, just maybe, we were on the cusp of uncovering the truth that could shatter the web of deception that had ensnared us.

The room was a mosaic of shadows, the dim light from the desk lamp casting an eerie glow over the papers strewn across the surface. My heart thudded in my chest, each beat echoing the growing tension in the air as I flipped through the documents, searching for any sign of the truth buried within. The stale scent of ink and old paper mingled with the faint hum of the air conditioner, creating an atmosphere that felt both claustrophobic and charged with possibility.

Jordan stood close by, his presence a steadying force. I could see the intensity in his eyes as he scanned the room, his posture alert, ready for anything. "You know," he said, breaking the silence, "if this were a movie, the lights would flicker right about now, and the villain would appear in a dramatic swirl of smoke." He shot me a lopsided grin, but I could see the tension in his jaw, the way his fingers twitched as if itching for action.

I smirked back, despite the flutter of nerves in my stomach. "Yeah, and I'd be the plucky heroine, rolling my eyes and delivering a snappy comeback right before we narrowly escape." I couldn't resist adding a wink, trying to lighten the moment, but the weight of the situation pressed down on us like a thick fog.

Just then, my gaze caught on a file tucked away in the corner, its edges frayed, like it had been hastily shoved aside. I reached for it, my fingers brushing against the worn surface, and pulled it closer. The name on the top sent a jolt through me—Adeline Mercer. She was the CEO of a rival company, but her connection to the web of deceit was murky at best. What was she doing in this place?

"Hey, check this out," I called to Jordan, flipping open the file to reveal a series of contracts, each one more damning than the last. "It looks like she was involved in some backdoor dealings with our suspect."

Jordan stepped closer, peering over my shoulder, his breath hitching as he scanned the pages. "This is gold. If we can connect her to the transactions... but wait, what's this?" His finger pointed to a name scribbled in the margins, barely legible. "That can't be right."

I squinted at the handwriting, feeling a chill race down my spine. "No way... it's not possible." The name was one I hadn't expected to see here—Travis Kane, a close associate of mine from years back, someone I thought I could trust.

"How does he fit into this?" Jordan's voice was low, the tension between us thickening as the implications settled over us like a storm cloud.

"I don't know, but we need to find out," I replied, my voice steady despite the whirlwind of confusion inside. The realization that someone I had once considered a friend could be tangled in this mess felt like a punch to the gut. I took a deep breath, forcing the whirlwind of thoughts to settle. "Let's keep looking."

We rifled through more documents, uncovering names and figures, the evidence painting a grim picture. Each revelation tied the threads of deceit closer together, and with every piece of information, a darker truth emerged. A new sense of urgency gripped me—this wasn't just about exposing a scandal; it felt personal now.

"Do you hear that?" Jordan suddenly whispered, his voice cutting through my thoughts. My heart raced as I strained to listen, catching the faintest sound of footsteps echoing in the hallway.

"Someone's coming," I said, adrenaline surging through me. My instincts kicked in, urging me to move. "We need to hide."

We scrambled to find a place, ducking behind the desk as the door creaked open, the shadows shifting in the doorway. My breath caught in my throat, the adrenaline coursing through me in hot waves. I could see the outline of a figure stepping inside, the silhouette illuminated by the dim glow of the hallway lights.

"Just stay quiet," Jordan whispered, his hand gripping mine tightly.

The figure moved cautiously, glancing around the room, their expression obscured by the dim light. I held my breath, praying we wouldn't be discovered. The tension in the air was palpable, each second stretching out like an eternity.

Suddenly, the figure paused, their gaze landing directly on the file I had been reading moments before, now partially obscured by the edge of the desk. I could hear the faintest of gasps as recognition flickered across their face.

"No!" the figure exclaimed, and in an instant, everything spiraled into chaos.

Jordan sprang into action, pulling me to my feet as we darted for the back exit, the urgency of the moment pushing us forward. "Go, go!" he urged, urgency threading through his voice.

As we burst into the hallway, the echo of our footsteps rang in my ears, a frantic reminder of the peril we were in. My heart raced, pumping adrenaline through my veins as we rounded a corner, desperate to put distance between us and the unknown threat behind us.

But as we dashed down the corridor, a sudden realization struck me—Travis was involved. My mind whirled, piecing together the fragments of our past, trying to comprehend how he fit into this chaotic puzzle. I felt a mixture of betrayal and fear churning within me.

We reached the stairwell, pushing through the door and racing down the steps, the air thick with tension and urgency. Each step felt like a leap into the unknown, a race against time. I glanced at Jordan, his expression fierce, determined, but also tinged with concern.

"Where's the exit?" I gasped, scanning the dimly lit staircase as we descended, my pulse pounding in my ears.

"Just a little further!" he shouted, pushing ahead. "We're almost there!"

But just as we reached the final landing, a figure emerged from the shadows—Travis, standing in our path, his face a mask of determination.

"Stop right there!" he commanded, his voice a low growl, echoing in the confined space.

I froze, my heart plummeting at the sight of him. This was the last person I expected to confront, and my mind raced with a mix of confusion and dread. "Travis, what are you doing here?"

He stepped closer, his expression unreadable. "You shouldn't have come here. You don't know what you're getting into."

"We need answers!" I shot back, the courage swelling within me despite the panic. "You're involved in this, aren't you? You've been lying to me!"

Travis's jaw tightened, a flicker of hesitation passing across his face. "It's not that simple, Adeline. You need to trust me. This is bigger than you realize."

But before I could respond, the sound of footsteps echoed behind us, a group closing in, their presence unmistakable. The walls felt like they were closing in again, and I knew we were out of time.

"Jordan, we have to—" I began, but before I could finish, the situation erupted into chaos.

The footsteps grew louder, a thundering chorus of impending danger as I glanced at Jordan, our fates intertwined in that single, breathless moment. We had come so far, but now, everything hung in the balance. With nowhere to escape and danger lurking at every turn, I felt the ground beneath me shift, teetering on the brink of a revelation that could shatter everything I thought I knew.

"Run!" Jordan shouted, and I turned to bolt, but just as I did, a shadow loomed, engulfing us both as the darkness threatened to swallow the light, the cliff edge of our lives looming perilously close.

Chapter 22: The Storm Breaks

Rain poured from a sky bruised with shades of gray, each drop hammering against the pavement like an urgent heartbeat. The wind whipped around me, carrying the scent of damp earth and distant jasmine, remnants of a summer that seemed long gone. I tightened the collar of my jacket, pulling it closer against the chill that seeped into my bones. It was an ironic twist that tonight, of all nights, I found myself standing before the hollow shell of what had once been a grand estate—Haverly Manor, a name whispered in hushed tones across our families for generations. It felt like the mouth of a beast, dark and inviting, waiting to swallow us whole.

Beside me stood Jamie, his presence a beacon amidst the encroaching shadows. He was a tangle of emotions, each one flickering across his face like the sporadic bursts of lightning overhead. "You ready for this?" His voice barely rose above the wind, but it carried an undercurrent of strength, grounding me as we faced the weight of our families' legacies.

"As ready as I'll ever be," I replied, forcing a smile that felt fragile on my lips. It was a lie, but one I hoped would lend me the confidence I desperately sought. We had spent too long skirting the edges of our pain, living in the remnants of our pasts rather than confronting them. This night was our reckoning, and though the fear clawed at my insides, a part of me thrilled at the prospect of finally untangling the threads of deceit that bound us.

Together, we stepped through the rusted gates, their creaks echoing like ghostly whispers of those who had come before us. The manor loomed larger with each step, a decaying titan that had once held opulence and splendor, now reduced to peeling wallpaper and shattered glass. Its presence was suffocating, the air thick with the scent of mildew and old memories, a reminder that every brick contained the weight of stories left untold.

Inside, the atmosphere buzzed with tension, the kind that prickled at the back of my neck. I could almost hear the echoes of laughter and the clinking of glasses from long-forgotten parties, now replaced by silence that pressed down like a shroud. As we moved through the grand foyer, Jamie's hand found mine, his grip firm and reassuring. The darkness seemed to pulse around us, a living entity that thrived on our fear.

"Are you sure we have to do this?" Jamie asked, his eyes darting to the long staircase that spiraled into shadow. "We could walk away, you know."

And there it was—the temptation to turn back. It would be so easy, to let the memories remain buried and untouched. But that wasn't why we were here. "No," I breathed, my voice steadying with purpose. "We need to face this. For ourselves. For everyone who came before us."

He nodded, the tension in his shoulders easing just slightly. We ascended the staircase, the wood groaning beneath our weight as if the manor itself resented our intrusion. Each step was a battle, a reminder of the burdens we carried. The upper halls were dimly lit, shadows playing tricks on our eyes, making it hard to discern what was real and what was merely a figment of our anxiety.

At the end of the hallway, a door stood ajar, the faintest glimmer of light seeping through the crack. We exchanged a glance, and without a word, pushed it open. The room was a study, filled with dust and memories—the air stale, yet thick with the sense of something powerful waiting to be unleashed. There, at the center, stood a figure silhouetted against the window, backlit by the storm raging outside.

"Welcome," the figure said, their voice smooth and dripping with familiarity, causing my heart to lurch in my chest. My breath hitched as recognition washed over me. It was my father.

"Why are you here?" I demanded, anger rising like bile. "After everything, you just...show up?"

He turned slowly, a wry smile playing on his lips, and for a moment, the resemblance was overwhelming. "Because, my dear, the past never truly lets go. It demands to be confronted."

Jamie stepped forward, protective and fierce. "What do you want from us?"

"Nothing more than what you owe yourselves," my father replied, his eyes narrowing. "To know the truth. To see the bigger picture."

The room seemed to shudder with his words, the storm outside echoing our inner turmoil. I glanced at Jamie, who was visibly on edge, and took a deep breath. "The truth? The truth is that you've caused so much pain, and now you want us to understand?"

"Understanding is the first step towards healing," he countered, an unsettling calmness lacing his tone. "You can't move forward until you reconcile with your past."

Lightning flashed, illuminating the chaos swirling in my heart. The storm was no longer just a backdrop; it was the embodiment of our conflict. "You think this is about you?" I shot back, my voice rising. "You don't get to dictate our healing, not after abandoning us when we needed you most."

His gaze hardened, but before he could respond, the walls seemed to vibrate, and an unexpected force rushed into the room, as if the storm outside had breached the boundaries of the estate. It rattled the windows, sending shards of glass cascading to the floor. The air thickened with tension, charged with a mix of emotions that threatened to explode.

"Run!" Jamie shouted, but my feet felt rooted to the ground, as if the manor itself was holding me captive. "We can't leave! We have to finish this!" I screamed back, desperate for resolution.

In that moment, I realized this confrontation wasn't just about facing my father; it was about reclaiming my narrative, about finding the strength within myself to confront the ghosts that had haunted us for far too long. The tempest outside roared in agreement, and I could feel the tide turning, the storm breaking around us as I prepared to shatter the silence that had bound us for years.

As the storm raged outside, the tempest within felt equally fierce. I stood, anchored by a mixture of fear and determination, the weight of my father's presence pressing down like the humidity before a downpour. Each breath I took felt laced with the electric charge of conflict, and I was acutely aware of Jamie's stance beside me, his body tense and ready, as if he could spring into action at any moment.

"I never abandoned you," my father insisted, his voice smooth but tinged with irritation. "I was protecting you from a truth too heavy for children to bear." The way he wielded his words was infuriating, like a magician trying to distract an audience from the sleight of hand.

"Protecting us? Or protecting yourself?" I shot back, my voice rising in pitch, matching the growing thunder outside. "You call this truth? This is just another lie cloaked in good intentions." The shadows around us seemed to writhe in agreement, as if the house itself recognized the futility of his excuses.

Jamie shifted, positioning himself slightly in front of me. "If you truly cared, you would have come back long before now," he said, his voice steady but carrying an undercurrent of fury that ignited the air between us. "You can't just walk in after years and expect everything to be forgiven."

I admired Jamie's strength in that moment, his fierce protectiveness. It was a reminder of how far we had come together, how we had forged our own path through the wreckage of our families. "You don't understand," my father said, frustration creeping into his tone. "What you think you know is just the surface. Beneath it lies a deeper betrayal, one that could destroy you both."

"Then show us!" I pressed, feeling the adrenaline surge. "Tell us what you've hidden all these years. We deserve to know."

With a reluctant sigh, he moved to the window, peering out as the rain lashed against the glass. "Very well, but understand—once you know, there's no turning back." He paused, glancing back at us, his expression somber. "Your mother wasn't just a victim; she was complicit in the darkness that enveloped our families. There were choices made that led to the tragedies you've endured."

The room fell silent, the air thick with the gravity of his words. My heart raced, a drumbeat of disbelief. "What do you mean? My mother? Complicit?"

He turned, and for a brief moment, I saw a flicker of vulnerability in his eyes, an echo of the man I had once wished to know. "Yes. Your mother was part of a pact—a deal made in desperation, with forces neither of us fully understood. Her actions had consequences that rippled through generations. I thought I could shield you from it, but in doing so, I merely allowed the darkness to fester."

Jamie let out a sharp breath, his hand squeezing mine tightly. "So, all of this—the pain, the family rifts—it all circles back to her?"

"Yes," my father admitted, his voice almost a whisper. "And I should have done more. But instead, I ran." The confession hung in the air like the distant rumble of thunder, punctuating the storm's fury outside.

"What does that even mean for us?" I asked, the words catching in my throat. "How do we move forward with this truth? What if it destroys everything we've fought for?"

"Moving forward is your choice, not mine," he replied, his expression shifting into one of resignation. "But you must confront your mother's legacy. You can't ignore the shadows any longer."

The tempest outside mirrored the whirlwind of emotions inside me, and I felt both liberated and trapped. "So, we're supposed to just accept this?" I demanded, my voice shaking. "After all the hurt, all the lies?"

"I can't take back the past," he said, his tone softening, "but I can help you understand it. If you want answers, I can provide them, but it will require a journey—a return to the roots of our families, where the pact was forged."

"Return? Are you out of your mind?" Jamie interjected, disbelief etched across his features. "You want us to wade through the muck of your mistakes? No way!"

"Do you have any better ideas?" I countered, surprising myself with the strength of my resolve. "If this is where we stand, I refuse to back down without knowing the full story. If there's any chance to break this cycle, to reclaim what's ours, we have to go back."

The room crackled with tension, my heart pounding in rhythm with the relentless storm. "I'll guide you," my father offered, his tone shifting from defensive to almost pleading. "But you must understand—the truth may hurt more than the lies."

I met his gaze, searching for any hint of the father I had longed for, the one who had abandoned us, but found only a shadow of regret. "Then we do it," I said, the weight of my decision settling heavily in my chest. "But know this: I won't forgive easily, and I won't forget."

Jamie's grip on my hand tightened, and I could sense his unease mingling with a flicker of determination. "We're in this together, right?" he asked, his voice low, filled with resolve. "No more secrets. No more games."

I nodded, feeling the fierce bond between us strengthen like the resolve in my heart. "Together."

"Good. Then we leave at dawn," my father stated, his demeanor shifting as if he had finally accepted the gravity of our situation.

"There's much to uncover, and we can't afford to waste any more time."

As he spoke, the wind howled outside, and the rain lashed against the walls like an impatient lover. I felt the storm raging both within and around us, each crash of thunder echoing the chaos that had ruled our lives for far too long.

The flickering candlelight cast long shadows against the walls, transforming the study into a theater of memories, both bitter and sweet. I could feel the past pulling at me, urging me to embrace the truth, no matter how painful it might be. "What if this journey doesn't lead to what we hope?" I whispered, my breath catching in my throat.

"It might not," Jamie said, his voice steady but filled with uncertainty. "But we owe it to ourselves to try."

I took a deep breath, the weight of our decision settling heavily in my chest, and nodded. "Then let's uncover this truth. Together." The storm continued to rage outside, but within me, a flicker of hope ignited—a belief that perhaps, just perhaps, we could find a way to break the chains binding our pasts.

The storm had settled into a rhythm outside, a relentless symphony of rain and wind that seemed determined to drown out our revelations. My father's words echoed in my mind, a haunting melody I couldn't shake. "The truth will hurt more than the lies." I glanced at Jamie, his expression a mixture of disbelief and fierce determination, as if he was trying to anchor us both against the tide of uncertainty that threatened to pull us under.

"Are you ready for what lies ahead?" Jamie asked, his brow furrowed with concern. The flickering candlelight played across his features, casting sharp shadows that hinted at the unease bubbling just beneath the surface.

"As ready as I'll ever be," I replied, forcing a steadiness into my voice that I didn't quite feel. "But there's no turning back now. We're committed to this path." The weight of our decision settled around us like the heavy air before a storm, charged with an electric anticipation.

My father's expression shifted, a glimmer of something—hope or perhaps regret—crossing his features. "There are secrets buried deep in the old family estate, hidden within the walls that have stood for generations. That's where we'll find the answers you seek."

The idea of returning to the place that had held so much pain was daunting, but it felt like the only way to carve a path forward. "When do we leave?" I asked, urgency fueling my words.

"First light," he said, the words hanging in the air like a spell. "But we need to rest. Tomorrow will be long, and the truth isn't easy to digest."

As we settled in the study, the storm outside raged on, its furious symphony echoing the turmoil in our hearts. I could feel the shadows creeping in, a reminder of everything we had to confront. Jamie and I sat on the worn couch, the fabric frayed from years of neglect, its history seeping into our skin.

"Can you believe this?" Jamie muttered, rubbing his hands over his face. "We're about to dig into our families' darkest secrets. It's like a plot twist in a bad novel."

I laughed, a short, bitter sound. "Except this isn't fiction. It's our lives."

He turned to me, his gaze intense. "We can't let their choices define us. We're stronger than that."

"Stronger," I echoed, the word tasting foreign on my tongue. "I hope you're right."

As night deepened around us, sleep became a fragile thread, tugging at the corners of my consciousness. I lay there, eyes wide open, thoughts swirling like the storm outside. Just when I thought I could drift off, a loud crash of thunder jolted me upright. Jamie stirred beside me, his hand instinctively reaching for mine in the darkness.

"Did that sound...off to you?" he whispered, his voice barely above a breath.

I nodded, unease creeping back in. "It's just the storm." But even I could hear the tremor in my own voice, the way it betrayed my anxiety.

A soft thud echoed through the manor, muffled but unmistakable. Jamie's grip tightened, and I could feel the tension radiating off him like heat. "That wasn't just the storm," he said, his voice steady despite the apprehension threading through his words. "We should check it out."

"Now? In the middle of the night?" I argued, but even as I said it, I could feel the instinct to investigate pulling at me. The shadows of the manor felt alive, the air thick with possibilities both wondrous and terrifying.

"Together," he insisted, his determination unyielding.

We crept through the manor, the darkness wrapping around us like a cloak. The floorboards creaked beneath our weight, and I could almost hear the whispers of the past echoing off the walls, urging us to retreat. But there was no retreating now.

We made our way down the narrow hall, pausing outside a door slightly ajar. A faint light flickered from within, casting an eerie glow that danced across the walls. I exchanged a glance with Jamie, my heart racing as we shared an unspoken understanding.

"On three?" I whispered, adrenaline surging through my veins.

"On three," he affirmed.

"One, two—"

Before I could finish, I pushed the door open, my heart thundering in my chest. The sight before us stole the breath from my lungs. The room was filled with artifacts, remnants of our families' pasts—old photographs, letters yellowed with age, and objects that seemed to pulse with memories long forgotten. But it was the figure hunched over a table that drew our attention.

"Hello, my darlings," the figure said, turning to face us, revealing a face I never thought I'd see again. "I've been waiting for you."

It was my mother. The storm outside howled with renewed ferocity as the recognition crashed over me like a wave. My heart raced, a whirlwind of confusion and emotions spiraling out of control. She looked the same yet different, a spectral version of the woman I had lost, cloaked in shadows and secrets.

"Mom?" I breathed, disbelief mixing with a surge of hope and fear.

"You're too late," she said, her voice calm but laced with an edge that sent chills down my spine. "The truth has already set its course."

"What do you mean?" I demanded, stepping forward, but Jamie held me back, his expression a mix of shock and protectiveness.

"Every choice has a consequence, and the pact we made—"

"Pact?" I interrupted, the word burning like acid in my throat. "What pact?"

She smiled sadly, a ghost of the warmth I remembered. "A pact to protect our family from the darkness. But darkness has its own rules, and it always finds a way."

The weight of her words hung in the air, suffocating and electric. "You need to leave now," she urged, urgency lacing her tone. "Before it's too late."

"What's happening?" Jamie asked, his voice strained.

But before she could answer, the lights flickered violently, plunging us into darkness. A loud crash reverberated through the room, and the floor beneath us shook.

"Run!" Jamie shouted, pulling me back as the walls began to tremble.

I felt the air shift, a rush of energy coursing through the room as if the very foundation of the manor was coming undone. My heart raced with a primal instinct to flee, but as I turned back, I caught a glimpse of my mother's face, her expression twisted between urgency and resignation.

"Find the truth!" she yelled, her voice barely audible over the chaos. "You must break the cycle before it consumes you!"

With those words, the lights exploded, sending shards of glass and sparks flying. I stumbled back into Jamie, his grip firm around my waist as we dashed for the door, the air thick with the scent of smoke and fear.

"Go, go, go!" he urged, and we barreled into the hallway, the ground quaking beneath us.

The storm outside roared, drowning out everything else as we raced toward the exit, the weight of our family's history pressing down on us like an anchor. Just as we reached the door, a deafening crash echoed behind us, the walls groaning under the strain.

"Don't look back!" Jamie shouted, his urgency echoing in my ears. But as we burst into the storm, the chaos of the manor behind us, I couldn't shake the feeling that this was just the beginning. The night was far from over, and the storm—both outside and within—was only just beginning to break.

Chapter 23: Rising from Ashes

The air was thick with the scent of charred wood and freshly turned earth, a bittersweet reminder of the night that had transformed everything we knew. My fingers brushed over the jagged edges of what was once a beautiful oak tree, now a skeletal silhouette against the pale light of dawn. I could still hear the echoes of laughter that had once danced through the branches, now replaced by an eerie silence that wrapped around me like a shroud. I inhaled deeply, forcing the memories of joy and warmth to mingle with the harsh reality surrounding me. It was a strange alchemy of loss, hope, and the resilience that flickered within.

Jordan stood a few paces away, his form framed by the rising sun, casting long shadows across the debris. I watched him for a moment, taking in the way the light caught the contours of his face, accentuating the lines etched there by worry and sleepless nights. There was a time when his smile could light up the darkest corners of my world, but today, it felt like a fragile thing, barely hanging on in the aftermath of our tumultuous battle. As he turned to face me, his eyes—those warm, expressive pools—betrayed a storm of emotions. Relief battled with the weight of our shared trauma, a duality that mirrored my own heart.

"Hey," he called softly, his voice carrying a hint of a tremor. "Are you alright?"

The question felt heavy, as if it were carved from the same wood as the remnants of our lives scattered around us. I offered a weak smile, one that didn't quite reach my eyes, and nodded. "I will be. We will be."

I took a step closer, feeling the cool breeze brush against my skin, almost as if it were trying to comfort me. "It's just... a lot to take in, isn't it? The ashes of everything we knew, everything we thought we could rely on."

He sighed, running a hand through his tousled hair, an endearing gesture that always made my heart flutter, even now. "Yeah, it's a lot. But maybe it's a chance for a fresh start? We can rebuild... or at least try to."

His optimism was a balm, soothing the jagged edges of my own despair. "You're right. A fresh start," I echoed, though I felt the twinge of doubt lurking at the corners of my mind. The idea of rebuilding was daunting, especially when the remnants of our past still burned in my memory. But I found comfort in the thought of us facing it together, forging a path out of the darkness hand in hand.

The sun continued to rise, casting golden rays across the landscape and illuminating the scars on the earth. I turned away from the wreckage and glanced toward the small gathering of people in the distance, our families and friends, their faces a mixture of concern and resolve. It struck me how much we all had been through, how connected we were by the threads of love and loyalty that would not fray, even in the wake of such devastation. But I couldn't shake the nagging feeling that we hadn't seen the last of the storm.

"What's next for us?" I asked, my voice barely above a whisper, filled with both excitement and trepidation.

Jordan stepped closer, his presence grounding me amidst the uncertainty. "We face it head-on. Together. We start with small steps—rebuild the garden, help our families find their footing again, and maybe..." He paused, his gaze locking onto mine, holding my attention with a gravity that made my heart race. "Maybe we take a leap of faith and finally pursue that dream we've been talking about."

My breath caught at the mention of our dream, the vision we had spun in the quiet corners of our minds—a little bakery where the smell of fresh bread mingled with the laughter of children and the warmth of community. It seemed so far-fetched amidst the ruins, yet the thought kindled a spark within me.

"Are you serious?" I asked, a hint of disbelief creeping into my voice.

"Absolutely," he replied, a teasing grin breaking through his serious demeanor. "We can't let this define us. We need to take control of our future. And what better way than with flour, sugar, and a whole lot of frosting?"

I laughed, the sound surprising me with its lightness. It felt like a lifeline tossed into the turbulent sea of my emotions. "Frosting, huh? You know that's my weakness."

"Exactly. I thought it might entice you."

The conversation flowed like a gentle river, winding through the tension and uncertainty that still clung to us. As we stood there, surrounded by the remnants of our former lives, I felt the weight of despair begin to lift, if only slightly. We were not just survivors of this catastrophe; we were dreamers, ready to transform our pain into something beautiful.

"Let's do it," I said, my voice firm with newfound determination. "Let's find a place for our bakery, one that smells of fresh bread and hope."

Jordan's smile broadened, lighting up his entire face. "Now that's the spirit! Together, we can rise from these ashes, and who knows—maybe we'll create something sweeter than we ever imagined."

As he took my hand, intertwining our fingers, I felt a surge of energy, as if the very act of holding on could weave a new future from the threads of our past. In that moment, beneath the brightening sky, I understood that our journey was far from over. It would be a road filled with challenges, but it would also be one paved with hope, laughter, and an unyielding love that could withstand anything the world threw our way.

The sun climbed higher, spilling its golden warmth across the landscape, coaxing life from the ashes. The wreckage, once a source of despair, began to feel less like an end and more like a canvas, waiting for our brushstrokes to transform it into something new. I took a deep breath, inhaling the crisp air that carried the scent of damp earth and the promise of renewal. With each passing moment, the heaviness in my chest lightened, nudged along by Jordan's unwavering presence beside me.

"Okay," I said, determination edging into my voice. "Let's get to work. We need to rally the troops, make a plan. I mean, a bakery doesn't start itself, right?"

Jordan chuckled, the sound deep and rich, lifting the tension between us like a balloon into the blue sky. "Exactly! But first, we might need to gather supplies. You know, flour, sugar, the essentials for a good old-fashioned stress bake-off."

I raised an eyebrow at him. "And you think that's going to fix everything? Flour and sugar?"

"Well, have you ever met a problem that cookies couldn't solve? I'm telling you, they're like little nuggets of hope."

"Is that what you tell yourself when you're eating them in bed?"

He feigned shock, clutching his heart as if I'd just accused him of a capital offense. "I prefer to think of it as a strategic culinary adventure. Cookies are my tactical comfort food."

We shared a laugh, and it felt as though the world around us began to shimmer with potential. As I looked into his eyes, I saw the flicker of shared dreams—a future that sparkled brighter than the sun overhead. "Alright then, tactical comfort food it is. But we'll need a location. We can't very well bake bread on a battlefield."

"True. What do you think about that little storefront on Maple Avenue? The one with the chipped paint and those rickety steps?"

"Perfect! It has character. Plus, I can already see the sign out front—'Kleszcz & Co. Bakery: Where Every Bite is a Hug.'"

"Now you're just making me hungry." He grinned, and together we plotted our next moves, filled with enthusiasm and the promise of a shared future.

As we began to gather our friends and family, the energy shifted. People who had once seemed crushed by despair now buzzed with excitement, rallying around us as we discussed our plans. My heart swelled at the sight of familiar faces, each one more vibrant than the last, infusing the air with a sense of unity. We shared ideas, sketches of what the bakery might look like, from the rustic wooden counter to the bright, inviting decor that would make anyone feel at home.

Just as we were ready to dive into the logistics of our plans, a voice cut through the cheerful chatter—a deep baritone laced with concern. "Are you sure this is the right path, given everything we've just been through?"

I turned to see my father standing at the edge of our gathering, arms crossed, a thoughtful frown creasing his forehead. His protective instincts were as natural as breathing, and I knew that beneath his concern lay a fierce love that sometimes manifested as worry.

"Dad," I began, my voice steady. "This is exactly what we need. We can't let fear dictate our lives. We've lost too much already, and starting this bakery feels like a way to reclaim our joy."

Jordan stepped up beside me, his stance firm. "We've been through hell and back. If we don't seize this moment, we risk losing ourselves completely. A bakery is more than just a place to sell pastries; it's a space for healing and connection."

I watched my father's expression shift, the tension in his shoulders easing slightly. "I just want to make sure you're not rushing into this. It's a big commitment."

"Maybe," I replied, choosing my words carefully, "but so is the commitment to our happiness. Every loaf of bread, every cookie will be a symbol of our resilience. We're not just baking; we're rebuilding."

"Alright," he relented, a hint of pride breaking through the concern. "If you're determined to go forward, I'll support you. But I expect a lot of taste testing along the way."

The laughter that followed was infectious, a joyful release that echoed around the gathering. I felt a rush of gratitude for the support surrounding us, for the warmth that grew like a wildfire as we shared our dreams.

As we dove into the planning stages, my phone buzzed insistently in my pocket. Pulling it out, I saw a message from Sarah, my best friend. "Hey! When's the bakery opening? I need a job—preferably the one that involves eating all the pastries!"

I typed back quickly, laughing as I did. "Well, if we can bake like we dream, it'll be a deliciously chaotic adventure! You're hired as chief taste tester."

"Perfect! I'll bring the milk! Can't wait to celebrate!"

Just as I was about to slip my phone back into my pocket, it buzzed again. My heart sank when I saw the name. It was from my brother, Matt, and the tightness in my chest warned me that it wouldn't be good news.

"Hey, we need to talk. Something's come up."

I glanced at Jordan, my heart pounding. "I have to take this."

"Go ahead," he said, his expression shifting to one of concern.

I stepped aside, the chatter of my friends fading into the background as I focused on my brother's voice. "What's wrong?" I asked, trying to keep the fear out of my tone.

"I just found out that there might be more fallout from last night's confrontation. I'm not sure how to handle it."

My stomach twisted as he spoke, the shadows creeping back into my thoughts. "What do you mean? Is it about the family?"

"Let's just say, someone's not pleased, and it could lead to more trouble."

My mind raced, the implications of his words igniting a flame of anxiety. "Matt, we can't afford any more drama. Not now."

"I know, but I'll figure it out. Just keep doing what you're doing with the bakery. Stay strong, sis. We'll get through this together."

The call ended, and I stood there, frozen in place as the reality of our situation settled over me. Just as we began to rise from the ashes, the specter of our past loomed larger, reminding me that not all battles were fought in the open. And though we had each other, I couldn't shake the feeling that the road ahead was still fraught with uncertainty.

As the sun climbed higher, illuminating the world with a warm embrace, the initial thrill of our plans began to settle into something deeper—a determination that filled the spaces left by doubt and fear. The vibrant colors of the day contrasted sharply with the shadows of the past, creating a surreal backdrop for the future we were daring to build. With every step back to the gathering, I felt an energy crackling in the air, a promise of hope that sparked between us like electricity.

Jordan had returned to the group, diving into discussions about flour sourcing and the best local ingredients, his enthusiasm infectious. I smiled to see him so animated, a stark contrast to the heavy weight he'd carried in the hours following our confrontation. As the chatter swirled around me, I marveled at the way our friends and family were coming together, knitting a safety net of support that felt solid beneath my feet.

Suddenly, the door creaked open, and our neighbor, Mrs. Whitaker, stepped into the clearing. A woman of petite stature with silver hair pulled back in a tight bun, she was a force of nature who had lived on our street longer than I had been alive. Today, she wore a yellow cardigan that seemed to pulse with sunshine, and I couldn't help but feel that her presence was a blessing.

"Is it true? You're opening a bakery?" she exclaimed, her voice rich with excitement.

"Yes, ma'am!" I replied, barely able to contain my enthusiasm. "We're going to bring some sweetness back to this neighborhood."

"Sweetness! That's just what we need." She clapped her hands, her eyes twinkling. "You must promise to make my favorite lemon tarts. I'll be your first customer!"

With the laughter and warmth from Mrs. Whitaker, a wave of optimism surged through me. This was it—the community was rallying, ready to embrace the new beginnings we had envisioned. Just as I was beginning to believe in the dream, however, the serenity shattered when a voice broke through the merriment.

"Are you really going to do this?" It was Matt again, his face drawn tight with tension, an urgent fire dancing in his eyes.

"What's wrong?" I asked, suddenly on high alert.

He stepped closer, lowering his voice. "I overheard some things. Not just idle gossip. There are people in town who aren't happy about what happened last night, and they're not going to let it go."

"What do you mean? Who?"

"Look, I don't want to freak you out, but there's a group—a faction, I guess you could call them—who think they can control everything around here. And they're not above using intimidation to get what they want."

I felt a chill creep down my spine. The warmth of our gathering, the laughter, the dreams—all of it began to feel fragile under the weight of his words. "What do they want with us?"

"Everything," he replied, his voice barely above a whisper. "They want to maintain their grip on the town. And they see you and Jordan as a threat to that."

Jordan had been watching the exchange, and now he stepped in, brows furrowed with concern. "We can handle this. We won't let them intimidate us into backing down."

"Easy for you to say," Matt shot back, frustration leaking into his tone. "But you don't know what they're capable of. We can't underestimate them. We have to be careful."

"Careful is my middle name," Jordan said, his tone a playful challenge, but I could hear the tension underneath.

"Your middle name is Michael," I retorted, trying to lighten the mood, but the moment felt heavy with uncertainty.

"Alright, focus," Matt interrupted. "This is serious. We need a plan. If they come after you, we have to be ready."

"What kind of plan?" I asked, feeling the weight of responsibility pressing down. "What do we do if they come after the bakery?"

"First, we gather information," he replied, his tone sharp. "If we know what they're planning, we can counter it. Then we make sure everyone in this group is on alert. They need to know we're not backing down."

As I looked around at our friends, their faces now serious and alert, I felt a sense of camaraderie solidify in the air. We were a collective force, bound not just by dreams but also by the determination to protect what we were building.

"Okay, then," I said, my heart racing with a blend of fear and adrenaline. "Let's do this. We'll become the best bakery in town, and we won't let anyone take that from us."

A cheer rose from our group, igniting a flicker of hope that danced in the face of danger. Yet, beneath the surface, an undercurrent of anxiety rippled through me, a constant reminder of the challenges lurking in the shadows.

With newfound resolve, we spent the afternoon hammering out details, assigning roles, and brainstorming strategies. But even as we filled the air with laughter and excitement, a tension simmered just beneath, weaving itself through our conversations.

As the sun dipped low, casting a golden glow that bathed everything in warmth, I felt a stirring in my gut. A nagging sense that we were not as prepared as we thought. I glanced at Matt, his expression serious, and at Jordan, who was fully invested in the conversation, yet I could see the tension in his shoulders.

Suddenly, a loud crash echoed from the back of the property, followed by the unmistakable sound of shouting. The jubilant atmosphere froze, a stark contrast to the chaos erupting just beyond our gathering.

"What was that?" I asked, my heart pounding in my chest.

"Stay here!" Matt ordered, his protective instincts kicking in as he rushed toward the sound, Jordan close behind him.

Panic surged through me as I remained rooted to the spot, uncertainty flooding my mind. Had they finally come for us? The bakery, our dream—it all felt perilously close to slipping away.

I moved instinctively, following them into the fray, adrenaline coursing through my veins. My heart raced as I rounded the corner, and what I saw sent a shockwave of disbelief crashing over me. A group of hooded figures stood in the shadows, their faces obscured, surrounding the remnants of our past like a pack of wolves ready to strike.

And at the center of it all was the unmistakable figure of a man I thought I'd left behind—a figure whose very presence threatened to unravel everything we had fought to build.

Chapter 24: A New Dawn

The morning light filtered through the curtains, casting soft, golden rays that danced across the bedroom walls like the laughter of children at play. I lay there for a moment, drinking in the warmth that spilled over the edges of the duvet, relishing the way it wrapped around me like an embrace. The air held a delicate chill, the kind that whispers of dawn and promise. My heart quickened at the thought of a day unshackled from the chains of the past.

Beside me, Jordan stirred, his tousled hair a dark halo against the crisp white of the pillow. I studied him in the gentle light, the way his brow furrowed slightly as he fought against waking, as if grappling with dreams that clung to him like cobwebs. I wanted to reach out, to brush those dreams away and wake him with a kiss, but instead, I savored this fleeting moment of tranquility.

Our journey had been anything but easy, a convoluted tapestry of love, misunderstandings, and the kind of pain that cuts deep yet stitches back together in unexpected ways. How strange it was, this feeling of anticipation tinged with hope, an emotion I had thought lost to the tumult of our past.

"Do you think the world is ready for us?" I whispered, unable to resist the urge to tease him awake.

He cracked one eye open, a lazy smile unfurling across his lips. "The world? Or just our world? Because I'm fairly certain my mother's still in denial." His voice was gravelly with sleep, yet the humor shone through, a reminder of the man I had fallen for, the man who could find light in the darkest corners.

"I'm sure she'll come around eventually," I replied, a chuckle bubbling up as I thought of his mother's exaggerated frown whenever our relationship came up at family gatherings. "But until then, we've got a whole new day to conquer."

As we both swung our legs over the side of the bed, the cool hardwood floor sent a jolt through my system, and I took a moment to breathe in the scents of fresh coffee and something baking—a subtle hint that Jordan had indeed risen before me. I peeked into the kitchen, my heart swelling at the sight. He stood there, clad in pajama bottoms that hung just low enough to draw the eye, pouring steaming coffee into two mugs that bore mismatched designs, each one a testament to our collective quirks.

"Breakfast is almost ready," he called over his shoulder, his voice warm and inviting. "I figured we could celebrate the new day with pancakes, if you're interested."

"Pancakes? You spoil me," I replied, joining him at the counter, my heart full of the kind of affection that made the world outside seem dim by comparison. "You know how to charm a girl."

"I have my moments." He flashed a grin that could have melted icebergs. "And by 'moments,' I mean every time I make pancakes. You should see how the neighbors react when I make those for you."

I laughed, picturing the collective sigh of envy that must have swept through the building. We had created a home—a refuge filled with laughter, teasing banter, and the aroma of Jordan's cooking, which was an acquired skill that had blossomed beautifully over our time together.

We shared easy conversation over breakfast, reminiscing about our adventures—the spontaneous road trips that had led us to quaint diners where we'd feasted on too much pie, the late-night talks that had uncovered the depths of our souls, and the countless moments when everything else faded away, leaving just us.

"Are you ready for the big meeting today?" Jordan asked, a flicker of concern threading through his playful tone.

"More than ready," I replied, though the flutter in my stomach betrayed me. The meeting was with a prospective client who had expressed interest in our joint venture, a project that could elevate both our careers. "I've been working on the pitch all week. If we get this right, it could change everything."

"I have no doubt you'll knock it out of the park," he said, lifting his coffee mug in a mock toast. "Just remember, don't take their first 'no' as gospel. It's just the beginning of a negotiation."

"Wise words from my beloved." I clinked my mug against his, reveling in the intimacy of the moment. "But honestly, I'm just excited to share our vision. I want them to see what we see—a world where we can create something remarkable together."

The sunlight grew stronger, pouring into our small kitchen, illuminating the scattered papers and half-finished drawings that littered the table. This was our life now—chaotic, yet filled with purpose.

The sound of my phone vibrating against the table shattered the peace, and I grabbed it, my heart racing at the thought of potential news. But instead of a message from the client, it was a text from my sister, a flurry of emojis punctuating her excitement about an upcoming family gathering.

"Looks like I'm back on babysitting duty," I said, rolling my eyes playfully. "She's convinced the kids are going to turn her house into a circus, and I'm the only one who can keep them in line."

Jordan chuckled, shaking his head. "You're a brave soul. I'd take a business pitch any day over a horde of children armed with crayons and glitter."

"Glitter is the true nemesis of adulthood," I agreed, the image of sparkles strewn across the floor flashing in my mind. "But family is important. And besides, it'll be fun to see them again."

We finished our breakfast, the warmth of the morning blending seamlessly with our playful banter. As we stood to clear the table, I caught a glimpse of the clock ticking steadily on the wall, a gentle reminder of the time slipping away. The day awaited us, brimming with possibilities.

DANGEROUS INVITATION

Hand in hand, we stepped outside into the crisp morning air, the sun now fully alight in the sky, bathing everything in a soft glow. I felt invincible, ready to take on the world and all its challenges, buoyed by the strength of our love and the dreams we dared to chase.

As we walked, the streets came alive with the energy of the day, a vibrant mosaic of laughter, footsteps, and the distant hum of city life. I could see our future unfolding before us, a tapestry rich with colors and textures, and I knew that with Jordan at my side, we were ready to weave our story anew, one thread at a time.

The street buzzed with life as we strolled hand in hand, the morning air alive with the sweet scent of freshly baked pastries wafting from the café on the corner. I glanced at Jordan, his expression reflecting a mixture of excitement and nervous anticipation. The rhythm of the city pulsed around us, yet in that moment, it felt like we were encased in our own bubble, isolated from the chaos that often marked our lives.

"Do you ever think we're living in a rom-com?" Jordan quipped, glancing sideways at me with a playful grin. "You know, the kind where the main characters are hopelessly charming yet somehow manage to make every mundane moment feel like a cinematic masterpiece?"

"Is that how you see us?" I teased, nudging him with my shoulder. "I'd say we're more like a quirky indie film—short on budget, but long on character development and spontaneous dance sequences."

He laughed, a deep, genuine sound that sent a thrill through me. "You've got a point. If this were a movie, we'd definitely have our fair share of montage moments, like preparing for the big meeting, only to realize I'm out of coffee and you're out of patience."

"I'd say that's an accurate depiction of our mornings," I replied, rolling my eyes in mock exasperation. "But we always pull through in the end, don't we?"

"Like superheroes in disguise," he said, puffing out his chest dramatically. "And what's our superpower? Making the best pancakes in town?"

"Exactly! And we save the day with flavor." I winked, feeling the warmth of our connection wrap around us as we navigated through the thrumming life of the neighborhood.

We reached the quaint little café that had become our weekend sanctuary, a place where the barista greeted us like old friends. The walls were adorned with mismatched art, and the air was thick with the scent of brewing coffee and sweet treats. I ordered my usual—a caramel latte with an extra shot of espresso, while Jordan opted for a black coffee that would put hair on his chest, or so he claimed.

"Are you going to order something sweet to go with that bitter cup of ambition?" I asked, leaning against the counter, my eyes sparkling with mischief.

He grinned, the light catching the dimple in his cheek. "You know me too well. Just a scone, I suppose. But I promise to keep the sass to a minimum this time."

"Promise? Because I thrive on that sass, you know."

As we settled into our favorite corner table, I took a moment to appreciate the blend of aromas that surrounded us—rich coffee mingling with the sugary scent of pastries, a small slice of heaven nestled in the busy city. Our chatter ebbed and flowed effortlessly, as natural as the steam rising from our cups.

But just as the conversation took a turn toward lighthearted banter about our favorite TV shows, my phone buzzed again, and a familiar knot of tension twisted in my stomach. The client's details flashed on the screen, an email reminder about the meeting that would take place in just a few hours.

I swallowed hard, the weight of expectation pressing down. Jordan noticed my change in demeanor and reached across the table, his fingers brushing against mine, grounding me. "Hey, you've got this," he said, his voice low and steady. "We've prepared for this. Just breathe."

I nodded, inhaling deeply and letting it out slowly. "I know. I just can't shake the feeling that everything hinges on this one meeting."

"Maybe it does, but that's not a bad thing. It just means we're on the brink of something amazing," he encouraged. "And if they can't see that, well, their loss."

His unwavering confidence soothed the flickering anxiety within me, and I managed a smile, a flicker of hope igniting. We spent the next few moments in comfortable silence, sipping our drinks while the world around us continued to hustle and bustle.

Then, just as I was beginning to relax, the café door swung open, letting in a rush of cold air that sent a shiver through me. I turned to see who had entered, and my breath caught in my throat. It was Claire, my former colleague, the one who had left abruptly a few months ago after a heated disagreement over our project's direction. Her eyes scanned the room, and I ducked my head instinctively, a wave of unease crashing over me.

"What's wrong?" Jordan asked, following my gaze.

"Uh, nothing," I stammered, though my heart raced at the thought of our last encounter. Claire had always been ambitious, her talent undeniable, but she had a tendency to bulldoze over others to get what she wanted. The prospect of facing her again was as appealing as stepping on a LEGO brick in bare feet.

"She looks like she means business," Jordan remarked, watching her with a bemused expression. "You sure it's nothing?"

"Definitely something. Just—" I hesitated, searching for the right words. "We had a bit of a disagreement about our last project. It was... intense."

Jordan raised an eyebrow. "Intense? You mean she didn't take your brilliant ideas and sprinkle them with a little fairy dust?"

"Something like that," I said, chuckling nervously. "Let's just say she's not my biggest fan."

"Doesn't mean she gets to dictate your mood. You're not letting her ruin our pancakes, are you?"

"Absolutely not," I declared, a newfound determination washing over me. "But if she comes over here, I might need a little backup."

He nodded, his expression turning serious. "I'm right here. Just remember, you're not alone in this."

As if on cue, Claire turned and strode toward our table, a confident smile plastered on her face. The moment she reached us, the atmosphere shifted, charged with unspoken words and lingering tension.

"Fancy seeing you here," she said, her voice dripping with feigned sweetness. "I didn't expect to run into you so soon after... well, you know."

"Nice to see you too, Claire," I replied, keeping my tone light, though my heart raced in my chest. "I hear you've been making waves at the office."

"Oh, you know me—always diving headfirst into new opportunities," she said, flicking her hair over her shoulder as if it were a golden trophy. "And I see you're still trying to play the small game."

My grip tightened around my coffee mug, but before I could respond, Jordan interjected smoothly, "We're actually gearing up for something big ourselves. A collaboration that could shake things up a bit."

Claire's smile faltered just a fraction, and for a moment, I caught a glimpse of the competitive spirit that had once driven her. "Oh? That sounds... intriguing."

I exchanged a quick glance with Jordan, who nodded slightly, silently urging me to take the reins. This was my moment to stand tall, to show that I wasn't intimidated by her presence anymore.

"Yes, it is," I said, keeping my tone steady. "We believe there's a lot of potential for growth if we're willing to think outside the box."

She leaned forward, her expression shifting into one of mild curiosity, perhaps even envy. "Is that so? I hope you're ready for the challenges that come with it."

"Oh, I thrive on challenges," I replied, meeting her gaze with newfound confidence. "In fact, I've come to find they're the best way to uncover our true potential."

Her eyes narrowed slightly, and I could almost see the gears turning in her mind, calculating her next move. "Well, I look forward to hearing more about it—if you're willing to share."

"Maybe over coffee sometime?" I suggested, my voice laced with a mixture of bravado and a hint of mischief.

"Sure. Just remember, the best ideas come from collaboration."

With that, she flashed a smile that didn't quite reach her eyes before turning to leave, the air between us crackling with unspoken rivalry. As she walked away, I let out a breath I hadn't realized I was holding.

"Wow," Jordan said, eyes wide. "You handled that like a pro. I could practically hear the fireworks."

"Thanks. I guess I've learned a thing or two about standing my ground."

"And if anyone can stand their ground, it's you." He lifted his mug in another toast, this one filled with celebration rather than mere anticipation. "To new beginnings, and to being fierce."

"To being fierce," I echoed, clinking my mug against his once more. In that moment, I felt a surge of confidence flood through me, bolstered by Jordan's unwavering support. The day ahead still loomed with uncertainty, but I was ready to face it, ready to claim my place in a world that had once felt daunting.

As we finished our coffees and prepared to leave, I couldn't shake the feeling that today was more than just another day. It was the dawn of something extraordinary—a chance to rewrite our story, one ambitious chapter at a time.

The walk to the office felt electrifying, the thrill of the morning still shimmering in the air like dewdrops on grass. Each step echoed with purpose, and I reveled in the newfound strength that coursed through me. With Jordan at my side, our conversation flowed seamlessly, laughter punctuating the air as we navigated the bustling streets. The anticipation of the meeting bubbled just beneath the surface, tinged with a sense of inevitability.

"Do you remember our first pitch?" Jordan asked, his eyes glinting with mischief. "You were so nervous you nearly spilled your entire presentation all over the client's lap."

"Hey, in my defense, they had that awful waiting room coffee," I retorted, my cheeks warming at the memory. "I was simply attempting to demonstrate how unpredictable life can be."

"Unpredictable? You could have passed for a circus act!" he teased, pretending to juggle invisible balls in front of me.

I rolled my eyes, fighting a laugh. "Only if the circus had a strict 'no clowns' policy. I've made my peace with the unpredictability since then."

"Thank goodness. I would hate to see what you'd do if you had to perform in front of a crowd now."

"Probably something involving interpretive dance and a lot of dramatic hand gestures," I shot back, grinning as we reached the office building.

We shared a quick kiss before stepping inside, the sleek, glass doors parting to reveal a flurry of activity. The energy of the office was palpable, a cacophony of ringing phones, clicking keyboards, and the low hum of conversation. I took a deep breath, feeling the familiar rush of adrenaline as I settled into the rhythm of my surroundings.

As we approached the conference room, I noticed a cluster of colleagues gathered nearby, whispering conspiratorially. I squinted, trying to catch snippets of their conversation. Something was off, a subtle shift in the atmosphere that made the hair on the back of my neck stand up.

"Hey, what's going on?" I asked, approaching the group.

Claire, who had been hovering at the edge, turned sharply, her expression veiled but her eyes gleaming with a hint of amusement. "Oh, just some last-minute drama," she said, a teasing lilt in her voice. "You know how it is—someone's been keeping secrets."

"What kind of secrets?" I pressed, trying to keep my tone casual even as my heart raced.

"Just a little birdie told me our competition might have a few surprises up their sleeve for today's meeting. I wouldn't want you to be blindsided," she replied, her smile devoid of warmth.

"Thanks for the heads-up," I managed, trying to shake off the unease that wrapped around me like a shroud. I shot a quick glance at Jordan, who stood just behind me, eyebrows furrowed in concern.

"Let's not let it distract us," he whispered, his voice a calming presence amidst the rising tension. "We've prepared too hard for this."

I nodded, but as we walked into the conference room, I couldn't shake the feeling that the ground beneath us was shifting. The long table was set up with sleek tablets and water bottles, the overhead lights casting a sterile glow over everything. I settled into my seat, my mind racing with thoughts of the unexpected competition.

The door swung open, and our clients filed in, all smiles and handshakes, their presence initially soothing. We exchanged pleasantries, and I felt the initial tension ebb slightly. But as the meeting commenced, I sensed a different energy in the room.

"Before we begin," one of the clients said, his voice booming, "we wanted to discuss a recent development."

The atmosphere shifted once more, and my stomach churned. "What kind of development?" I asked, my voice barely above a whisper.

The client shared a look with his associate, and then he continued, "We've decided to open up the proposal to include other teams as well, a few of whom have experience that might be... beneficial."

Claire's smirk returned, a shadow of triumph passing across her face. "Interesting," she chimed in, her tone innocent but laced with underlying tension. "Sounds like a thrilling opportunity."

"Thrilling indeed," I replied, forcing a smile even as the knot in my stomach tightened. "But we believe our vision is uniquely positioned to deliver exceptional results."

Jordan placed a reassuring hand on my knee, grounding me as the clients continued to discuss their options. The room felt increasingly constrictive, the air thick with unspoken words. The conversation danced around topics that were all too familiar, yet the stakes felt heightened, as if I were teetering on the edge of a precipice.

Finally, I cleared my throat, summoning every ounce of courage. "While we respect your decision to consider other teams, we believe our combined talents and experiences offer a distinctive edge that can propel this project forward. We're committed to delivering not just results, but innovation."

There was a moment of silence, the weight of my words hanging in the air. The clients exchanged glances, their expressions inscrutable. I glanced at Jordan, who nodded encouragingly, and I felt a rush of adrenaline coursing through me. This was my moment to seize.

"Let's be clear," I added, my tone firm yet composed. "We're not just offering a service; we're proposing a partnership built on trust and shared goals. If you give us the opportunity, we will exceed your expectations."

DANGEROUS INVITATION

The lead client leaned back, arms crossed, a glint of interest in his eyes. "That's quite the promise."

"Consider it a challenge," I replied, my heart racing.

The meeting pressed on, each presentation slide showcasing our vision, our strategy, our commitment to excellence. I poured my heart into each word, each graph, eager to convince them of our worthiness. But just as I felt the momentum shift in our favor, the door creaked open once more, drawing everyone's attention.

In walked a figure I hadn't expected to see. It was my former boss, the one who had fired me just a few months ago. His presence loomed large, an unmistakable aura of authority following him as he stepped inside.

"Sorry to interrupt," he said, his tone smooth yet somehow dismissive. "I wanted to share some insights about the competition."

The tension in the room morphed into something tangible, an electric current that crackled in the air. I exchanged a glance with Jordan, whose expression mirrored my shock.

"What is he doing here?" I whispered, my heart racing.

"Maybe it's time for you to show him what you've got," Jordan urged softly, his eyes filled with determination.

As the meeting continued, I fought to maintain my composure. My former boss launched into a critique of our approach, his words slicing through the air like a knife.

"While I respect your efforts, I believe there's a certain level of expertise missing from your proposal. Experience counts for everything in this industry."

Each jab felt personal, a direct hit to my confidence. Yet I sensed a shift within me, an ember of resilience igniting as his condescension fueled my determination.

"I appreciate your input," I said, my voice steady despite the rising tide of emotions. "But what we bring to the table is fresh insight and a unique perspective that seasoned professionals might overlook."

The room fell silent, and the tension intensified, the clients glancing back and forth as if weighing their options.

"Perhaps we can arrange a follow-up discussion," the lead client suggested cautiously, but the finality of his tone felt like a cliff's edge.

"Absolutely," I replied, fighting to mask the storm of emotions brewing inside.

The meeting wrapped up, but the uneasy atmosphere lingered. As everyone shuffled out, I felt Jordan's hand slip into mine, a tether of support.

"Whatever happens, you held your ground," he said, his voice a low murmur as we stepped into the corridor.

"Did I? Or did I just unleash a tempest?" I countered, trying to quell the whirlwind of thoughts racing through my mind.

Just then, my phone buzzed again, and I glanced down, the screen illuminating my face. A message from Claire: "Nice try today. Just remember, there are more ways to win than just your pitch."

A chill swept over me, and I met Jordan's gaze, the uncertainty hanging in the air like a dark cloud.

"Did you see that?" I whispered, dread pooling in my stomach.

Jordan's expression hardened. "We need to find out what she means by that."

Just as I turned to leave, the lights flickered ominously, plunging us into semi-darkness, and a sense of foreboding washed over me. The day had promised new beginnings, yet it felt more like the calm before a storm.

"Stay close," Jordan said, his voice tense.

And just then, the fire alarm blared, shrill and relentless, echoing through the halls as people began to surge toward the exits, panic rippling through the crowd. My heart raced as I grabbed Jordan's hand tighter, the chaos swirling around us.

"Let's get out of here!" I shouted over the cacophony, but a sudden loud crash echoed behind us, sending us both spinning.

The door swung open, revealing a shadowy figure at the entrance, the chaos behind us fading into a deafening silence. My breath hitched in my throat as recognition dawned, dread pooling deep in my stomach.

There, silhouetted against the blaring lights, stood someone I had thought I'd never see again.